THE TERRIFYING TEACHER

A MURDER IN MARIN MYSTERY – BOOK 4

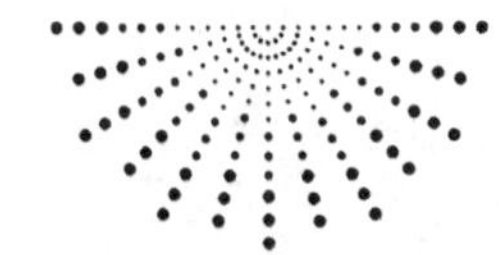

MARTIN BROWN

A BOOK BY

SIGNAL
PRESS

CHAPTER ONE

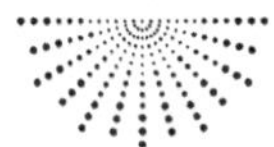

On Friday afternoons at five, Sheriff's Detective Investigator Eddie Austin and his two closest friends, Rob Timmons and Holly Cross, have a standing date to meet at Smitty's, Sausalito's neighborhood dive bar.

Their work—Eddie in law enforcement, Rob, the owner and publisher of Marin County's Standard Newspapers, and Holly, his crime and gossip-loving assistant editor— required they perform at their best, from the first moment of each workweek to the last. By week's end, they were always ready to relax and swap stories.

All the more reason Rob and Holly were surprised when come half-past five, Eddie still hadn't arrived.

"This is a first," Rob muttered as he looked at the screen display on his phone to be sure he hadn't missed a text or call.

"Maybe something big came up," Holly suggested, as she eyed Rob from over the rim of a cocktail glass that contained what she called her "Friday night liquid relief," a very dry vodka martini. Like most of her weeks, the one just concluded would require a minimum of two martinis.

The moment Rob placed his phone back down, it began to vibrate its way across the small cocktail table's fading laminate finish.

"Hang on," Eddie said before Rob had a chance to ask where he was. "I'm on my way over to Smitty's right now. Wait until you hear what kept me! Tell Holly to order herself a second martini on me. She'll need it when she hears where I've been."

After Rob repeated Eddie's declaration, Holly grabbed Rob's phone. "Really, Eddie?" she asked.

"If it weren't a department no-no, I'd put on my light and siren just to get there faster. This is a full OMG alert!"

Not wanting to blurt out his news, Eddie clicked off.

"Sounds like Eddie's got some pretty big news," Rob said as he waved down Gail, their usual waitress, and ordered a second martini for Holly, a second Guinness beer for himself, and one for Eddie.

"We could use some excitement around here. This town's been unusually quiet for too long," Rob said making no attempt to cover his disappointment. The biggest story we've had in the past few weeks was the inebriated tourist stepping off the ferry from San Francisco, tripping and falling into the bay. We're going to need more than that level of excitement to keep the paper's readers hanging on."

"Makes me miss our old friend, the gossiping gourmet. When nothing exciting was going on, he'd make something up. God bless the old busybody."

"Making stuff up is a good way to get yourself killed," Rob warned.

"He certainly proved that point," Holly said as she glanced around Smitty's, sniffing the air and curling her mouth into a disapproving frown. "Speaking of things that never change, how come this place still smells of cigarette smoke? It's been so many years now since California banned smoking in bars."

"Give the owners time to do one of those deep steam cleanings, Holly. That'll get the smell out."

"If they haven't done it by now, I'm guessing it's not going to happen. And this place needs a lot more than steam cleaning! A new coat of paint would be a good start. Maybe that's why it's so empty during 'happy hour,'" Holly said complete with curling her fingers to make air quotes.

"Stop griping. You know why we keep coming back here."

"I forget. Enlighten me!"

"First, nearly all the places downtown are tourist rip off joints. Second, you've got the No Name Bar, which has a great local vibe, but way too crowded and way too many nosy locals. They see the three of us together, and they figure something we're gabbing about is worth overhearing. Look around this place, it holds a few old sailors cozied up to the bar. Otherwise, it's just wide-open space. We could sit here planning a bank robbery, and no one would be the wiser."

"Yeah, it's wide open until nine or so on Friday and Saturday nights. "Then they push the tables aside and start dancing. Once that happens the crowd extends out into the street," Holly said.

Rob nodded. "True, one more reason to be here now: quiet, private, and happy hour prices."

Holly giggled. "I know you, buddy. The quiet and private might get you in the door, but those happy hour prices keep you coming back."

Engaged in their debate over Smitty's good and bad points neither of them noticed Eddie walking in carrying his suit jacket by one finger over his shoulder on what was an unusually warm, early April afternoon. He winked at Gail—his signal that he was ready for his usual Guinness.

"Rob's already got you covered big guy," Gail said with a wink of her own.

Holly looked up and noticed Eddie steps away. "So, what's the big news, pal? Oh, and by the way, this is my second martini—the one you insisted on buying, thank you very much."

"You're welcome very much. Now, hold onto your seats, boys, and girls. This bit of news is going to rock your world." Eddie sat down and leaned in as Rob and Holly edged their chairs closer. "Earlier this afternoon Henrietta Hammer was found dead in that old house she's lived in since the stone age."

"The Hammernator? Dead!" Holly gasped.

"I don't believe it!" Rob said, staring blankly back at Eddie.

"Ding dong, the old witch is dead," Eddie said as he used his freshly poured Guinness to clink glasses with the two of them.

"Whoa! I better stop after two martinis," Holly murmured. "My head's already spinning."

"I've been around you long enough to know your head

doesn't start spinning from one and a half martinis," Eddie said. "I think my news about Henrietta passing is what's made you lightheaded."

"You're right. This is certainly oh my God worthy," Rob said as he and Eddie bumped fists. The two had known each other practically all their lives. They'd met in elementary school, and became best friends as basketball teammates back in high school over twenty years ago. Putting his beer down, Rob added, "As kids, all of us thought Mrs. Hammer ran on battery acid. It never occurred to me she would die one day. That just seems too ordinary a thing for her to have done."

"Well, it's been a while since she was our fifth-grade teacher," Eddie said as he shook his head in wonder over how quickly time passes.

Holly shrugged. "It's been a lot fewer years for me, I'm not nearly as old as the two of you."

"Holly," Rob said. "We've been over this before, five years is not exactly a huge age difference."

Holly pointedly ignored Rob as she moved her chair closer to Eddie. "So, what killed the mean old thing?"

"Probably some kid she made repeat the fifth grade finally went after her with an ax would be my guess," Rob muttered.

"Nothing as messy as that," Eddie explained. "Right now, they're not certain. Probably a stroke, or a heart attack. I was in my car heading back here from San Rafael when I heard the call go out for the EMT crew and a couple of squad cars. I knew the address. I don't think a kid who grew up in Sausalito had the nerve to go anywhere near that old place of hers."

"Certainly not on Halloween," Holly added with a shutter. "It's been a spooky looking place for as long as I can remember."

"That old Victorian had to be the scariest place in town," Rob said as the memory still caused the hair on the back of his neck to rise. "And it's not as if we don't have a bunch of creepy looking old houses in the hills above downtown."

"Remember how much fun it was to scare the fourth graders by telling them that kids Hammer didn't like were hanging as skeletons in the attic of her house?" Holly asked as she stirred her drink.

"Either that, or we would tell them about all the kids buried under Hammer's house," Rob added.

"Great stuff," Eddie said. "Particularly when you could make one of the third graders cry. I think there had to be some kids who got their parents to transfer them out of the district they were so scared of spending one day in Henrietta's classroom."

"So true! Kids were scared to death of getting Hammer when they reached the fifth grade," Rob said. "Those were some good times."

"I don't think there was ever a kid who didn't come close to wetting their pants when Henrietta pointed one of her long bony fingers and asked, 'What do you mean you don't have your homework assignment with you?'" Eddie said doing his best to mimic his late teacher's high-pitched squeal, which caused Rob and Holly to laugh uproariously.

"We might laugh now," Holly said, catching her breath, "but we didn't think it was funny then."

"Who found the poor dear's body?" Holly asked, hungry for details.

"Hammer's old cat, Misty had been whining at the back door of Henrietta's neighbor, Marilyn Roswell. You both should remember her? Her husband, Mike, was the city's director of maintenance from the time all of us were kids. He's been retired for several years now. Up until today, I probably hadn't seen Marilyn in years. Anyway, she finally picked up the cat and brought her back over to Henrietta's place. Marilyn gets to the back screen door and sees Henrietta sprawled across the kitchen floor with a broken teacup and plate lying beside her. She was probably having a little tea and cake when Gabriel came to blow his horn. Dear old thing gone, just like that," Eddie said with a snap of his fingers. "Gone to that little red schoolhouse in the sky."

All three sat silently for a few moments as they imagined their once fearsome teacher dying in such an ordinary way.

"Poor Marilyn," Eddie added. "The sight of Hammer sprawled across the floor scared her half to death. In a complete panic, she drops the cat and runs back to her place, shouting to her husband, 'Call 911, Call 911!' She still had not calmed down by the time I got there."

"Was Henrietta alive when the EMT crew arrived?" Holly asked.

"Nope, she was already cold as a block of ice," one of them told me. Probably died well before Marilyn first heard Misty meowing outside her back door."

"How old was Hammer?" Rob asked.

"Everyone in my class guessed she was well over a hundred," Holly said with a laugh.

"At age ten, all of you were off by decades. Hammer was in her late seventies. The coroner got in touch with her nephew, guy by the name of Scott Silva," Eddie said as he checked his notepad to confirm his memory. "Actually, Marilyn met the nephew not long ago. Nice guy, she tells me, apparently grew up down in Pasadena. Now he's living up here, head of the math department over at Marin Academy. Henrietta and her husband Elijah never had children.

"Any chance she was killed by one of her former students?" Holly asked.

"Probably not. There was no evidence of a struggle, and no evidence of an intruder."

"I suppose the broken cup and plate were the result of her hitting the floor when she collapsed," Rob suggested.

"That would be my guess," Eddie said. "I know you two would like to get your hands on a story about a former student taking out his vengeance on the teacher all her students loved to hate, but I don't think that's going to work out. Nine chances out of ten, this is just another story of an aging ticker gone bad or a blood vessel in her brain going pop. Spend some time hanging out in the morgue, and you'll see those cases come in and be processed nearly every day of the week. We're all more fragile than we care to consider."

"So is that it?" Holly asked, clearly disappointed by the routine nature of it all.

"It is for now. The coroner will do a quick check, looking for signs of injuries, and so on. They'll also take a look at her most recent medical records. They'll probably speak with her physician, but no big production, no autopsy, nothing dramatic. It's not too suspicious when a woman her age dies suddenly. Sorry to disappoint. By now even the last of her students is through high school, college, or like us, well beyond. I think they've recovered from the slings and arrows of having Mrs. Hammer as their fifth-grade teacher."

"I didn't know she kept teaching for so many years," Rob said with surprise.

"Marilyn told me she retired around five years ago. I guess she liked teaching kids a lot more than kids liked having her as their teacher."

"Well, Eddie, you've got your theory as to how she died, and I've got mine," Holly said. "Mine comes with a long list of suspects. I'd put Billy Muntz as my top suspect."

"Okay I'll bite," Eddie said. "Who is Billy Muntz?"

"Muntz was in my fifth-grade class. Hammer was on his case constantly. Incomplete homework, unfinished book reports, sloppy locker, you name it. Even by the loose standards of fifth graders, we all thought Billy was a screw-up. When he didn't return to class after our Christmas break, all of us thought Henrietta had killed him and buried his body under her house. Maybe we were wrong. Maybe he just transferred out of the school district."

"Gosh, ya think?" Rob said loud enough to stir two besotted ancient mariners sitting on their usual perches at the far end of the bar. "Eddie, on a more serious note, the guy Henrietta married left her a very wealthy widow. We did a story about him not too long ago when he passed away."

"The husband's name was Elijah Hammer. After the EMTs did their thing and the coroner's staff took over to tag and bag the body, I chatted with Marilyn." He glanced down at his notebook. "She told me that Elijah was older than his wife by about five years. They'd been married over forty years. Died four or five months ago. Went fast. Pancreatic cancer, and let me tell you, that's some bad stuff."

"He left her pretty well off," Rob said.

"Sure did. Henrietta's father-in-law started a tool company up in Fort Bragg. When he retired, Elijah took over. He sold the tool company many years after he moved the business down to San Francisco."

"You mean if her husband had not moved his company down from Fort Bragg, we would have never had Mrs. Hammer for a teacher?" Holly asked.

"That's a safe bet since it's a hundred and fifty mile-drive each way," Eddie replied. "Even the thrill of meeting us at age ten would not have been enough to justify that kind of commute."

"After he sold the tool company, he had a second very successful career buying and selling commercial and residential real estate," Rob added. "I remember putting that into the story."

"That fits what Marilyn told me," Eddie added. "And of course, The Hammer home in and of itself is worth millions. It's in pretty sad shape, but it sits on a great piece of property near the top of Sausalito. Incredible views! It's worth big bucks, even if the new owner bulldozes the place and starts from scratch."

"Wow!" Holly said as she nearly choked on the last of her martini. "Millions? I would have been better off getting out of the news business and taking care of my favorite teacher in her sunset years!"

"You would have sacrificed your dignity in the hope she left you a piece of that fortune?" Rob asked.

"Sure, I'd sacrifice both of you for that kind of money.

Friends come and go. If you're smart, a nice inheritance can last a lifetime."

"No one could accuse you of being a sloppy sentimentalist," Eddie said with a laugh.

"She had all that money, and nowhere to go," Rob added as he shook his head in wonder.

"Marilyn told me she was very involved with the Fine Arts Association, the Sausalito Preservation League, and that nutty opera society."

"You mean the group that puts on all those awful opera nights down at Gabrielson Park?" Holly said as her nose wrinkled up in disgust.

Eddie laughed. "That's the one, my dear. And don't forget our favorite band of local do-gooders, the Ladies of Liberty. Maybe she left some or all of her money to them, or some other favorite cause—perhaps the Marin Animal Rescue Shelter. Marilyn claims she was very active with that group as well. It's where she adopted her one faithful companion, that old gray cat, Misty."

"Damn, I could have been her faithful companion!" Holly announced with a regretful shake of her head.

"Cheer up," Rob retorted. "A good part of her fortune might go to enhance the cultural life of our community."

"Oh goodie, just what I wanted to know. The Sausalito Opera Society will be able to continue their 'Operas by the Bay' for the rest of my life. Eddie, take out your gun and shoot me, just shoot me now!"

Eddie shook his head. "Not in here, Holly, too many witnesses. I'll take you out back in the ally later and finish you off."

"Very funny, copper."

"Okay you two," Rob said. "I think we should go to Henrietta's funeral service. It would be interesting to see who shows up."

"I'll go, provided it's held somewhere near here," Holly announced quickly. "Now that I'm all grown-up, I suppose I feel bad for Henrietta—but not bad enough to drag myself up to Petaluma, or out to Walnut Creek."

"I suspect her service will be here," Eddie said. "Her husband's service was held up at the Episcopal Church on Santa Rosa Avenue, Marilyn said. Chances are her service will be there also."

"It would be nice for the three of us to attend a funeral service that doesn't involve someone who has been murdered," Rob said.

"Yeah," Eddie added. "No need to go snooping for clues, just three former students paying respects to their least favorite teacher. What could be nicer?"

For a few moments, the three of them were lost in their own recollections of the elementary school teacher whom many years earlier had caused each one of them several uneasy nights and stressful days.

"When we were kids, we would have all danced a jig to hear the Hammernator had died," Holly declared. "Now it doesn't seem like the right thing to do,"

"In time, we all grow up," Eddie said as he patted Holly's hand. "Even you, my dear."

"Not our Holly," Rob insisted. "She's like one of Peter Pan's gang! She'll never grow up."

"Very funny, you two," Holly said as she stuck her tongue out at both of them.

"It's strange at our age to think how terrified we once

were of old Henrietta," Rob said recalling some of his own difficult times.

"You're right," Eddie agreed. "And before long, we'll have kids of our own in the fifth grade. It all seems pretty silly now, but she certainly scared the bejesus out of us! The last thing you wanted to hear was your name coming out of her mouth. It made you hold your breath. And if you just got dropped off at school and your mom drove off with your homework assignment still sitting on the back seat of the car, you wanted to dig a hole and disappear into it!"

After another few moments of quiet reflection, Rob murmured, "But, really, was she as bad as all that?"

Eddie and Holly looked at each other. Then in unison, they nodded and said, "Yes!"

Rob raised the last of his beer and tipped his glass toward his two friends. "Here's to one of the few people who knew how to keep the three of us in line—no small accomplishment for a woman who was probably about five-five and maybe a hundred and ten pounds."

"I'm sure there was a lot more to her story than we ever imagined," Eddie said.

Holly raised a nearly empty martini glass and declared, "To Mrs. Hammer. Now that we're all grown up it's time to say, 'Henrietta, we hope you had a happy life.'"

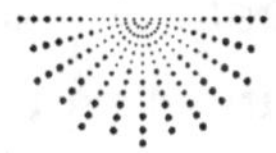

CHAPTER TWO

Christ Episcopal Church, often called, Sausalito's "Little Church on the Hill, sits high above the city's small downtown. The chapel, accented by dark woods and brightly colored stain glass windows, transports visitors back to the late Nineteenth Century.

The Wednesday morning service for Mrs. Hammer was a drab affair. After it concluded with Father Michael Louis speaking of the "generous gifts given to the church by Elijah and Henrietta during their years as members of the congregation," he invited attendees to, "share their memories of the dearly departed."

Few took the reverend up on his offer. Apparently, the dislike of Henrietta extended beyond her students, Holly thought as she squirmed uncomfortably in an old wooden pew sandwiched tightly between Rob and Eddie.

After a long, awkward silence, the principal of the local elementary school came forward and spoke briefly of

Henrietta's "consistent success in achieving the school's highest test scores."

"I'm not surprised by that," Rob whispered in Holly's ears. "I imagine she scared the bejesus out of her students. Some things never change."

Contrasting the principal's lack of fond memories, were the comments of representatives of the five local charities, all of which had their founders, presidents, directors and or board members in attendance.

Michael Palmer of the Marin Animal Rescue Shelter, MARS, spoke briefly of the constant support Henrietta gave to the society since the adoption of her beloved cat, at one of the society's fundraising luncheons. "At the time, Misty was just a ten-week-old kitten," the bespectacled, pinched-faced man explained. "That adorable kitten went on to have an eighteen-year friendship with the kind woman who welcomed an orphaned kitten into her home. I am told that on the day Henrietta left us, her faithful companion went in search of a neighbor for help. It's this kind of story that makes the hard work we do at the shelter so rewarding! Henrietta was devoted to the extraordinary creatures with which we share our increasingly fragile planet. She showed that devotion through her generous gifts to our annual fund."

Holly poked Rob in the ribs and muttered, "I wish she had adopted me! I would have been happy to be her faithful companion."

"Don't do anything to get us tossed out of here," Rob responded in a soft growl.

Palmer was followed by Amy Oliver, the newly elected president of the Sausalito Ladies of Liberty, SLOL, who commented on Henrietta's "kind and giving nature, her extraordinary leadership, and her unstinting generosity. I wish our founder, Mrs. Alma Samuels, could have been in attendance today, but she has been a bit under the weather."

"Most people nearing the age of one-hundred are," Eddie whispered into Holly's ear, which led to her guffaw and Rob squeezing her knee as a reminder to stay quiet.

Francis Phillips, the longtime executive director of the Sausalito Preservation League, SPL, followed. Rob stared up at the ceiling, praying silently that the usually long-winded Phillips would keep his comments brief.

"Henrietta Hammer's generous gift to the SPL's essential work will help safeguard the treasured history of our fragile community. She knew that the work we did today would determine how future generations valued the enduring but delicate fabric of our past."

"I hope they bring this to a close pretty soon," Eddie wrote in a note he passed to Rob.

"Supposedly they're serving sandwiches from Venice Gourmet in Campbell Hall after the service. Hang in there. Those guys have the best cold cuts in town," Rob wrote quickly on the flip side of Eddie's note, which he slipped to Holly, who in turn poked Eddie before handing it back.

Pulling Rob close, Holly said softly, "I'm not sure how much more of this I can stand."

Chris and Ruby Reese, husband and wife co-chairs of the Sausalito Fine Arts Board, SFAB, acknowledged Henrietta's "generous support," as well. Ruby, dressed dramatically in black leather pants, with a snug-fitting black blouse, wrapped in a dark red shawl, took the podium first. "We will always be grateful for Henrietta's unstinting generosity to Sausalito's artists' community. It helped to establish our organization as a source of funding for emerging artists," Ruby explained with an implacable smile.

Chris, the man Holly noticed outside the church taking a quick hit from a silver flask, followed with one brief comment: "Henrietta's support will help countless artists for generations to come. Along with my wife, I will forever cherish her memory."

Laurie Chase, founder and president of the Sausalito Opera Society, SOS, cried dramatically as she shared the details of her last meeting with her patroness; an encounter which occurred only three days before Henrietta's death. Pulling a long white handkerchief from the sleeve of a black velvet dress, Chase, a woman of substantial proportions, waved it about as though it was a flag signaling her surrender to a grief so powerful it could have been the finale of a grand opera.

"Our dearly departed patroness was determined to share the grandeur of opera with the masses," she intoned gravely. "If Henrietta were here today, she would insist I sing a few bars from the final moments of Tosca. Before hurling herself over the edge of the castle wall our beautiful heroine, having heard of the death of her brave hero sings, 'O Scarpia, Avanti a Dio!' which means, 'We shall meet before God!'"

Mourners familiar with Laurie's impromptu, but rarely requested, performances steeled themselves by taking a deep breath as the diva took one dramatic step closer to the congregation and began to sing.

Holly leaned into Rob and hissed, "This woman is Sausalito's Florence Foster Jenkins! If she goes on for more than two minutes, I'm out of here. There's only so much I can take!"

It took Laurie just a few minutes longer than Holly's stated time limit to conclude her performance before a captive audience, many of whom winced on more than one occasion.

Twice Rob and Eddie sensed Holly was ready to bolt from their pew. When she finally attempted to make her move both of them clasped Holly's arms below the elbow to hold her in place. Their quiet struggle went on until Chase's unrequested and unappreciated performance ended and the minister invited mourners to, "Step across the road to Campbell Hall for a luncheon buffet, which has been generously provided by Mrs. Hammer's devoted nephew, Scott Silva."

Eddie, Holly, and Rob joined the other congregants on the walkway outside the small church. They smiled and nodded as the last of the mourners headed across the narrow, winding road, which separated the church from the reception hall.

"I don't know about the two of you, but I'm ready for lunch," Rob said happily. "Let's go over, grab something to eat, and then take off."

"I'm up for that," Eddie replied.

The two of them started on their way toward the reception when Holly said, "I thought you two sports were going to treat me to lunch! It's the least you can do after manhandling me in there. You know, I might have suffered hearing loss because of that woman's bellowing."

"What did you say? I'm having a problem hearing you," Eddie said, unable to keep himself from laughing.

"Come on it will be fun," Rob added. "We haven't snooped around a funeral since the murder of our phantom photographer. We all need a little practice even if dear Henrietta died of natural causes."

"You sure this isn't just about the two of you being too cheap to buy me lunch."

"Us, cheap?" Eddie said, poking his finger into his chest. "Don't be ridiculous."

"You two really know how to show a girl a good time," Holly complained. But the two of them were already out of earshot hoping to make sure they hit the buffet before the roast beef, turkey, and ham disappeared.

Campbell Hall, an elegant space often used for a variety of community and church functions, looked particularly charming on this early May afternoon.

As with many of the town's vistas, the view from the reception hall's large brick patio was breathtaking. Devoid of fog that day, the hills surrounding Sausalito were etched sharply against a dark blue sky. Looking east across Richardson Bay, sailboats and the vast estates of Tiburon all sparkled in the noonday sun.

Inside, Scott Silva greeted mourners as they walked into the reception. All professed their grief over the loss of Scott's generous aunt.

The representatives of the five nonprofits the Hammers supported were, not surprisingly, the most effusive in their comments. They slowed the reception line considerably as

Eddie, Rob, and Holly anxiously eyed a remarkably generous buffet of sandwich meats, sliced cheese, fruit, accompanied by a wide variety of dessert plates.

Eddie extended his hand to Scott, explaining briefly that he was a detective with the Marin County Sheriff's Department adding, "The reason I'm here today is your aunt was one of my favorite elementary school teachers," Rob explained. Additionally, as the publisher of The Sausalito Standard, he was hoping to do a profile on Henrietta.

Holly explained she too was a "pupil of Mrs. Hammer's, but I was her student many years after Eddie and Rob."

After speaking briefly with Scott, Holly reached the buffet table just as Rob and Eddie were leaving it. Their plates were filled with thick sandwiches they had hungrily slapped together.

Rob's already had a bite missing "Quite the spread!" he exclaimed, through a mouthful of turkey, ham, and cheese.

Eddie nodded. "All these different slices of bread! The ham is outstanding!"

"Venice Gourmet has the best cheeses," Rob added, as he took another large bite.

Holly rolled her eyes. "My God, you two will do anything for a free meal. How do you both manage to stay so thin?"

"Pickup basketball games two-nights a week," Eddie explained. "Try the coleslaw!" He pointed to it then gave a thumbs-up.

"The potato salad is killer too," Rob added enthusiastically.

Holly shrugged. "Yeah, yeah, okay. But first I'm going to go wander around. There's got to be something better for me to do here than watch you two polish off an entire table of food."

Holly was circling the room when she spotted Ruby Reese.

Why does she look so familiar? Holly wondered. Then it hit her:

My God, that's Ruby Smoot! Well, she's undoubtedly upped her game from the ten-year-old who loved putting black ribbons in her dark red hair.

Holly walked up behind Ruby and tapped her on the shoulder.

Ruby looked her up and down, but there wasn't a glimmer of recognition. Finally, she murmured, "Have we met before?"

"It's Holly. Holly Cross. We were together in Mrs. Hammer's class."

"Oh yes, of course! It's wonderful to see you again." Ruby grabbed Chris's arm. Pulling him in close, she announced, "This is my husband, Chris."

Holly smiled as she took the gaunt man's hand. Her brain flashed, oddball, but her warm smile hid that reaction.

"Chris, you should join my friends who are standing by the buffet table. Rob Timmons and Eddie Austin, they're both a lot of fun," Holly added, thinking he could use a good meal. "That would give your wife and me a chance to catch up, I don't think we've seen each other in more than twenty years!"

"That's okay," Chris said. "I think I'll go outside and enjoy the sun on the patio."

Ruby grimaced as a sign of disappointment, but Chris

ignored her reaction and took the opportunity to avoid chatting with Holly, or any of the other guests.

"I had no idea you're an artist." Holly declared.

"I'm not, I'm a supporter of the arts. Chris is the artist in the family. He's a sculptor, and a painter—just a pure soul!"

Holly nodded. "What's the focus of his work?"

"Like all the best artists, his passion is for the world around him. He loves to paint everything Sausalito! The houseboats, the headlands, the bay waters, and the people. We have such interesting people living here! Chris is a very creative soul. Henrietta was quite taken with him."

"Sausalito is such a small town, I'm surprised in all these years we haven't run into each other," Holly said.

"After college, I moved to San Diego. It's where I met Chris. I didn't move back here until two years ago."

"Was it strange reconnecting with Mrs. Hammer? As I recall you weren't one of her favorites."

Ruby's eyes narrowed. "As I recall, neither were you."

"To be honest, I'm not sure Mrs. Hammer had any favorites. I don't know if I even saw her much around town over the years since she was our teacher. I thought maybe she just came out for Halloween."

"Holly, really? How immature! Surely, your opinion of her must have changed since we were children."

"Not really. I didn't give her a thought for years until I heard she had died. How did you reconnect with her?"

"Henrietta was very interested in supporting the work of local artists. She helped Chris with the purchase of several of his works. Henrietta did the same for many others," Ruby explained. "She suggested we consider starting the fine arts board, as a private, nonprofit organization. The city's art commission fell apart after all that unpleasantness with Grant Randolph, the commission chair, and the murder of Warren Bradley. With her backing FAB has been a great success. Have you attended one of our open studio events?"

Holly shook her head. "I work such long weeks. By Friday night I'm ready to tune out the world. I go to my yoga class on Saturday, take a hike or a bike ride on Sunday, and get ready for work again on Monday."

"Where do you work?" Ruby asked attempting to show interest in someone she had no interest in.

"I'm the number two person at Standard Community Newspapers."

Ruby shrugged dismissively. "Oh yes, the Sausalito newspaper."

"Along with weekly editions in Mill Valley, Tiburon, and Ross Valley. So much news, so little time."

"We always list open studios in your newspaper's event calendar. You should come sometime to one of our events," Ruby suggested.

"I'll certainly do that," Holly replied with a smile, doubting she ever would.

As if reading her mind, Ruby declared, "I'm glad we had a few moments to reconnect. I better find Chris. We have another commitment this afternoon. Come to one of the studio events and be sure to say hello to us when you do." Ruby gave Holly a quick hug, an air kiss, and then walked quickly away.

She turned into a cold fish Holly thought, as she watched Ruby fade into the crowd. To hear Ruby speak so highly of Henrietta, who as Holly recalled was number two behind Billy Muntz on their late teacher's least favorite student list, was unexpected. Holly wondered how many sticks of chalk Ruby went through writing, "I must not talk in class," countless times on the blackboard.

***

"God," Eddie said as he patted his stomach, "I think I ate too much!"

Rob groaned in agreement. He pulled at the belt on his pants and backed it off by a notch. "Tell me about it! Those lemon tarts on the dessert tray were to die for."

"Poor choice of words, pal."

"I hope you two had enough to eat," a voice said from behind them.

Eddie and Rob turned around to find a heavyset older woman picking up their used plates. She had a pale complexion, but her cheeks had a healthy pink glow.

"I'm Eddie Austin—"

"...and I'm Rob Timmons," the two well-fed mourners said, as they put their hands out.

"I'm Eloise. I was Mrs. Hammer's housekeeper. I enjoy seeing two young men with healthy appetites," she said in a noticeable Swedish accent.

"Well," Eddie said, with a laugh, "follow the two of us around, and you'll see a lot of healthy eating. I hope we didn't take more than our fair share."

"Don't worry about it. Most of these people eat like birds," Eloise said as she waved her hand at the nearby crowd.

"I was up at Mrs. Hammer's home the day she died, I'm a

detective with the county sheriff's department. "I didn't see you there."

The woman shook her head and looked down. "I wish I had been. Fridays have always been my one day off."

"Well, from what we could tell Mrs. Hammer died very quickly. Most likely, there would have been nothing you could have done."

"I understand," Eloise said as she pulled a handkerchief out from her sleeve and dabbed her eyes. "Probably, that is true. Still, I would like to have been there with her. She was always very kind to me. Very kind."

Having said that, Eloise smiled, nodded, and walked off.

"Wow," Rob said, breaking their momentary silence. "I never thought of Henrietta as being kind to anyone. I suppose there was a side to her we kids never recognized."

"Maybe as fifth graders, we weren't all that good at assessing a person's character," Eddie said as he gave his best friend a light punch in the arm. "We should do a little floating around, Rob. I don't want people thinking we came here only for the food."

"But we did!"

"Sure, but we don't have to make it that obvious!"

The first person they came upon was Francis Phillips. He was a head shorter than Eddie and Rob, both of whom stood six-three. His frame was slight, but his stomach slipped over the black belt he wore against a neatly pressed pair of beige slacks. He wore a white shirt, thin black tie, and a black jacket, hoping that was enough black for a somber occasion. Wisps of his blond hair stood straight up on his head, defiant of the slick gel he used to tamp it down.

After introductions, Rob said, "Sad occasion."

"Sad indeed," Phillips intoned. "Mrs. Hammer's legacy gift to the Sausalito Preservation League, if it indeed comes our way, will help us accomplish several goals. Most importantly, assisting us in safeguarding the community's historical treasures and preserving Sausalito's small-town character."

Phillips' remarks were a rehash of those he had made less than an hour earlier from the pulpit. Rob had heard many of these same preservation pitches over the years.

Amy Oliver joined their threesome. After introductions, she too emphasized, mostly for Rob's benefit, the significance of Henrietta's financial support of the Ladies of Liberty.

"So, the five organizations represented here today were all supported by Mrs. Hammer?" Eddie asked Phillips and Oliver, already knowing the answer.

"Indeed," Oliver responded enthusiastically.

"And I imagine there will likely be an additional bequest from the Hammer estate providing for the future support of your organizations?" Eddie asked.

"We certainly hope so, detective!" Phillips exclaimed with an awkward laugh. He looked to Oliver, who quickly nodded in agreement.

Rob thought things were going from bad to worse when Laurie Chase joined their foursome. She had a cherub's smiling face, green eyes, a dramatic sweep of brown hair, which seemed a bit overdone considering her modest stature.

After introductions, Chase placed both her hands on Rob's forearm and pulled him closer to her. "Henrietta's sudden death is like a great operatic tragedy," Laurie opined in a whisper.

"How so?" Rob asked, immediately regretting he had.

"Well everyone thinks she died of something so mundane as a stroke, but in classic opera, she would have been poisoned by a jealous lover or a greedy, wicked man."

Rob smiled innocently, but could not help imagine how much better a lead story Henrietta's murder would have made. Nevertheless, he resisted adding fuel to Laurie's already overactive imagination.

When Laurie offered to favor the group with a piece written by Verdi, Rob immediately declared, "I don't think that will be necessary. But thank you for treating us to your gifted voice during the church service, your performance was one I'll long remember."

"You're too kind, dear sir!" Laurie said flirtatiously. I hope Henrietta is in heaven now listening to performances by Maria Callas and Luciano Pavarotti. She and her husband were incredibly generous souls. I don't know what we will do without them."

Probably live off of the money Henrietta gifted you, Eddie thought while presenting a sympathetic smile and nodding his approval.

"Did she support any other nonprofit groups?" Rob asked suspecting he knew the answer, but knowing it never hurt to dig.

"You see those two gentlemen over there" Phillips nodded toward the two undistinguished looking men. They were dressed in nearly matching dark gray suits. "They're here representing the Animal Rescue Shelter. Mrs. Hammer has been a loyal supporter of their organization as well."

"The kitten that laid the golden egg, you might say," Amy Oliver added in what sounded to Eddie like a soft growl. Suddenly, her eyes widened—proof she immediately regretted her quip regarding Hammer's support of the county's animal shelter.

⁂

Holly made a quick stop at the buffet table, curious to see what if anything was left of the food after the twin tornadoes, Rob and Eddie, touched down.

Not much, apparently.

Sighing, she turned back toward the gathering—only to bump into Scott Silva.

"Hi, Scott. I'm Holly Cross," she smiled as she reintroduced herself and thrust her hand forward.

Holly guessed Scott to be in his mid-forties, but he had a handsome face and a youthful vigor that made it hard to be sure. He had thick blond hair and dark blue eyes, which Holly thought were features that must have come from his mother's side of the family. Indeed, he was more Swedish than his Portuguese surname would cause one to believe. To this day, Holly remembered one of Mrs. Hammer's lessons on geography, where she explained that her family came from a fishing village along the western coast of Sweden. She turned the giant globe on her desk and pointed with one of her long fingers to the town and said a name Holly thought would be impossible to pronounce.

"Thanks for coming," Scott said, as he shook Holly's hand. "Do you live here?"

"Yes, I'm one of a vanishing breed: born and raised in Sausalito. That's how I came to have your aunt as one of my elementary school teachers. Most of the locals have cashed out over the last couple of decades as property values went through the roof."

"I've seen home prices go crazy in Pasadena as well."

"Is that where you grew up?"

"Partially. I was born in Fort Bragg, along the Mendocino County coast. That's where my mom, Ruth, and my aunt Henrietta were born and raised."

Holly nodded. "I've been up there several times. I love it along the north coast! Just as pretty as the Marin County coast with a lot fewer people and tourists."

"My mom was just a couple of years older than Henrietta," Scott explained. "Their dad was a minister sent by his church in Sweden to help tame the frontier—or at least that's how Europeans thought of it back then. My mom and dad moved to Pasadena before I turned ten."

"I heard you teach at Marin Academy, up in San Rafael. What do you teach?"

"I'm the math guy."

Holly laughed. "I was terrible at math."

"I hear that from a lot of people. But numbers can be fascinating if you spend some time learning how to use them to your advantage. Anyway, I taught at a private prep school in Pasadena but got an offer to come up to Marin Academy. It was a chance to be closer to my aunt and uncle, and I have always loved this part of California."

"Is there a Mrs. Silva?" Holly asked boldly.

Scott laughed, wondering if the attraction he felt was mutual. "Not yet. And is there a Mr. Cross?"

"There was," Holly purred. "But my father passed away several years ago."

Hearing this, Scott's grin grew even wider. Somewhat embarrassed by his reaction, he rushed to say, "I'm sorry to hear that."

Holly blushed, as she considered unexpected possibilities.

All too soon, Rob and Eddie appeared.

"Oh, there you are," Rob said. He held out his hand to Scott. "Thank you for hosting this gathering. By the way, Holly and I work together, Rob Timmons."

Scott shook his hand then turned with an extended hand to Eddie as well.

"Eddie Austin. I'm with the Marin County Sheriff's Department.

"They also had Mrs. Hammer in school—many years ago," Holly explained. "Long before me. I was in Kindergarten when Rob and Eddie were in the fifth grade."

Scott nodded. "It's great to meet some of Henrietta's students. I'd only met one other—Ruby Reese, the one with the arts group."

"Ruby Reese and I were classmates," Holly announced. "

" I understand you're living up here now, working at Marin Academy," Eddie said.

"Yes. I'm the lead teacher for the school's math department."

"Marin Academy has a great reputation," Rob added.

"From everything I've seen it's a well-run school. I've been happy there. And it was nice having a chance this past year to reconnect with my aunt. I was sorry to lose her. It happened so soon after Uncle Elijah died."

"Scott, why do you say a chance to reconnect?" Holly asked.

"My mom and Henrietta never got along. I have no idea why. I think things unraveled when my parents left Fort Bragg."

Rob, Eddie, and Holly nodded but said nothing. The thought occurred to each of them that Scott's mother had as difficult a time staying on Henrietta's good side as they did as children.

Rob's way of covering the awkward silence was to declare, "I'm doing a story about your aunt for next week's edition of The Sausalito Standard. Any chance you have some old photos of your aunt as a kid, or as a young woman?"

"There's not much in the way of photos that I recall. As I said, my mother and Henrietta were estranged. If they exist, I suspect they haven't seen the light of day in many years."

After a pause, Scott added, "After my Uncle Elijah died, Henrietta asked if I would help her clean out that huge house she lived in for so many years."

"Was she planning on getting a smaller place?" Holly asked.

"Absolutely. With no kids of their own, I'm amazed they stayed in that huge place as long as they did. Anyway, I'm going to clean it out so the estate can get ready to put it on the market. Have any of you ever been to her house?"

Holly, Rob, and Eddie all shook their heads to indicate they had not as each of them felt a shiver go down their spines over the very idea.

"This weekend, I was planning to start the job of

cleaning out the place. I'm happy to share any old photos I come across. You can take your pick."

"So, I guess you've been up there?" Eddie asked.

"I have, but only a handful of times."

"Cleaning out that place is going to be a big job," Holly said. "I'd be happy to help if you think I could be of any use."

"That would be great," Scott replied quickly. "I'm still not sure how many rooms are in the old place. The good news is I don't think either of them was pack rats. At least I hope not. I've been in the downstairs, but never in any of the bedrooms upstairs. In any event, with a house that size, you're right in saying it will be a big job."

"I have no doubt it will be a lot of work," Rob said. "But it would be great if you could find any old photos. So many people in this town knew your aunt, I bet they'd enjoy seeing photos of her that go back to when she was a child and a young woman."

"Was she popular with her students?" Scott asked.

All three of them hesitated in offering an answer.

"That's a long story, which we should leave for another day," Eddie explained as he glanced down at his watch. "Look at the time, all of us should be getting back to work."

"I'm sorry for the loss of your aunt. She was a wonderful person." Holly said as she held onto Scott's arm and raised herself up on her toes to pull Scott down for a kiss on the check.

Just as the three of them were about to leave, an older woman approached in a rush. She had a full head of white hair, bright dark eyes, and red lipstick that looked as if it had been applied too quickly. The woman was wearing a simple black dress adorned with a string of pink pearls. In a nearly frantic voice, she asked, "Are you, Scott?"

Before Scott could answer, the woman offered a quick apology. "I'm sorry to have arrived so late! Traffic coming down Highway 101 from Santa Rosa was just awful! My name is Jeannie Newberry." She took a needed moment to catch her breath. "Your mother Ruth and I were friends in high school. In fact, your aunt Henrietta and I shared an apartment when she was a student at Santa Rosa College, studying for her teaching certificate. I was afraid I'd miss you altogether," she quickly added, sticking out her hand to shake Scott's as she gulped in another breath.

Scott seemed flustered by the woman's sudden appearance. By the way he looked at her, it was apparent she was not someone he recalled. Nevertheless, he said, "It was very nice of you to come all this way. I'm sorry you missed the service, but please come and have something to eat and we can visit for a while."

Scott introduced the woman to Holly, Rob, and Eddie. They quickly made their apologies for not being able to stay longer, explaining that they were already late getting back to their jobs.

Feeling bad for the woman, Holly offered to make her a plate of food. Quickly, she made her way over to the buffet table.

Eddie said his goodbyes and hurried off.

For a moment, there was an awkward silence. Scott filled it by asking, "Ms. Newberry, has it been a long time since you've seen my aunt?"

She nodded. "No, my dear, not that long. We had lunch together up in Petaluma about six months ago."

Holly returned with a plate holding a few remaining scraps along with some bread and a few pieces of fruit. "There wasn't much left, Ms. Newberry. Some people have pretty big appetites," Holly said, eyeing Rob, who returned an innocent shrug.

"That's alright, dear. I came to pay my condolences, but I appreciate your effort." She said, turning back to Scott. "I'm sorry I missed the service, but I am so pleased I have this chance to spend a little time with you! I remember how excited your mother and your aunt were when you were born. You were their prince!" She shook her head sadly. "I'm so sorry you've now lost them both."

Rob stepped in, putting a firm hand on Holly's arm, "I'm sorry, Ms. Newberry, but I'm going to have to steal Holly away. Our weekly deadlines are unforgiving. I do want to write a feature story for our Sausalito edition on Henrietta as I told Scott just before you arrived. Could you write down your contact information on the back of my card and we'll be in touch in a few days." Rob handed her a pen.

Newberry nodded. Writing down her phone number and name, she handed the card back to Rob. "Feel free to call me anytime. I'd be happy to tell you all I know about Henrietta and her sister Ruth."

CHAPTER THREE

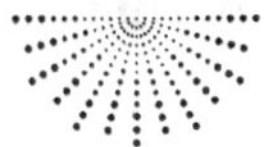

Two days later, at Smitty's on Friday evening, Holly suspected she would be the target of teasing by both Rob and Eddie.

Eddie was the first to raise his glass. "Here's to our dear Holly and her future happiness."

Not missing a beat Rob added, "Here's to the future mistress of Henrietta's haunted house."

"I was sure you two were going to gang up on me for offering to do a simple kindness: helping Scott clean out his aunt's humongous house. I'm just trying to be kind, you know!"

"She's a saint, this one is," Eddie said taking his first big gulp of Guinness and trying out, for the umpteenth time, his faux British accent.

"A saint! You're certainly right about that, governor." Rob said, tipping his glass in another toast.

"What is it about drinking Guinness that gets you two going with your awful British accents?" Holly asked.

"Don't know, love. Just seems to be part of the experience," Eddie responded.

"I hope we don't have the wrong end of the stick, dearie," Rob said with a mischievous smile.

"Well, knock it off. It's annoying."

"Oh, come on Holly," Rob pleaded. "You've got to admit you were laying it on pretty thick up there."

Eddie chimed in with an awful impersonation of Holly: "'Let me help you with that, Scotty!'"

As Holly took the first sip of her Friday night martini, she replied, "I did no such thing!"

Eddie put down his nearly finished Guinness and signaled to Gail for another. Then, flipping open his notebook, he read, "Holly Cross, last Friday night at this very establishment, you expressed a theory that the decedent, one Henrietta Hammer, had likely been murdered by a former pupil. One possible suspect, a former student and classmate, Billy Muntz." Eddie pointed to a random blank page in his notebook and continued. "You further referred to the late Henrietta Hammer as, and I quote, 'the Hammernator.' Just forty-eight hours ago, you told the victim's nephew, one Scott Silva, that the decedent was, and I quote, 'A wonderful woman.'" With that Eddie flipped his notebook closed and placed it back in his jacket.

"Are the taxpayers of this county well served by the amount of time you spend scribbling notes in that little notebook of yours?" Holly asked.

"That's for my boss, Sheriff Jack Canning to decide," Eddie countered.

"Alright, you two! Holly was just her usual sweet, helpful self." Rob said.

"That's one theory," Eddie said with a raised eyebrow. "But, I would suggest to the jury that her motives are suspect in the presence of a gentleman whose name is likely to appear in the will of a very wealthy woman."

"No such thought ever occurred to me," Holly replied. "Since when is it wrong to be helpful to someone in need?"

"If that's your story, that you're simply doing an act of kindness, I'll let you off with a warning this time," Eddie said. "But if you become the queen of Hammer Manor, you're going to have several more questions to answer."

Rob shook his head. "Now that we've had our fun at Holly's expense, let me ask you both a question. Was I the only one who noticed that everyone at the reception, other than the three of us and that Newberry woman, had an interest in the disposition of Henrietta's will?"

Holly nodded. "It made me feel like the only people she socialized with had their hands out for a donation. Not that I can't say the same thing about myself. I was thinking how much better off I would have been had I been her faithful companion instead of that cat of hers."

"Don't feel bad about that, Holly," Eddie said. "Having money can make life a lot easier than not having money. We're not the only ones to feel that way. That's why millions of lottery tickets are sold every day. The word jackpot certainly catches our attention."

"You have a lot better chance of having money when you're around people who have money," Rob added.

"What did the two of you think of Francis Phillips?" Eddie asked.

"Gave me the creeps," Rob and Holly said in unison and then laughed over their identical assessment.

"This town has a long history of con men coming here and saying they want to save the 'unique character of this special place,' when what they're really looking to do is line their pockets with a good chunk of whatever they can fleece people for in the name of preservation," Rob explained.

"And that guy, Chris Reese?" Eddie continued.

Holly and Rob looked at each other, then back at Eddie. "Even creepier," Rob muttered.

Holly nodded in agreement.

"And that opera diva, Laurie Chase?" Eddie asked.

"That one I'd say is more crazy than creepy," Holly replied.

"Ditto," Rob added.

"And then, of course, there's Alma's latest lap dog, the lovely Amy Oliver," Eddie said.

"She's just another run of the mill, Ladies of Liberty, social butterfly," Rob replied. "Whenever old Alma Samuels says jump, Amy has only one question, 'How high?'"

"I would agree. She's a bit on the mousey side, but I wouldn't turn my back on her," Holly declared.

"Our dear departed teacher kept quite a collection of friends," Eddie said as he finished his second Guinness.

"You're thinking one of them knocked off old Henrietta, aren't you?" Holly asked, looking carefully at Eddie and moving her chair a little closer.

"Well, it's certainly possible. You're always going to think twice when there's a rogues' gallery of suspects standing to benefit from the death of their patroness. Don't either of you ever read any cozy mysteries?" Eddie asked, shaking his head while both Rob and Holly gave a shrug. "At that reception, I kept thinking of the board game we always played as kids. You know, the one with the professor in the kitchen with the wrench. All of them had a motive—and, I suspect, numerous opportunities."

"But you could probably say that about a lot of friends of old rich people," Holly said.

"I agree to an extent," Eddie replied. "But this group struck me as particularly untrustworthy."

"I thought you said that there was not going to be an autopsy," Rob reminded Eddie.

"Max Brownstein, the county's medical examiner, has been on vacation. He's always the curious one when it comes to each and every death. I think he dissects frogs on slow days, although I've never gotten him to admit it."

"What happened when they brought her body up to the morgue?" Rob asked.

"I didn't follow the disposition of it, but like I said last week, I'm quite sure her body was processed through normal channels by the coroner. I doubt that the guy who works under Max, the assistant ME looked at her or at the coroner's report."

"According to the program notes handed out at her service," Rob offered, "Henrietta was scheduled for burial up at Mount Tamalpais Cemetery after the service on Wednesday."

"If we can show some cause to actually suspect that Henrietta's death was not the result of natural causes, I'm sure we can get Max's office to go along with a court order to have her dug up."

Holly finished the last of her martini and started on a second. Stirring her fresh cocktail with a long toothpick that anchored three oversized olives, she added, "I don't like the smell of this whole thing."

Rob chuckled. "Must we remind you that you were having an affair with a guy who was later convicted of murder? I think your nose for sniffing out a killer might be a little suspect at this point."

"Amen to that," Eddie added clinking glasses with Rob.

Holly rolled her eyes. "Let a girl make one little mistake, and you two never let her forget."

"That was one hell of a little mistake!" Eddie said in a louder voice than he intended.

Rob looked around to see if anyone had noticed Eddie's comment. Apparently not. "Wouldn't it be cool if the three of us, all of whom at one time or another, thought of killing our fifth-grade teacher, unraveled a more sinister cause of death?"

Eddie snorted. "Sounds like you're already dreaming up a front-page story. What's wrong, Rob? Getting tired of stories about drunk tourists falling off the town's ferry dock?"

"You have to admit, Henrietta getting knocked off by a greedy beneficiary in waiting would be one heck of a story," Rob said as he finished the last of his second Guinness. "But where would we start?"

"Holly, are you still meeting Scott tomorrow to help him get started on cleaning out Hammer's place?" Eddie asked.

"Yup. We're meeting up there at eleven."

"Start snooping. And be sure to write down some notes when you get home." Eddie said as he pulled his notebook out of his jacket pocket. "Believe me, it helps you to keep track of all those little details you might overlook or simply forget."

"Henrietta is going to stay dead and buried unless we find something that looks suspicious enough to get her dug back up and given a second look," Rob added.

"Second look?" Eddie said with a laugh. "I'm guessing she barely got a first look!"

"Okay, I'm in," Holly said. "It's really kind of ironic when you think about it."

"What is?" Eddie asked.

"All the nights we lost sleep wondering what kind of trouble we'd be in the following day when Mrs. Hammer went over our test pages or our homework. Now it might be us who disturb her eternal rest."

"If she was given a shove into the great beyond," Rob said, "she would be thankful to us for raising relevant questions."

"Rob, if someone nailed Mrs. Hammer," Holly suggested, "that's a story that will keep our readers coming back."

"I like that," Eddie said. "Nailing Mrs. Hammer."

"Good. So we're all in," Rob said. "One last homework assignment from our old teacher; find out who killed me and why?"

CHAPTER FOUR

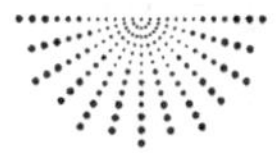

Scott was fumbling his way through a set of keys when Holly's aging white Honda Civic pulled into the circular driveway to Henrietta's home the following morning.

She had dressed casually, but with care. Her usual Saturday attire—jeans, tennis shoes, and a loose-fitting flannel shirt—had been replaced by a form-fitting black sweater atop her best jeans, and beige kitten-heel slingbacks.

After the teasing she took from Eddie and Rob the previous night, she was reluctant to admit to herself the attraction she felt for Scott. Did it have anything to do with the possibility that Henrietta's only nephew might receive a significant bequest from his aunt and uncle's estate? Of course not, she angrily told herself.

As she walked closer, she noticed how Scott's light blue cotton sweater matched the color of his eyes. In spite of his age, he had a youthful, vigorous demeanor. His horn-rimmed glasses complemented his position as an academic. His thick blond hair no doubt had thinned a bit on top, but despite his subdued appearance, it was apparent that he must have been a strikingly handsome young man.

Had he never been married? Is he indeed interested in women? What is his real story? Those questions and others raced through Holly's mind.

Scott, who looked up and gave her a welcoming wave. "Right on time. This is so nice of you to help."

Holly glanced up at the house that frightened her as a kid. Children knew to keep clear of the place for fear of running afoul of their current, future, or former teacher. Nearly all of them were convinced the house was haunted. If you were a witch, a ghost, or a ghoul, they reasoned, this house would certainly meet your needs.

Holly wondered if Henrietta, with a carefully prepared basket of treats, waited each Halloween for the doorbell to ring. She felt certain only a handful of children, likely prompted by a dare, would have knocked on the dark gray front door with the imposing brass knocker.

Scott finally hit on the right key. Suddenly, the aging door opened emitting an angry creak.

Naturally, a chill ran down Holly's spine. To offset the reluctance she felt, Holly's first instinct was to make a joke. But she resisted. Instead, she said, "I'm sure we'll have a lot to do, this is a big place. Although I've never seen Mrs. Hammer's home from the inside."

As Scott took her on a tour of the downstairs, Holly felt increasingly foolish that she'd allowed her childhood fears to fill her with such trepidation.

The house's large windows filled it with light and afforded it straight-on views of the bay. The high-ceiling foyer led to a spacious living room—perfect for accommodating a growing family.

When Holly walked through the kitchen, Holly saw a small table for days when the formal dining room was not needed, Holly thought of Misty, meowing over her mistress' lifeless body. Thank goodness Mrs. Roswell came to investigate. Who knows how long Henrietta might have laid here?

The home's tidiness prompted Holly to ask, "Is the housekeeper, Eloise, still working here? I met her after the service on Wednesday. "

"No. But she kept it neat as a pin. And no one has been inside since she locked up the place the afternoon of the funeral. I hope Henrietta left her something generous in her will. She was a hard worker and very loyal."

Even though the furniture had been dusted and tidied, the floors vacuumed and cleaned, there was still a feeling of decline and decay about the place.

"Gosh, I had nightmares about being in this house when I was ten," Holly said as she quickly regretted her candor.

"Why is that?" Scott asked.

"Well, let's just say your aunt wasn't the type of teacher you wanted to disappoint—you know, forgetting to bring in a homework assignment on its due date, doing poorly on a quiz, that kind of stuff."

"I never thought about whether she was popular or not with her students," Scott said. "I saw her so rarely as a kid. And after my parents moved to Pasadena, I hardly saw her at all. I never knew what happened between Henrietta and my mother, Ruth. But it must have been pretty bad considering how many years they were estranged."

"They never reconciled?"

"Not from what I know. My mom passed a couple of years ago. She never reached out to her sister before she died. Weird, I know."

"I wonder what drove them apart," Holly murmured.

"I should know more about that. I tried broaching the subject with Mom on a couple of occasions, but she didn't want to talk about Henrietta. She waved me away and just said, 'I don't want to talk about that ridiculous woman.' Odd, huh? I have to admit I was curious, but, in time, I just let it go. I'm a lot better at figuring out math equations than reasoning out why people behave as they do."

Holly continued to follow close behind Scott as he showed her the downstairs library, the formal living room, the solarium, and the formal dining room. Each room had been painted in various shades of green, gray, or rose. Wisely, this was mitigated by white ceiling molding, wainscoting, or both.

A long rectangular table made of dark mahogany dominated the dining room. A dozen high back wooden chairs surrounded it. Two tall display cabinets, filled with expensive looking china pieces faced each other from opposite walls. Two crystal chandeliers hung over the table.

Holly was surprised by the degree of elegance. This room could have been used for one of the sets in Downton Abby, she thought. "I suppose they entertained a lot," she offered.

"Not from what I could tell," Scott replied with a shrug.

"Perhaps in earlier times. In any event, they certainly accumulated a lot of things during the forty-five years of their marriage. You'll better appreciate my point when I take you upstairs."

Holly stepped carefully, as she followed Scott up the long straight staircase. She winced each time one of the steps creaked, precisely as they did in nightmares she'd had of being held prisoner here: a fitting punishment, she reasoned, for not bringing in her homework in on time.

Only one of the upstairs rooms looked like Scott's aunt, and uncle regularly occupied it. One, perhaps on occasion, while two others were set up as guest bedrooms. And it appeared to have gone untouched for years.

Holly found it hard to imagine a home this large with so much unused space. One room, devoid of furniture except for a table in its center had been set up to accommodate a variety of wrapping papers, folded boxes, ribbons, and gift notes.

Holly whistled. "Your aunt must have been big on buying and giving gifts to have a wrapping room like this."

"Not that I ever saw," Scott said with a shrug as he turned in a circle while standing in the room's center. "I remember a fire engine she gave me when I was six, maybe seven. I kept it for years on a shelf. It was a cool toy! It had lights, a siren, and even a ladder that went up and down. But no gifts ever came after that, not for me or my parents."

"Something must have happened between Henrietta and your mom. Being a kid at the time you probably paid little attention to anything adults were talking about."

"There were times I wondered about it as a teen, but

you're right, as a child I never gave it a second thought. I pressed my mom about it a couple of times. She would just sigh and say, 'life is complicated.' It was pretty clear she wanted to leave it at that. From that point on I thought it best that I mind my own business."

The final upstairs room served as a private den, with bookshelves, a fireplace, and a stereo system.

"Well this looks like a cozy room," Holly suggested. "It strikes me as a hideaway."

"I agree. It's less formal than many of the other rooms. I wonder if this was my uncle's favorite room. Maybe his man cave."

"Do you think they were a happy couple?"

"Sometimes I wonder if there is such a thing." By Scott's half smile, it was evident he was only partially joking.

Holly let the comment pass and thought it better to stay on point.

"Would you like to live here one day?"

"I don't have any plans to do that. It's been a busy month at school. I'm sharing in an honors project with the chair of the health sciences department. We're working with our students on understanding the statistical likelihood of different genetic strains revealing themselves."

Boring, was Holly's first thought, but she resisted the temptation she felt to express that opinion.

"So, what will happen to this old place?"

"Nate Beasley, my aunt and uncle's attorney asked me to keep an eye on the place. We've only been in touch by phone. Henrietta gave him my phone number in the event of an emergency, and he contacted me the afternoon that she passed. For now, I can't imagine that I would ever live here. I know nothing about any provision in her will as to what she wanted to do with this place. Even if she gifted it to me, the stepped-up property taxes would likely be a good deal more than my annual salary."

"Really?"

"I'm sure that Elijah and Henrietta had an annual tax bill that's a fraction of what it will soon be. It's called a stepped-up basis or something like that. California properties are heavily restricted in how much their property taxes can rise until such time that homeowners move away or die. You can pass on your property but not your vastly reduced tax bill. I would guess that a place this size is going to be valued in the ten million dollar range in today's market. When all is said and done, the new owner, nephew or stranger, is going to have an eye-popping tax bill. Anyway, what does a single man need with all this space?

My mom told me that her sister lived in this big house because when they bought it, they were both in their thirties, and planned on having a big family. Therefore, the five bedrooms."

"Wow, I never thought of Henrietta as a parent! All the kids thought that she slept in a crypt!" Seeing Scott's shocked face, she added, " I mean—well..."

"I think what you're trying to tell me is that the kids were scared to death of Henrietta."

"That's one way to put it," Holly said softly, relieved that Scott didn't appear offended by her comment. "Your mom ever say anything about why your aunt and uncle never started a family?"

"Not a word. I never asked Henrietta about it. I figured it was none of my business. But it seems logical that at one time they must have planned a big family. They certainly didn't buy a place this size because they were thinking of taking in borders."

Scott and Holly looked around at the expansive master bedroom taking note of the scope of the project before them. Many of the deceased couple's belongings seemed decades old.

Finally, Holly said, "I know you want to clean out the place. Any idea where you want to start?"

Scott sighed. "Their bedroom is as good a place to start as any. Let me run out to the car. I loaded the back seat, and the trunk with boxes folded down flat."

Left alone in her deceased teacher's bedroom increased Holly's sense of discomfort. She was determined, however, to follow through on her commitment to help. Besides, there was a certain perverse joy in cleaning out the belongings of the woman who once told her she was, "A disappointment in so many ways!"

When Scott returned, he found Holly opening the master bedroom's double door closet. "Any idea what you're going to do with her coats, dresses, jackets, shoes, and all this other stuff?" Holly asked.

"Not really. Do you want any of it?"

Holly laughed. "Thanks, but no. I'm not into vintage clothing." She opened another closet. It held Elijah's ties, shirts, suits, leisure clothes, and shoes.

"Wow!" Scott exclaimed. "I guess it was wishful thinking on my part to imagine that my aunt would have cleaned out a lot of this stuff in the time between my uncle's death and her own. It looks like I'm going to be making a lot of trips to the Salvation Army, Goodwill, and anyone else interested in having this stuff."

"There are some very nice vintage pieces here. You should check with one of the consignment shops that benefit various groups. For example, Repeat Performance, on Fillmore Street in the city supports the San Francisco Symphony."

"That's a smart idea. I guess we can start by boxing up some of this stuff. What's the ancient Chinese wisdom?" Scott asked.

"The longest journey begins with the first step?" Holly responded.

Scott smiled and nodded. "Let the journey begin."

Two hours later, over a dozen boxes had been packed and sealed. Scott and Holly both felt somewhat discouraged knowing they'd barely made a dent given the size of the house and all Elijah and Henrietta had accumulated over the years.

They separated donations from other things they considered to be of little or any value. Occasionally, they came across a third type of item: one that caused them to pause and think of the sentimental value it might have represented to the Hammers.

These included an old black and white photo of Henrietta and her older sister, Ruth. They couldn't have been more than seven and five at the time. They smiled as they pushed baby dolls in toy strollers.

Scott's grandparents stood behind their two girls. "Grandpa Johannes was a preacher sent to America by his church in Sweden," Scott explained. "My grandmother, Sara, was widowed at age sixty-five when he died suddenly of a heart attack. I was still a little guy when my grandmother came to live with us in Pasadena."

"Would you mind if The Standard scanned a few of these photos to accompany the story that Rob wants to do?"

"Absolutely! I think it's great that Rob wants to write a story about Henrietta. Even if the memories students have of her aren't so great, people will look at these pictures and see a different side of her."

Holly's cheeks flushed with guilt. "You know, Scott, this is all pretty weird for me. As a kid, I never dreamed of being inside Henrietta's home, no less going through her things. I'm glad to help, but I'm not sure she would have approved."

"My aunt is no longer here, and I greatly appreciate that you're here helping," Scott said smiling brightly. "It makes the job easier, and a lot more fun."

"Henrietta was a bit of a hoarder," Holly said as she looked through another dresser drawer. Here are some more old photos. Gosh, these must go back decades!" Holly handed one black and white photo over to Scott and asked, "Is this one of your uncles? He looks a lot like you, don't you think?"

Scott stared down at a three by three-inch photo that had yellowed with age. "I don't know who he is. At least, I don't recall ever meeting him. My mom never mentioned another uncle living up in Fort Bragg. It was my understanding that the rest of her family never left Sweden. Maybe this was a photo Ruth and Henrietta's mother or father held onto." As with all the other photos, Scott flipped it over to see if there had been any notation made on the back.

In faded blue ink he could make out, "Mikhail Orlov." Underneath the name was a phone number that began with a "707" area code.

Holly stood next to Scott with the top of her head touching the side of his shoulder.

"That's an area code that starts up in Napa and Santa Rosa and goes through straight up the coast to the Oregon border. A lot of territory, but as you go further north, not many people. Maybe this was someone Henrietta knew in Fort Bragg, Mendocino or Ukiah. Why did you think he was my uncle?"

Holly snatched the photo out of Scott's hand, turned to face him, and held it up to his face. "There's a definite family resemblance Scott," she declared. "Maybe this guy was a cousin you never met."

"I might share some of his features, Holly, but Orlov is a Russian surname. It's not Swedish, and it's certainly not Portuguese."

"Scott, I don't know, maybe I'm imaging this. Eddie and Rob, sometimes think that I imagine a whole bunch of stuff. But, wow! It's black and white, but I'd guess that's your hair color, your jawline, even your eyes, and high cheekbones. I can't be certain with an old black and white photo, but the resemblance looks pretty clear to me."

As Scott turned back to the closet to box the last of Elijah's shoes, Holly continued to study the photo. She placed the bottom edge of the picture on the nightstand and noticed that the photo leaned toward one side.

"The bottom of this photo was trimmed off, probably with a pair of scissors," Holly announced.

"What do you mean?"

"Come here and see for yourself."

Scott stood beside her. He too looked down at the photo. "You're right. Why do you think someone did that?"

"I'm guessing that back held the last seven digits following the 707 area code. Maybe someone wanted the rest of that phone number to disappear."

"I wonder why?" Scott asked.

"They didn't want anyone to see the whole phone number would be my guess."

After some silent thought, Scott shrugged and said, "I guess we should keep packing. I'm sure we'll come across other mysteries before we're done."

Holly got the message: it was time to let the matter drop, at least for now.

The day plodded along. By late afternoon, only the master bedroom and the upstairs den were packed up.

"Fortunately, the three other rooms up here will be easy," Scott said. "I'm going to get back to it later this coming week. In the meantime, I've got a full day tomorrow grading student test papers. I've also got to complete my lesson plans for this coming week. I'm off on Friday, so I'll be back up here then."

"I'll be working Friday, but I'm happy to help you again next Saturday."

"That would be great!" Scott said and smiled. "Hey, let me take you out now for a bite to eat—that is if you're free."

"Sure. Let me take a shower. We can meet up a little later."

Scott reached in and gave Holly a kiss on the check. "Thanks. If this was our first date, it might have been the oddest one ever."

Holly laughed. "Trust me; I've had stranger dates than this."

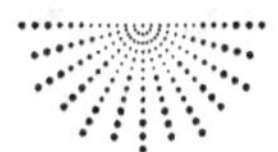

CHAPTER FIVE

Scott suggested burgers and cocktails at Marin Joe's. Holly was happy to agree with any plan that included Marin County's best place for a great hamburger.

They enjoyed great meals, drank martinis, and had enough in common to laugh or commiserate over through their time together.

The night ended on a more serious note when Scott gave Holly a lingering kiss.

After, Scott said, "I hope I wasn't too forward. I'm not great at reading a situation."

"You don't give yourself enough credit. You read me perfectly,"

When they parted, Holly realized for the first time, her relationship with Scott could actually be more than just a friendship.

The following Saturday Scott and Holly met again at the Hammer home. By now, they were determined to continue their efforts regardless of the size of the task.

From the moment Holly stepped out of her car, she could see that something was troubling Scott. But before she could ask, Scott suggested that they both sit for a few moments in the solarium off the living room.

Seeing that the room was filled with bright morning sun, Holly happily agreed.

"Have you had any coffee?" Scott asked.

"Nope. I overslept, so I threw something on and got myself up here."

"Let me put some up for both of us."

It didn't take long to find what was needed to make the coffee. There was no sugar or milk to be found, but both agreed that any coffee was better than none.

Together, they sat close to one another. Confident that something was pressing on Scott, Holly asked, "How was your week?"

"Amazing." He hesitated, then added, "And shocking."

"Wow, how so?"

My accelerated math class is doing a joint project with students in an advanced biology program. Do you remember I mentioned to you about reviewing sequencing for DNA samples and the measurable outcomes that are possible in finding a match?"

Holly nodded and smiled.

"I understand a great deal more about this process now than I did before we started the project."

"What got you thinking about DNA testing?"

"That photo you dug out of Henrietta's drawer. The one that said Mikhail Orlov on the back."

"You mean because I asked if he was your uncle and you replied that you had never heard of him?"

"I didn't tell you last week, but it has always bothered me that I looked like my mom's side of the family, but not at all like my dad's."

"Scott, genetics can throw some real curveballs. Perhaps you got more of your mom's features on the outside, and a lot of your dad's on the inside."

"True. But let me explain. Ruth and Henrietta's parents, my grandparents, were all of Swedish descent. From what I know, going back generations. My dad, Scott, Sr., was Portuguese on both sides. Silva is a common Portuguese name. I should show you a picture of my dad as a young man. He was a truly handsome guy: dark complexion, dark eyes, and dark hair. I always thought it odd that in appearance, I only favor my mother's side of the family: blond, fair complexion, blue eyes. I realize genetics is a crapshoot, but while I could name a variety of ways in which I have my mom's physical characteristics, there isn't a single way in which I can physically identify with my dad or my paternal grandparents."

"So you're wondering if Orlov might have been your father?"

"Holly, the first two nights after we came across that photo, I could hardly sleep! Maybe Orlov was my mother's lover! If so, perhaps I was their little accident."

"That's a pretty big assumption based on nothing more

than a random photo and cockeyed me thinking that the guy in the picture looked like you."

"If I thought I remotely resembled my dad, I would not have given any of this a second thought. I finally mentioned it to the woman who chairs the health sciences program—the one who is sharing the honors class project with me on statistical probabilities and genetic outcomes. Apparently, the Y chromosome carries the story of our lineage. If half my bloodline is not of Portuguese descent, I can say without a doubt that my dad was not my biological father."

"Genetic testing can pinpoint your heritage?"

"Yes and no. For example, if your bloodline comes from one of the Balkan countries, DNA can't differentiate one side of a border to another, particularly in parts of the world where maps change dramatically in as little as fifty years. But recognizing the genetic differences in Swedish and Portuguese origins is a snap. So I thought about it and decided to get the test done."

"Don't keep me in suspense, Scott! What did you find out?"

"Just a small amount of my saliva proved that the two bloodlines I have carried since conception are Russian and Scandinavian. I never resembled my father or his family, and now I know why. It wasn't just by genetic chance that I had none of his physical traits. I was my father's adopted son. I'll always love him. He was a fantastic dad. Still, it would be wonderful to know something about my biological father. Starting with the most important question of all: Is he still alive?"

"I guess you can't be sure that your mother was your real mother, either?"

"Not from a simple test like the one I had performed this week. The only thing I can be sure of is that, like my mom, I am of Swedish descent. The half that is Russian, however, is a mystery. I do have facial characteristics in common with both my mom and my maternal grandfather, so chances are, Ruth was my actual mother."

"But you think your dad might be this Orlov guy?"

"Who knows? I've been in something of a stupor since I discovered my dad was not my biological father—and more than a little embarrassed that it was so easy to reveal such a simple fact. That's also why I wanted to talk with you before we got back to work. I wanted you to know that I'm a little distracted right now and not simply because I'm a math nerd or a space cadet. Now, I'm a little nervous over what else we might stumble upon in this old place."

Holly reached over and put her hand on top of Scott's. "What you're going through can't be easy. First off, your mom dies not very long ago, then your aunt and uncle die in quick succession, then you find out you were deceived about the identity of your father. All of that would be unsettling to me, and I suspect it would knock anyone for a loop."

For a few moments, Scott said nothing. Then he stood up and pulled Holly up out of her seat so that they were facing each other.

"I want to kiss you," Scott said.

"Can you tell the feeling is mutual?"

They stood, kissed, and held each other for a long time.

"Holly, I've not had anyone in my life for a long time. I don't think I'm great at relationships."

"Why do you say that?"

"I think I'm a bit of a nerd and I'm no superstar when it comes to being romantic."

"Why don't you let me be the judge of that; I'm not looking for Romeo, a kind, decent, considerate man is more than enough."

They kissed again. This time, it was more prolonged and more intense.

"Should we take this upstairs?" Holly asked.

Scott laughed. "I was thinking the same thing, but I'm a little too shy to ask."

"Life is too short, and we're both a little too old for shyness," Holly said as she took Scott by the hand and led the way.

Later, after their passion was spent, both Scott and Holly looked up at the ceiling of the guest bedroom.

Holly broke the silence first. "Was this a foolish thing for us to do?"

Scott was silent for a few moments. Finally, he replied, "Possibly. But I don't think so. I felt a connection with you when we first met after Henrietta's service. I like those green-brown eyes of yours. You know they have gold flecks?"

"So I've been told."

"And that curly black hair. Not to mention your little, upturned nose."

"Stop you're embarrassing me," Holly said as she laughed.

"But, most of all," Scott added, "I like your honesty. If you hadn't said what was on your mind about that photo, I might not have had the courage to answer a question I've thought about often."

Holly flashed the smile that first caught Scott's eye.

"You don't mind that the top of my head barely reaches as high as your shoulders?"

"No! Why should that matter?"

"I don't know. I thought tall guys like tall girls."

"Not me. I'm tall by genetics, not by choice. Ruth's dad, Grandpa Bratten, was six-three, that's probably where I got my height. Or perhaps I get it from both him and my dad. But as far as tall or short, I always liked what Lincoln said that a person is tall enough if their feet reached the ground."

Holly smiled, fell back into Scott's embrace, and said, "I don't know about you, but I'm starved! That cup of coffee we had downstairs is all I've had today."

"Let's get dressed. You can tell me where you like to eat here in town. You know Sausalito a lot better than I do."

"We haven't made any progress on getting this place packed up today."

"That's okay. Right now, I just want to spend time with you. Not to mention, I'm starving!"

"Okay, let's get something to eat. I'm not good at thinking or working on an empty stomach."

"I can tell you something you do great on an empty stomach," Scott said as he kissed her passionately.

Coming up for air, Holly said, "You're not so bad yourself."

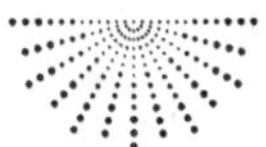

CHAPTER SIX

It was a lovely day, so Holly, anxious for Scott to better know her hometown, walked him down through Sausalito's winding hills to Bridgeway, the city's main north/south road in and out of town.

Approximately a half mile north of the city's ferry landing is the Lighthouse Cafe. After the two of them settled into one of the small restaurants' large booths, they ordered stacks of pancakes with sides of bacon and coffee. Scott took Holly's hands and said, "Happy?"

"Absolutely," Holly answered with a smile.

"Any thoughts about how I might find Max Orlov?"

"Have you got that photo of him with you?" Holly asked.

Scott reached around and pulled his wallet out of his back pocket. He slipped out the black and white photo and placed it in the center of the table.

"Over the last five years, I've learned a lot hanging around a news reporter and a cop. The first lesson: never ignore the obvious. Scott, you and I agree that probably someone trimmed off the bottom of this photo. The likeliest guess would be that was done by Henrietta or Ruth. And the obvious conclusion is that the missing piece contained the seven digits of Orlov's number since the three numbers on what I assume was the top line contained only the name Mikhail Orlov and the 707 area code."

It took Holly only a few minutes on her cell phone to identify five different Orlovs listed in area code 707.

"I don't know if you're aware of this, but there is and has been for a very long time, a substantial Russian heritage population along the entire Northern California coast," Holly explained. "They were early settlers along the Pacific Northwest as far south as the Sonoma Coast. Of course, now, the epicenter for Russian families has moved to other parts of California, principally the Bay Area and the LA Metroplex.

"Before we start looking far afield, let's stick with this clue of the 707 area code. We'll check cities like Mendocino, Ukiah, Santa Rosa, and Healdsburg. We'll also research the name in towns along the Russian River, like Guerneville, Monte Rio, and Jenner. It's a shot in the dark. Still, it's obviously worth the effort. The guy in this photo looks pretty young, in his early twenties, I would guess. Perhaps it's a duplicate of a class photo that appeared in his high school yearbook.

"It's also a reasonable assumption, given his age, that whatever number Orlov wrote on the back of this photo could have belonged to his parents. It's all but certain his parents have passed by now, and the number has been reassigned. So our having, or not having, the full number may not have mattered."

"What's your guess as to why the number would have been cut-off?"

"Maybe Ruth gave it to Henrietta for safekeeping because she didn't want to make it easy for your dad to find the photo, but at the same time, she didn't want to part with it. If he'd found it, he might have called her lover and asked him to explain himself."

"What would be your guess as to Orlov's age today?"

"Probably early eighties. If he was your mother's lover, it's reasonable to assume that they were approximately the same age. Perhaps, two or three years apart. I'll see if Rob and or Eddie have some ideas on how we might locate him."

"That would be great," Scott said with a growing sense of confidence. "I know we could be chasing a dead man, but if Orlov is still alive, I'd sure like to find him and learn what he knows."

"Agreed. And if Orlov is gone, maybe we'll be lucky enough to find one of his children and secure a DNA sample."

"Holly, you think he might have made a deathbed confession about the child he left behind?"

"The one thing you learn in the newspaper business is just about anything is possible."

Late on Monday, when their work for the day was complete, Holly asked the question that had been on her mind since Saturday afternoon: "What would you do to locate Mikhail Orlov?"

She filled Rob in on the details of both Scott's suspicions, as well as his discoveries over the past week concerning his parentage, and his hopes of finding Orlov.

Rob took a few moments to consider the situation. "At some point," everyone has thought of what it would be like to find out that one or both of your parents is not the person you always assumed them to be. Suspicions aside, however, I'm sure, Scott was thrown by all this. Particularly the DNA results regarding his father's bloodline. I would think that would shock anyone. How exactly did you get yourself into the middle of this?"

"Remember, I offered to help him clean out his aunt and uncle's place? I found this photo going through Henrietta's stuff." Holly smiled and shrugged innocently. "We've spent a lot of time together in the last couple of weekends."

"Have you gotten involved with Scott?"

Holly's eyes went skyward. "Well…sort of…YES!"

"Holly, isn't the guy, like, fifteen years older than you?"

"Yes, but if that doesn't matter to me, why should it matter to you?" Holly asked.

Rob raised his hands in surrender. "You're right. Who you date is certainly none of my business."

"We agree on that. When I found the photo, I said to Scott, 'Is this your uncle?'"

"Why would you say something like that?"

"I know you think I should have kept my yap shut. But how was I to know a simple question would start all this."

"And that's why Scott started looking into DNA proof of his parentage."

"I guess I should have kept my opinion to myself."

"Normally, I'd agree with you. But everyone has a right

to know who their birth parents are. So, what have you done to try to find Orlov?"

"Not all that much. Someone—my guess Henrietta's sister, Ruth— cut off the phone number on the back of the picture except for the area code: 707. I found a handful of Orlovs in that area code, but I've had no luck locating a Mikhail Orlov."

"Did you try San Francisco?"

"Why the city?"

"It might be a wild goose chase, but the Richmond District has the largest Russian population in Northern California. Check any address on or near Geary Avenue west of Presidio, all the way out toward 48th Avenue and Land's End. The densest population is likely around Holy Virgin Cathedral. It's the largest Russian Orthodox Church in the entire state. The cathedral is on 26th and Geary if I remember correctly."

"Rob, you amaze me! How did you come to know all this?"

"When I was in elementary school, my parents were friends with a Russian family that settled in Sausalito. After they moved to San Francisco, we came into the city every now and then to share in their Sunday dinner. We even went with them a couple of times to Sunday service at Holy Virgin. It's an incredible place. We had no idea what the priest was talking about during his sermon. It's nearly all in Russian. Probably still is. But they had a big reception afterward, in their community room. I'll wager it's still like that to this day. Old World ties can last for generations. Modern American families are not like that. It's a pretty cool thing to see."

"Are you saying, If Scott and I start asking questions we might find a connection to the Orlov family?"

"Orlov is a pretty common Russian name. But, if the Orlovs lived in Fort Bragg or some part of Mendocino County, that at least narrows your search."

"It still sounds like a long shot for finding the right Orlov."

"I agree. Your odds aren't great. At least you know he's pretty old if indeed he's still alive. Perhaps he lives with his kids. I mean it when I say Russian families tend to be pretty tight. Three generations, all living under the same roof is not at all unusual."

"I'll pitch the idea to Scott and see if he wants to give it a shot."

"If there is one thing we learn in the news business it's this: The answer to every question never asked is, 'NO!' Did you hold on to that contact information you got from that woman, Jeannie something or other?"

"Newberry—yes! Of course! That totally slipped my mind." Holly said as she smacked her forehead. "We could ask her if she knows anything about Orlov. She said that Henrietta, Ruth, and she were very close growing up."

"Send her a copy of the photo of this mystery man you found. Better yet, take a picture of it with your phone. If she's crossed that bridge into the Twenty-First Century, maybe you can send the photo to her cell. If she recognizes the guy, she'll let you know right away. Holly, you might be looking for a needle in a haystack. Still, dive in. You never know when you might fall onto that needle."

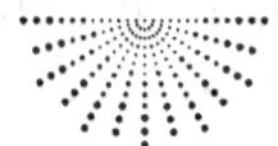

CHAPTER SEVEN

The following day, Holly learned that Jeannie Newberry did have a smartphone.

Better yet, after Holly sent a phone camera picture of Orlov, Jeannie claimed to recognize the person in the photo.

"He was a friend of Henrietta's, and Ruth's as well, I believe," Newberry texted back to Holly. "I don't know how well either of them knew this fellow. I think he lived up near Fort Bragg. But that was over four decades ago. I have no idea where he would be now. I can't, however, recall the name Mikhail. Sorry not to be of more help."

Holly was tempted to engage Newberry with a follow-up text perhaps hinting at a possible liaison Mikhail had with Scott's mother. After a moment's thought, however, she decided first to discuss the matter with Scott.

That night, Holly and Scott met at Sausalito's F3 Restaurant on Caledonia Street. It was just two blocks from Holly's apartment and a favorite hang for her.

As she dove into her burgers and sweet potato fries, Holly exclaimed, "I know it's not much, but at least Newberry has seen this guy's photo before. According to her, he did have some role in the lives of your mother and Henrietta."

"Did she remember who first showed her Orlov's picture?"

"She said she wasn't certain. A few moments later, she replied that it might have been Ruth or both of them."

"Do you think her recollections are reliable?" Scott asked.

"I do, up to a point. Jeannie might know more than she's letting on right now. If we learn more about Orlov, I think it would be smart to take a ride up to Santa Rosa and pay her a visit."

"Could she be holding something back?"

"If Orlov is your biological dad, and you know Scott, Sr. could not have been, it's hard for me to square her not having any idea that her good friend was pregnant with another man's child. I honestly don't know what she knows, but I think she knows more than she has shared to this point."

"Perhaps she knew my mom had an affair with Orlov? And Henrietta likely knew about this as well?"

"Who knows? One thing you learn in the news business, people are not nearly as forthcoming with the truth as most of us would like to think. It's fun watching Rob and Eddie. Both of them are born snoops. They're a classic case of brothers from other mothers. Only one pursued a career in criminal justice and one in journalism."

"Did they go to the same college?"

"Yep. Both are graduates of San Francisco State. They've been thick as thieves since high school when they played for Tam High's basketball team."

"Digging stuff up that other people would prefer to keep buried must be exciting," Scott said with a sense of admiration. "I'm probably like most people, a little too shy around people to push for honest answers. But it would be hard to stay in the profession of reporting the news if you felt uncomfortable asking difficult questions."

"You have to set at least some of your inhibitions aside if you want to get closer to the truth. Where it gets interesting is when you start finding stuff you never expected to find, and you have no idea where it will lead."

"Any examples of that?"

"Rob and I were working a story a couple of years ago in which this rich Sausalito guy, Mack Mulligan, died and left two different wills. One neatly typed, and the other was this screed written out in cursive, on blue lined white pad paper. No one could figure out which was real, and which was fake. People who knew the deceased thought both read like they could have been from him, although one written when he was sober and the other…when he was not. None of this would have mattered very much if his estate hadn't been valued at over ten million dollars."

"Did the story get a lot of reaction from readers?"

"Absolutely! Besides the old guy's wealth, mostly from

real estate investments, he had run a bar in town called Mackie's. Over half of the people in town knew him." Holly paused, took another healthy bite of her burger, and then continued. "We put an investigative piece together, hoping to get to the bottom of these two very different wills. My favorite part of our coverage was when we put a photo box on the front page of the scribbled will with the headline, 'Real or Fake? A Ten Million Dollar Question!' A few days after the story broke, someone—we never knew who—pushed a handwritten note inside an unmarked white envelope through our front door's mail slot. Our office is on the second floor of an old two-story Victorian walk up on Princess Street. Every workday around noon, I go down the steps and pick up the mail. So here's this one blank envelope. I open it. Inside, there's a note that looked like it was written with a red crayon. It's clipped to the article we had published about the old man's will."

"What did it say?" Scott asked in a rush.

"Eight words… 'Good story! But you haven't dug deep enough.'"

"Wow, that must have gotten you thinking. Did you ever find out who dropped the note?"

"Never. And, unfortunately, like a typhoon out in the Pacific, the story just blew itself out."

"What do you mean?"

"We sure tried to keep moving it forward, but all the leads we had turned into dead ends. In our business, you have to face the fact that you're not the law, and you have limited resources. And even if you're the cops, there's still a chance you'll run smack into a dead end. People get nervous, they clam up, and you find yourself with no place to go. We're a two-person weekly community newspaper with a group of volunteers who feed us local society coverage and some photographs. At the same time, you'll always have some readers who treat you like a cross between the New York Times and the FBI. But that's just their fantasy. We push, and we work hard. Sometimes we get to the answers, and sometimes we come up short. That's the news business. Limited resources, and limited time. Still, you have to give it your best shot."

"You must have had a hunch as to how it happened—the two different wills."

"Rob and I were convinced that near the end of his life, the old guy was hoping to redirect the bulk of his estate to his boozy, younger girlfriend. Therefore, the final will. In the end, to the relief of his heirs, the court threw out the screed, saying its validity could not be determined. But the story upped our readership—at least for the weeks that the probate court tried to figure it all out and come to a final decision."

Scott dipped two of his sweet potato fries into a cup of ketchup. "I'll tell you one thing about this town: Sausalito has a bunch of interesting characters."

"That's for sure! And besides Mill Valley, Tiburon, Belvedere, we also report on the towns that make up Ross Valley: Larkspur, Corte Madera, Ross, Kentfield, and San Anselmo. They all have their own collection of eccentrics!"

Scott chuckled. "The longer I live in Marin, the better I understand its eccentric nature. I suppose that keeps life interesting."

"Speaking of colorful characters, some of them are likely

included in bequests your aunt left in her will," Holly replied.

"Really? Like who?"

She leaned in. "My vote for number one nut job is Laurie Chase. She founded the Sausalito Opera Society. According to Chase, your aunt donated to her organization several times."

Scott raised an eyebrow. "I'm not a big fan of opera, but I assume you think Ms. Chase has a couple of loose screws because she loves opera."

"No, it's not that! I mean, yes, I dislike opera as much as the next person. But, the real problem is Chase has the annoying habit of stopping people on the street and favoring them with an aria."

"Really?"

"Hand to God, she actually does that."

"Her singing had a few people squirming at my aunt's funeral service, including me," Scott acknowledged with a laugh.

"Trust me, that was nothing compared to some of the other stunts she's pulled. Just last week, right across the street from our office, I saw her stop a couple of tourists coming out of one of the little art galleries. She started telling them about some opera she had been listening to with her earbuds. The next thing you know, she starts singing it to them. I lowered my window, but that does no good! Her bellowing comes right through that thin glass."

"Just stops a couple of tourists and starts performing; that is odd. Doesn't she have anything better to do?"

"Laurie doesn't have a day job, other than making a public nuisance of herself."

"Does her husband support her? Or is she an heiress?"

"From what I know, the answer would be, none of the above. Laurie's father left her the family's house up on Channing Way. That's a really nice street. Up in the hills, however, I'm guessing only natives and longtime residents know the street is there."

"I wouldn't have a clue where to go find it without a map. I've been doing some biking starting out from Henrietta's place, and I've never come across it. So how does Miss Songbird get by?"

"Other than the value of her home, my guess is she's what people call, 'house poor.' Of course, depending on what your aunt gifted her from the Hammer estate, she might not be cash poor for long."

"…and there's no Mr. Songbird?"

"Nope."

"Gosh, Holly! I hope Henrietta found some better causes than the Sausalito Opera Society to support."

"I don't know, Scott. Except for the Marin Animal Rescue Shelter, and the Ladies of Liberty, nobody knows all that much about any of these other groups."

"I met some of these people at the reception after the funeral service, but the whole event is kind of a blur now. Way too many people for me to remember."

"Many of them came up to speak before the service concluded."

Scott frowned. "In all honesty, I kept nodding off. I remember that woman with the dark red hair—what was her name?"

"Ruby Reese. She was there with her husband, Chris. I introduced you to Ruby at the reception after the service."

"Right, they're the couple that runs the Sausalito Fine Arts Board?"

"Yep. Ruby was in my fifth-grade class. She's an odd duck. For that matter, so is Chris. Speaking of odd ducks, there's also Francis Phillips, who runs that Sausalito Preservation League. I wouldn't trust that guy as far as I could throw him."

"Are you sure all these years working in the news business hasn't made you a bit of a cynic?" Scott asked with a curious smile.

"I wouldn't say that. I mean hanging around people like Rob—and particularly Eddie—has made me more aware of some of the shenanigans people get themselves into. But you'll just have to take my word for it: the people behind these organizations are an odd collection of characters!"

"I wonder why Henrietta didn't pick up on that? Not that I ever knew much about Henrietta. To be honest, there's almost nothing I knew about her likes, dislikes, or interests."

"Scott, you could tell me to mind my own business, but I have to ask: What if anything did Henrietta leave you in her will?"

"Don't think I haven't wondered about that." He shook his head in frustration. "I went most of my childhood without seeing her. As an adult, I saw her even less. Just two weeks after Uncle Elijah died, Henrietta invited me over to her house. She told me that she would like to leave me her house."

"You must have been pretty bowled over when you heard that!"

"That's putting it mildly. It was certainly out of left field."

"Surely she must have explained something to you about her decision."

"Yes, but she didn't make a big deal about it. It was almost as if she was embarrassed by the whole thing," Scott said with a shrug. "Her rationale was now that I'd relocated to Marin and was happy with my new teaching position, it made sense for me to have the house."

"You must have been surprised to hear that."

"I was! I wondered if Henrietta felt guilty that after falling out with her sister, she was absent from my life. She did say that Elijah had a substantial portfolio of properties he had left her, as well as a good deal of stocks and cash. The house, she explained, would be her one and only gift to me.

"But, like I explained when we met up at the house for the first time if she did leave me the property, I'd probably sell the old place. Take the money and run, you might say."

After a few moments of silence, Holly worked up the courage to raise Rob's suggestion about using the Russian Orthodox Church in San Francisco as one approach to begin their search for Mikhail Orlov.

"I know it's farfetched, but why not give it a try? It'll be an adventure. And when I talk about snooping, it's all about following a hunch and seeing where it takes you. Regardless of what happens with Henrietta's estate, you're not going to be able to set Orlov aside. Particularly not after that DNA test you took. Hell, I can hardly get him off my mind, and I know for certain he's not my daddy."

Scott sat in silence as he considered Holly's suggestion. Finally, he said, "Yeah, why not? If nothing else it gives us an excuse to spend a day together in the city." He leaned in to give her a soft kiss on the lips, and then happily added, "Let's make a date of it and have lunch in the city as well."

"Only if you promise to take me home afterward," Holly said with a smile.

"Deal!" Scott declared as they sealed their plan with a kiss.

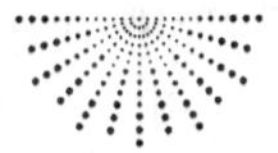

CHAPTER EIGHT

Sunday Mass at Holy Virgin Cathedral was unlike any service Holly ever attended. From the look on Scott's face, he felt the same way.

The church, massive on the outside and breathtaking on the inside, was filled with Eastern Orthodox icons and paintings of the Holy Virgin, Christ, and his disciples.

The smell of incense filled the air. Blue smoke curled upward, into the rounded nooks and other sections of the painted ceiling. The streaks of sunlight piercing through it gave the sanctuary a mystical and intimate feel.

The priests, several with ponderous beards of black, gray, and white, were draped in elaborate black, gold and silver garments. The large, heavy crosses, which hung around their necks, reached well below their chests.

Most of the service was delivered in Russian. Although neither Holly nor Scott understood it, the cathedral provided an "etiquette summary," for visitors, so at the very least they knew when to sit, stand, and join the congregation in prayer.

Scott and Holly were equally impressed by the strong sense of community evidenced by the congregants. Happily, a majority of them stayed after the service for a community reception held in a large room which comfortably held the two hundred plus who attended the Sunday service.

Holly, never one to allow shyness to impede her progress, began telling people she was looking for a gentleman named Mikhail Orlov. Pointing to Scott, who smiled shyly, Holly explained, "I believe Mr. Orlov knows the identity of my friend's father. He just recently learned he was adopted!" Holly knew her depiction of these facts was not entirely accurate. But, in pursuit of the truth, she didn't hesitate in taking shortcuts.

Her presentation of Scott's story caught the imagination of every listener. Most were open and sympathetic to Scott's desire to find his biological father. The story spread from one member of the congregation to another as various versions of Holly's inquiries made their way around the reception.

Soon, people sought out Holly and Scott, wanting to learn more about him in the hope they could be of help.

"We're quite sure that at one time the Orlov family we're seeking lived near Fort Bragg, in Mendocino County," Holly explained with a smile. "We suspect they moved to San Francisco, but we're not sure when or exactly where in the city they settled. Any clue you could provide might provide the information we need to locate him."

That Mikhail or the Orlov family moved to San Francisco was pure speculation. But having come up empty in

Mendocino County, they had nothing but hope they might be right.

Many of the congregants were enthusiastic about helping and began searching their memories. One older woman stared at Scott. Finally, she proclaimed, "There was a Yuri Orlov, who might be a son of Mikhail. You look like Yuri. Perhaps he is your brother?" She said with a smile and a soft laugh.

From another congregant, the same theory was put forward regarding a Dmitri Orlov.

Scott and Holly showed anyone interested the two-by-two-inch photo with the name "Mikhail Orlov" written on the back.

One older couple came up to them. "You know, the Orlovs were Royals in the old country. There was a Count Orlov, and a Princess Orlov."

An older woman took Scott's arm and pulled him close. Conspiratorially she explained, "There were five famous Orlov brothers, all of whom served her Majesty, Catherine the Great." Looking around to be certain no one overheard, she added, "One was thought to have been the queen's lover!"

It was all fascinating, but Scott and Holly realized that none of this was getting them any closer to discovering the Orlov they hoped to find.

Amid a growing tumult, everyone turned as a woman with a heavy Russian accent called out a name neither Scott nor Holly had heard, "Rimma! Rimma Orlov!"

The room went still for a moment as all the congregants appeared to consider this new clue. A renewed buzz filled the reception, one in which the name "Rimma" was spoken a dozen times, mostly in the form of a question. To Scott and Holly, the name in question sounded like "REE-MA?"

Suddenly, a short, heavyset woman came forward. She was at least seventy-five, perhaps older, and dressed elegantly in black, with a large gold cross hanging around her neck. The curious onlookers parted to let her through. She walked slowly but intently toward Scott and Holly.

Extending their hands, the woman touched each of them lightly and gave them a shy smile as she balanced herself with the help of a dark, wooden cane.

The congregants closed in, hoping to hear if the old woman had indeed solved the mystery.

She spoke slowly with a heavy Russian accent. "My daughter's friend, Rimma, runs a bakery," she began. "The girls have known each other for many years. The bakery is called Baku. You will find it very close to here on Twenty-Third Street, just off of Geary. Rimma and her husband, Alexey, moved here from the town of Mendocino. That was many years ago." Then, with a dramatic pause, the woman added, "Rimma's papa's name…is Mikhail Orlov!"

"Do you know where Mikhail lives?" Holly asked. She was overwhelmed by the thought that this hundred to one shot might have indeed paid off.

"Not certain, but I believe Mikhail lives with Rimma and the rest of the family, in the apartment above their bakery."

"Go over there now," one of the listeners insisted excitedly. "This bakery, Baku, is a few blocks east of here!"

"Are they open today?" Scott asked.

"Open today, open every day."

"Russians work hard!" Another in the group called out enthusiastically.

"Thank you," Holly all but shouted, as she gently took the old woman's hand for the second time and gave a satisfied smile.

"Thank you all," Scott added happily to the entire room.

Holly realized that in Scott's excitement, his natural shyness had disappeared.

Hand in hand, they hurried away. Their spirits rose even higher as the shouted good wishes from the congregation added to their growing sense of excitement.

It was a typically busy Sunday at Baku Bakery. As Scott and Holly walked in, they were struck immediately by a blend of wonderful aromas. At that moment, the realization hit them that they hadn't eaten since early that morning.

Scott looked at the woman working behind the counter. To many of her patrons, she spoke perfect English. But when needed, she comfortably switched to Russian. Given her thin frame and tired gray eyes, Scott guessed her age to be in the early forties. She appeared accustomed to hard work. Could this be Rimma?

Holly yanked Scott toward the nearest table. "Go ahead," Holly nodded toward the woman. "Go up there and ask her name."

"If she answers to the name of Rimma, I can't come out and ask her if she's my sister?"

"Of course not, start slow. Ask her if Mikhail Orlov is her father."

Seemingly as a loss for words, Scott approached the counter.

After the woman had finished serving the customer before him, she turned with a weary smile to Scott and said what she said countless times each day: "How can I help you?"

"Are you Rimma?" Scott said softly.

"Yes. Do I know you?"

"No, but I'm trying to locate your father, Mikhail. He was a friend of my aunt, who died recently. I found this photo of him in her belongings. I think they may have been friends when they were growing up. There's actually a possibility we are related." Suggesting Rimma might be a cousin was pure speculation, but as Scott learned watching Holly, one had to be a bit bold to prompt a response.

In a city with as many eccentrics as San Francisco, anyone who deals every workday with the public is accustomed to hearing a variety of odd questions and comments. For Rimma, however, this was a first. This well-dressed, middle-aged man seemed too sincere to be making some bizarre joke. Mikhail had not worked in the bakery for many years. The fact that this stranger knew her father's name added to the surprise Rimma felt when she heard him use the word "related."

And then, of course, there was the photograph he showed her. Rimma only glanced at it quickly, but it was evident that the picture was decades old and apparently the man in the photo resembled the man holding her in pictures of her as a small child. Clearly, Rimma was curious to know more. In a traditionally tight-knit family, the sudden appearance of an unknown relative was an all but unheard of event.

"My shift ends in thirty minutes, let me get you coffee and a slice of Medovik cake," Rimma said in a daze. "When I finish, we can talk."

"That would be nice, but I'm here with someone and…" Scott said, taking out some money.

"No, no. I don't want your money," Rimma insisted as she handed him two pieces of Medovik, a traditional Russian cake, and two mugs of black coffee.

"I will come over soon. Just sit and wait a bit," Rimma asked as she nodded and gave a faint smile.

I cannot imagine my father having a relationship with any woman other than Mama, Rimma thought, as she watched Scott walk back to a table where a short woman with dark curly hair sat waiting for him to return. Is that his wife? Rimma wondered. Perhaps my family is growing by the minute.

"I'm guessing that went well, considering how much time you spoke with her. Was that Rimma?"

Scott was feeling a little light headed and needed a moment to steady himself. "I think I'll get a glass of water to have with this cake. I don't need to be anymore amped-up than I already am."

When Scott returned and drank half of his water in a single gulp, he said, "Yes, that's Rimma. I showed her the picture of Mikhail, and I got the impression that she thought it was her father. To be honest, she seemed rattled by the picture and by what I said."

"Well, that's a good sign. What did you say?"

"I told her that I was looking for the man in the photo and I explained to her what little we know. I said there's a chance she and I are cousins."

"There's a chance she's your half-sister."

"She seemed rattled enough by my suggestion that we might at least be cousins. She gave me these pieces of cake and two coffees and asked that I wait thirty minutes until her shift ended."

"Good God Scott, I'm starting to think that Rob's crazy idea of going to the Russian Orthodox Church might have been spot on. I've got to be honest, I thought it was a long shot at best."

"Agreed! I'm just hoping when I go to sleep tonight I'll know more about how I came into this world than I knew when I woke up this morning."

Holly put her hand over Scott's and said, "I hope you do too. I know it would bring you a certain peace and happiness that money could never buy."

In spite of enjoying their cake and the intimate surroundings of the busy café and bakery, time passed slowly while they waited for Rimma.

When her relief arrived, Rimma went into the back kitchen, washed her hands, looked at herself in the mirror, pulled a comb out and did her best to look a little less frazzled and tired after what had already been a hectic Sunday.

She smiled in the mirror and convinced herself that she was ready to hear whatever Scott had to say.

Rimma reintroduced herself to Scott, who stood to greet her. Rimma shook his hand and smiled. She then turned to Holly, who introduced herself as "a friend of Scott's."

"First, let me ask you, where did you find this photograph of my father."

"So you think this is your father?"

"If not, it's someone who looks a good deal like the photos of my father as a young man that are in our family album. Obviously none of those pictures are like the photos we're accustomed to seeing today, but even so, I would guess that's him."

"Where is he now?"

"It's a Sunday afternoon during the baseball season so I'd guess that he's upstairs in his recliner watching the Giants game."

"I'd love to meet him," Scott said anxiously.

"First, could you tell me a little more about what brought you here?"

"Absolutely," Scott said enthusiastically. Above all else, he wanted to assure Rimma that there was nothing more to his visit than natural curiosity and a desire to get to the bottom of a mystery. He began by explaining, "Up until recently I thought my father was Scott Silva, Sr., then all that changed when Holly discovered this photo…"

Scott briefly recapped the journey they had taken over the past two weeks that brought both of them to the door of her bakery. He concluded with, "My bloodline is Russian and Sweedish, there's not a chance in the world that the loving man I knew as my father, was my biological father. I don't know if your father is also my father, but given what we know now, there's a reasonable chance that's the case."

There was an awkward pause that was broken by Holly, who asked, "Is your mom still alive?"

"No. Mama died years ago. I was just a teen at the time. It was a terrible time for all of us. Breast cancer. They probably could have saved her today, but not back then. So we lost her. Papa found it too depressing to stay in Mendocino after she passed. Our cousins all live nearby. It was time to have family close. So we moved into the city."

Rimma stood up. "I think it's time we go up to the family apartment so that Scott can meet my father. Maybe he has some answers to all this."

"How is your father's health?" Scott asked.

"Not perfect," Rimma said. "Age is taking its toll. He loved working in the bakery because he has always enjoyed being around people. He's a very nice man. But arthritis got into him, and it became difficult to use his hands. In a service and food prep business, it's hard to get by without the constant use of your hands. But he's always an optimist, so his spirits remain high."

Moments later, Scott and Holly followed Rimma into the small but comfortably furnished apartment.

Mikhail sat in a recliner, shouting at the television and pleading with the Giants to pull their pitcher.

Excitedly, he turned to Rimma and exclaimed, "They're going to lose another game! Unbelievable!" Suddenly realizing that she wasn't alone, he attempted to maneuver himself out of his chair to give these two guests a proper greeting.

"These are friends of yours, Rimma?" Mikhail asked, then immediately added, "Sit down, please!"

"Please sir, don't get up on our account," Scott insisted. Suddenly confronted with the man Scott doubted they would ever find, he felt uncertain about their entire mission. What if this old man they imposed upon was nothing more than a complete stranger?

Just as his confidence slipped, he remembered that the man he was seeking was the handsome young man in the photo: A man his mother Ruth had perhaps once loved. Cleary, this was no longer that man. But with the passage of so many years, that, of course, was to be expected.

"Papa," Rimma began, "Scott and his friend Holly have been looking for you because of a photo they found after Scott's aunt died."

"What photo?" Mikhail asked as he grew increasingly bewildered.

Feeling more than a bit foolish, Scott took the photo from his shirt pocket and pushed it forward on the small dining table at which they all sat.

Mikhail put on a pair of reading glasses he pulled from the pocket of an aging flannel shirt. Silently, he studied the photo for what Scott felt was a very long time.

Then with complete confidence, he said, "This is not me, this is my brother, Max!"

"Turn it over," Scott said.

When Mikhail saw his name and the partial phone number, he raised his head, "How did you get this picture?" He asked in a surprisingly urgent tone.

"My aunt's maiden name was Henrietta Bratten. Her

father was a minister in Fort Bragg, a long time ago. Her sister, Ruth, was my mother."

"Henrietta? Henrietta! Oh, my God!" Mikhail declared as he got up from the table and walked back to his recliner. What little color he had in his aging face drained away. "I can't believe this," Mikhail muttered softly. The old man looked as though he had seen a ghost.

"What's happening, Papa?" Rimma said as she, Scott and Holly followed the old man back into the living room. Mikhail grabbed the remote he kept on the arm of his recliner, pointed it toward the television and clicked it off.

Whatever was happening must be serious, Rimma thought. Papa never does that in the middle of a Giants game.

"Scott," the old man said, "The part of you that you see in this photo, has to be my brother Max. He was three years younger than me."

"Was?" Scott said as disappointment settled over him.

"Yes, Scott. Max died a very long time ago. He worked up at a timber-processing mill, along the Noyo River, near Dolphin Cove. I suppose none of you know that terrible place ever existed, do you?"

Scott, Holly, and Rimma shook their heads, confirming the old man's suspicion. But all by now were at the edge of their seats anxious to hear more.

"When Rimma was born, her uncle Max was already long gone," Mikhail explained, as he turned to look at his daughter. "It's a story I should have told you years earlier, but the memories were always too painful for me to look back on," Mikhail explained as he shook his head sadly. "The mill was just outside of Fort Bragg. Max died there, in an accident. Two others died that day as well. I can promise you this, there was never a better man than Max. I miss him to this day."

"Do you have any idea how Scott's aunt wound up with this photo of your brother?" Holly asked with a level of curiosity that had her perched at the edge of her seat.

"Yes, I do. But so you understand, I should start from the beginning." He bowed his head as if weighed down by countless memories. "I'd had breakfast with Max on the morning of the day he died. He was already late for work. He told me that he had spent the night with a girl with whom he was madly in love. He called her Henrietta. He told me she was a beautiful Swedish girl—the daughter of a minister in Fort Bragg."

Scott's hands gripped the arms of the aging wooden chair in which he sat. His mouth went dry, his feet went cold, and his heart began to thump.

For Scott, the unthinkable suddenly came into focus:

Was Henrietta my mother? His mind shouted as he made a desperate attempt to appear calm.

"Several days after he died, we had a service for him at the Russian Orthodox Church in Mendocino. I'd put that photo of Max in my pocket. I wondered if I'd see this girl, this Henrietta he told me so much about. I never said a word about this to my mother or my father. I was the only one in the family that knew.

"Several times, I looked around the old church, but all the young women were our own people. Cousins, aunts, nieces, high school friends. Then, near the end of the service, I looked once more. There she was! She looked like an angel. She was dressed all in white. Such pretty eyes, and such a pretty face!" Mikhail paused to drink a bit of tea from the cup that sat on the small table next to his recliner.

"When the service ended, your aunt slipped out the back door of the church. She was walking through the dirt parking lot toward her car. I knew I had to act right then, or I might never see her again. I caught up to her as she was opening her car door. I remember saying 'Henrietta,' and she walked a few steps further. So I repeated her name, this time she turned around. There were tears in her beautiful eyes. I think she was embarrassed, certainly surprised, to have been recognized. When I told her that Max was my brother, she hugged me and said, 'I'm so sorry.' Her tears just kept falling. It was clear my brother's death had overwhelmed her."

Scott felt tears welling up in his eyes. He glanced over at Holly and noticed her eyes were damp as well.

"We didn't say another word. She kissed me on the cheek, turned, and walked up to the door of an antique car. I mean old, even for those days, so I thought it probably belonged to her parents.

"I said, please we must talk before you go. So we sat down on the running board of the car. Fortunately, my family was all still inside the church, probably with a line of people waiting to talk to them. I was thankful that we had time alone. Your aunt was so pretty. I was jealous that Max had won the heart of such a beautiful girl. Before she left, I took out that photo of Max you just handed me. I asked if she had a picture of my brother. She said 'no,' then began to cry again, just looking down at the photo. I felt so sorry for her! I thought if Max had lived, Henrietta might have become my sister-in-law. I wrote my name and phone number on the back, and I told her to call me if she ever needed to talk." He frowned. "She seemed a little upset that she had been recognized, but relieved to have been able to talk with someone about her loss."

"Did you ever see her again?" Holly asked.

"No," Mikhail replied, "She never called my parents home; at least not that I knew. But about a year later there was a picture of her and the man that she married in the county newspaper."

"My uncle, Elijah Hammer," Scott explained.

"That's right, Scott. I was happy for her that she had found love again. And such a successful man! Everyone in Fort Bragg—in fact, most of Mendocino County—knew of the Hammers. Their tool company was one of the county's biggest employers."

The room was silent. No one was sure what to say.

Mikhail began to cry softly. Rimma sat down on the side of the oversized recliner. She wrapped her arm around her father's shoulders and held him tight.

"This is hard for me. Max was such a good brother, such a good friend," Mikhail murmured. "I still miss him."

Rimma handed her father a few tissues. Watching the pain that swept over him, she wept as well.

Scott and Holly had also been overwhelmed by the story of the two young lovers, separated forever by a sudden, tragic accident. At the same time, however, they were stunned by the possibility that Henrietta was Scott's birth mother.

For the first time in his life, Scott experienced the pain of missing a father he never knew and deep anger over the apparent deceit of his mother and his aunt, who appeared to have switched roles.

For a few moments, they sat silently as they all tried to reason out how all this occurred.

"You have my brother's eyes," Mikhail said aloud as if looking at Scott for the first time. "I think you must be my brother's boy," he said as he began to sob.

With that, the old man stood, and the newly expanded family joined in a group hug. Holly sat there not sure what to do as she watched the three of them embrace until Scott said, "Holly get in here we're not doing this without you. None of this would have happened without you!"

Holly was happy to join in.

"Rimma, let us drink to the miracle that brought Max's boy back to us," Mikhail exclaimed excitedly, "Let's have some of the good stuff!"

Before they left, Scott asked if Mikhail would give a DNA sample

Mikhail laughed and said, "I'd be happy to do anything to know for certain that Max lives on in you." With that, Mikhail gave Scott a kiss on each check.

Rimma then hugged Scott, and Holly, and asked, "How long have you two been married?"

Feeling that he had unintentionally put Holly in an awkward position, Scott quickly jumped in and said, "Holly and I aren't married, but we are dating, and she is very special to me. She knew it was important to me to learn who my father was, and it was her encouragement that helped me find the two of you."

"Wait... Cousin, what do you mean, 'find the two of us?'" Rimma asked with a playful smile.

Scott was apparently confused by the question. But Rimma quickly explained, "Scott, you have a huge family now! I think your uncle and I should make a party for you. Don't you think so, Papa?"

"Absolutely! And we'll serve only the good vodka. Holly, you must come too."

After another round of hugs and kisses on both cheeks, Scott and Holly were on their way down the stairs and back out onto the city's busy streets.

None of the passersby appeared to notice that Scott Silva had undergone a profound transformation. Nevertheless, Scott knew he had. His mind lapsed back into stunned silence, but his heart was racing over the possibilities. While he felt a bit shocked, he had no doubt that from this moment forward, his life would never be the same.

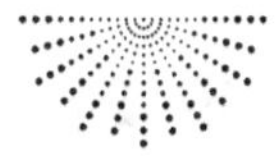

CHAPTER NINE

"There's somebody I have to call right now," Scott announced moments after leaving Mikhail and Rimma.

"Oh," Holly said, curious as always. "Do you need some privacy? I could stop and look around inside one of these shops. There are so many places in this neighborhood I've never seen."

"You're not going anywhere. Stay by my side." Scott declared as he put his arm around Holly and pulled her close. "I'd planned on speaking Monday with my teaching partner, Patricia Michaels, who has worked with me on the academy's joint math/science program. But now I'm too excited to wait. I've had a critical question regarding genetics and DNA that cannot wait any longer."

Without saying another word, Scott found his colleagues number in his contacts list, tapped it and stopped for a moment hoping he would reach her.

After just two rings, Patricia answered. She insisted that

she did not mind the Sunday afternoon call considering the amazing news Scott shared about finding Mikhail and the fantastic story he told. "I have a family I never knew I had," Scott explained with obvious excitement. "But now I want to go a step further."

"I assume you want to run a DNA workup on Mikhail?" she asked.

"Yes, but that's not why I called. Based on Mikhail's story, it's reasonable—logical actually—to assume that it was Mikhail's brother Max who impregnated my aunt, Henrietta. If that's indeed true, it will follow that my aunt is my mother and that Ruth—who I always thought was my mother—is really my aunt."

"Wow, a pretty dramatic turn of events."

"I'll say! But here's the question I called you about: would my DNA prove my mother was one sister as opposed to the other? Don't they have the same genetic composition because they both share the same parents?"

"Hold on, Scott, are you telling me that Ruth and Henrietta were identical twins?"

"No. Henrietta was the younger of her parents two children. They were born two years apart."

"Then the results will be clear," she assured him.

"But don't they share the same DNA?"

"They do, but only identical twins share the exact same DNA sequence. And yes, while siblings get approximately fifty percent of their genetic makeup from each parent, the traits they have, or don't have, will be different for every child. It's like splitting a deck of cards down the middle and reshuffling the deck each time the same two people create a new life. Two children, or a dozen, it doesn't matter. Whenever you put those same two halves back together, they will be aligned differently; in other words, each child will have his or her own genetic sequence. One sister could resemble her mother's mom; the other sister might be the spitting image of her dad's mother. The basic ingredients are the same, but the result is unique every single time."

"So then, my DNA would differ from Ruth's, and have certain markers unique to Henrietta?"

"Correct. You don't need a sample of Ruth's DNA. That would only prove that she is closely related. But you will need a sample of Henrietta's DNA to prove that her genetic sequencing is uniquely similar to yours."

"I don't know how easy it will be to get that sample."

"Since, as you've told me, both your mother and aunt are deceased, it would be preferable to have Henrietta disinterred to prove your case."

Scott winced at the thought. "There's no easier way?"

"Perhaps hair of Henrietta's if anyone has an old brush that she once used. Hell, today you can pick up DNA from a tissue you pull out of the trash. Pretty iffy, however, considering an old brush in her house might have been used by a friend as well. I would start by seeing if the coroner kept any blood or tissue samples."

"Okay," Scott sighed. At this point, it all seemed overwhelming, but at least he had a solid idea of what needed to be done.

Scott was surprised to look at his watch and realize it was nearly four. He and Holly were walking back to where Scott had parked his car. "I'm so amazed by everything that has happened today that I forgot we haven't had a real meal since breakfast," Scott said. "I nibbled at the slice of honey cake Rimma gave us, but I was too anxious to eat."

"I felt the same way," Holly added."

"I don't know how I survived that vodka they poured. I guess I was too excited by what Mikhail said to notice any effect."

"Where do you want to go?" Holly asked. "The Richmond District has food from just about every country on the planet! Thai, Italian, Chinese, Ethiopian, Japanese, Cajun —we have a lot of choices."

"Given what just happened, I'm feeling like some Russian food. Do you think we can find anyone open at this hour? It's early for dinner and too late for lunch." Scott gave Holly that engaging smile that Holly was quickly coming to love.

"Let me look on my cell." After scrolling through a few choices, Holly said, "Got it, Katia's Russian Tea Room it's in the Inner Richmond, over on Balboa and Fifth. About a twenty minute walk if you're up for that."

"Sure, beats moving the car and then driving around for fifteen minutes looking for another parking space," Scott replied.

The morning fog they encountered driving across the Golden Gate Bridge had vanished, leaving behind a perfect day in more ways than one.

Scott entered Katia's with a new sense of confidence. He might speak just a few words of Russian—Da, Nyet, and Nostrovia, being the only three that came quickly to mind—but he felt at home, which was easy to do given the delicious scents that greeted them as they walked through the front door.

They ordered two Baltika beers and shared an order of the Shashlik (marinated strips of lamb) with an order of potato cutlets. They were pleased with their choices, and hungrily attacked their food.

Given the odd hour, the typically busy restaurant was unusually quiet. "That woman at the church was like a royal out of a Tolstoy novel," Scott said. "Very grand, and a bit intimidating. I might go back to the church in a week or two to thank her and tell her how things turned out."

"I tried to read War and Peace, but I kept falling asleep," Holly explained. "Then I tried Dostoyevsky's The Brothers Karamazov, and I got the same result. Now that I have a boyfriend who is half Russian, I might give both authors a second try."

"Ha! I might give them a first try. I guess it's time I started learning more about Russian culture. I hope I stay close to Mikhail, there's a lot about my dad and his family, I mean my family, that I want to learn."

"Such as?"

"When did they come to America? Why did they settle in Northern California? I don't know if my grandparents were born in Russia or here in America. And that's just for starters."

As hungry as they both were, it wasn't long before their plates were cleaned. Holly jokingly told the waiter, "I guess you can see we didn't like the food very much."

Both of them passed on dessert, but each ordered a second lager. With food done and the second round of beers in hand, the two fell back to what was most on their minds: Mikhail's certainty that Max's lover was not Ruth.

"I'm shocked, almost beyond words," Scott said. "If Mikhail's story is correct, it's almost certain that Henrietta was my mother, and Ruth was my aunt."

"True, but if Ruth was recently married, she might have used her sister's name with Max. Given the times, and the fact that your grandpa was the town's preacher, Ruth being recently married and having an affair with another man would have been a huge scandal."

"I suppose so," Scott muttered. "I just can't imagine my mom—I mean, Ruth—being that devious."

"At the funeral, Mikhail only knew the name, Henrietta. He didn't have a photo of Henrietta, so it's possible that Ruth deceived both of them."

"I never thought of that, but I suppose it's a possibility."

"And perhaps Ruth simply told her husband that she was pregnant with his child," Holly added. "In fact, if she were having a tryst with Max, that would make keeping the child—"

"You mean keeping me?" He pointed out teasingly.

"Yes, keeping you, a lot easier than it would have otherwise been. Perhaps her husband never knew he was not your actual dad!"

Silently, both of them pondered the possibilities.

"But consider this as well, Scott. Henrietta died

suddenly, and just a few months after your uncle, Elijah, passed. If you assume that she never told Elijah that she had gotten pregnant, had a child, and her sister raised that child as her own, perhaps she was hesitant to name you in the will and leave the bulk of her estate to her child, because it might have caused her husband to be more than just a little curious. Especially when you consider that Ruth and Henrietta had been estranged for years. They have a relationship in tatters, and for some inexplicable reason, she wants to leave her sister's son, who is now an adult, a substantial bequest."

"That's certainly possible. If Henrietta is my mom, there's a good chance she wanted to continue the charade of my being her nephew even though her sister predeceased her."

"Elijah only predeceased Henrietta by two months.

"The more I think about it, the stranger the whole story gets. But as Patricia told me a couple of hours ago, sequencing Henrietta's DNA would settle the issue."

For a while, both of them sat in silence.

"Even when you settle the question of whether or not Henrietta was your mother, there are still going to be unanswered questions," Holly said.

"You're right. Questions that Mikhail, despite however helpful he would like to be, won't be able to answer."

"Scott, every instinct I have tells me that Newberry woman in Santa Rosa knows a good deal more than she's told us. She did say something about knowing Ruth in high school. And that at one time she and Henrietta shared an apartment."

"That whole reception was something of a blur for me,

but I do remember that, and she said something about Henrietta sharing an apartment with her in Santa Rosa while she and Henrietta were pursuing her teaching certificate at the local college."

"She also told us how excited Henrietta and Ruth were when you were born. Something about your' being their little prince.' Whatever it takes, we need to get a sample of Henrietta's DNA. I suppose you'll need to get a lawyer involved as well."

"I'm sure that pulling in an attorney won't come cheap. But, I'm not going to worry about the cost right now."

"Let's go after Newberry first," Holly suggested. "Whether she wants to share the truth with us is anyone's guess. But I'll bet the bank she knows which sister is your mother—and which sister is your aunt."

"What if she won't open up?"

"Do you remember she was so flustered over arriving so late driving down from Santa Rosa that she missed the funeral and nearly all of the reception?"

"Sure, Holly, I remember that. The poor thing looked so frazzled. I really felt sorry for her."

"Yes, you're right. And Rob gave her his card and said that while we were both late for getting back to work, he would like to interview her to fill in parts of Henrietta's story."

"At this point, I'd say a lot more is missing than either of us imagined," Scott added with a laugh.

"Well, I'm going to call her and set up the interview. Let her think I need her help to get Henrietta's story straight. I'm guessing Newberry is trying to stay faithful to a promise she made to Ruth and Henrietta, but I'm also guessing she's pretty conflicted about all these secrets she's had to keep for so many years; particularly now that both Ruth and Henrietta are deceased."

"If you're right Holly, Newberry's been sitting on a huge secret for decades! A secret that, at this point, means much more to me than it does to her."

Both felt the weariness of a day filled with excitement and remarkable discoveries.

Scott asked for the check and grasped Holly's hand after pulling out his credit card as she said, "Let me pay my share."

Scott shook his head, adamantly. "You've got to be kidding! After what you did today? I would have never had the nerve to walk into a community reception at a Russian Orthodox Church and started asking people if they had ever seen or heard of a man named Mikhail Orlov! Holly, in a single day, you turned my entire life around."

"I hope for the better," Holly said with a smile.

"From the start, this has been an adventure. I'm happy I've been able to share it with you."

"I suspect that we've got some more surprises ahead of us," Holly said as a note of caution. "Putting everything else that we have learned aside, the fact that the woman you always thought was your aunt is most likely your mother, would throw just about anyone for a loop."

"Agreed. I'm going to have to take time to process all this."

"Remember, Scott, once you start digging, you never know where it might lead."

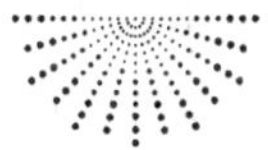

CHAPTER TEN

The following morning Holly reviewed with Rob the remarkable events of Sunday.

"Holly, this information could be way bigger than our story about that crazy old coot with the hand-scribbled will!"

Holly shook her head. "You're right Rob. I like Scott, and this is more than just a great story for me. I wouldn't want to do anything that embarrasses him."

"I understand. But, if Henrietta Hammer had a secret love child, we can't sit on a story like that. When it comes out, we need to make damn sure it will be The Standard's scoop!"

"I know. I just don't want Scott to feel as if he was used by me—or us—in pursuit of a good story."

"Listen, Holly, you've got half the crackpot charitable organizations in this town waiting to see what share of the Hammer estate they're going to receive. If she had a love child that she kept secret from everyone—most notably her husband of God knows how many years, as well as from her child—it could throw the validity of any bequests she made regarding the disposition of her estate into question!"

"Why is that?" Holly asked as her eyes squinted in puzzlement.

"It's a long story, but I'll tell you this. When we spent weeks working on that crazy Mack Mulligan inheritance story, I learned a lot about California law regarding the disposition of an individual's estate. Secrets kept by the deceased—most important secrets regarding offspring—can derail a will faster than you can say Bob's my uncle."

"Not sure I'm following you, Rob."

"You know what? Friday I'm going to invite Bob Ivan to join you, me, and Eddie, for happy hour. I'll let Bob explain how and why. The guy is a walking law library. In the meantime, get a hold of this Newberry woman and see if you can drive up there one afternoon this week."

Holly snorted. "You mean you're going to let me out of here early?"

"I'll pull double duty and get your assignments done as well while you're out of the office. The potential of this story is well worth the sacrifice."

"Okay. I guess Thursday is the best afternoon for me to be gone. Can you let me go by two?"

"How about if you leave at two-thirty? That's as good as I can do," Rob replied.

"You are tight as a screw!"

"I prefer to think of myself as running a tight ship," Rob said with a grin. "Come on, Holly. You know how tough it is to get done early, any day of the week around here. And you've got to be anxious to talk to this woman. God only knows what she might say."

"Okay, it's a deal."

Thirty minutes later Holly received a text back from Scott saying that he could meet her at the San Rafael Transit Depot at two forty-five on Thursday to share a ride north with her to Santa Rosa.

Next, Holly placed her call to Jeannie Newberry. She picked up on the third ring.

Holly took a deep breath. Her primary goal was to get Newberry to agree to see her. The best way to do that was to remind Jeannie that The Standard wanted to interview her for their story on Henrietta's life.

"Absolutely! I'd be delighted."

"Would later this week, perhaps Thursday afternoon work for you?

"I'm here all day. What time works well for you?"

"Can we say four? I'll plan on leaving Sausalito at two-thirty, so hopefully, I can make it to your place by four.

"I know how bad traffic can be on 101 at that time of day. If you're running late, don't worry. I have nothing on the calendar all afternoon."

Holly ended the conversation quickly, not wanting to give Newberry any additional time to rethink her commitment to being interviewed.

Three days later, Scott was waiting when Holly slid into the pick-up and drop-off area at the transit depot.

After getting into the car and giving Holly a kiss on the cheek, Scott asked, "How do you want to handle this conversation? And by the way, did you tell Mrs. Newberry I would be there?"

"The most important thing is to see if she knows a lot more than she has told us previously," Holly reminded him. "As usual, we're flying by the seat of our pants! I told her that we'd gotten some photos of Henrietta that we wanted her to see, for the story. That's at least partially true."

"I guess in Holly-speak that means, no, you didn't tell her that I was coming along."

"I sort of left that out," Holly said with a shrug. "Quit worrying. It could be a bit awkward at first, but we've got one important fact on our side: Elijah, Henrietta, Ruth, Scott, and Max are all deceased. And other than you, there are no kids to be embarrassed over all this. Actually, the only person who would be harmed by her not telling us what we suspect she knows is you."

"That's true—if we're right, then I was the one most harmed.

"Scott, remember when I sent her a phone camera shot of Mikhail's photo, she admitted to recognizing Mikhail's image, but not recalling his name. What none of us knew at the time is the photo might actually have reminded her of Max. Someone who you and I knew nothing about."

"Any thoughts about how you want to approach Newberry?"

"None, other than being very kind—and putting the squeeze on her when and if needed. Scott, I really think this is going to work. Why would Newberry want to carry this secret with her to the grave? Ruth and Henrietta, as best as we know, already have. I believe she's going to take the opportunity to get all of this off her chest. Having you there, I think, is going to seal the deal."

"After what you pulled off locating Mikhail, I have no business doubting you," Scott said with a laugh. "Still, you're going to have to come up with something to explain how I showed up, and it needs to be better than you bumped into me while walking to your car."

Holly shook her head. "Actually, I want her to be caught off guard. Once you've made your case, you have to give the person you're interviewing as much time as they need to formulate what it is they'd like to say. If you say something at that point, it's no different than taking a hook from a fish's mouth and tossing it back in the water."

"Isn't that a bit mean?"

"Probably. But a few awkward moments are a small price to pay for learning the truth."

Opening the front door and seeing Scott standing there, Jeannie Newberry was indeed surprised.

But, in a moment, her surprise turned into a smile as she reached up, put her arms around Scott and pulled him down for a kiss on the cheek. "I'm so happy to see you, Scott! I felt awful that we had such little time to visit when I saw you at Henrietta's service. I wanted to call and invite you up here or to meet for lunch so we could have the chance to visit."

Holly was relieved by Jeannie's reaction. "I had a feeling you would enjoy seeing Scott, so when I told him that I was driving up to see you, I suggested he come along."

"I'm so glad you did."

After tea and homemade cookies had been set out, Holly began by reviewing a dozen different photos she and Scott had placed aside while working on the house.

The final photo was the one that started their quest: the small black and white photo of Max Orlov that they had shown Mikhail on Sunday.

"Does this face look familiar to you?"

"You sent me this photo over my phone last week. I recalled the face but didn't recognize the name."

"When I sent you the photo, there was some confusion about the name of the man in this photo. Mikhail Orlov was the younger brother of the man in this photo. This is a photo of Max Orlov." Holly watched Jeannie's face intently to gauge her reaction.

"I do remember that name, but I never met the gentleman. I heard a lot about him from Henrietta. She thought the world of him."

"I see," Holly said. Although not her greatest strength, Holly kept reminding herself to be diplomatic. "Just a few days ago, we met Mikail Orlov. From him, we learned that Henrietta and Max were more than friends. We're quite sure they were lovers. We also learned that what ended their romance was Max's sudden death in an accident at the lumber processing plant on the outskirts of Fort Bragg.

Most surprisingly, we discovered that Scott was deceived all his life about who his birth parents were."

Jeannie shifted in her seat but held an innocent and surprised look on her face.

"We already know for certain that Scott's father, Scott, Sr. could not possibly have been his actual father because of his Portuguese heritage. A recent genetic test shows that Scott is of Swedish and Russian descent. We located Mikhail, just a few days ago. He lives with his daughter and son-in-law in San Francisco. He has agreed to a DNA workup that will confirm that Scott and Mikhail are closely related. At this point, our only remaining question is whether Scott's birth mother was Ruth or Henrietta. Given the fact that apparently Henrietta and Max were lovers, it would seem logical that the woman he thought was his aunt in truth was his mother."

"Oh my," Jeannie murmured. As she blushed and shifted uncomfortably in the floral print wingback chair she sat in, Holly realized this was not the conversation Newberry expected to have when she opened her front door.

"Mrs. Newberry, since you were friends with both women, we were wondering if you might help us better understand what happened?" Holly said in a soft voice.

Jeannie removed a handkerchief from a pocket of the sweater she wore. Suddenly, she seemed older to her two guests. Without saying a word, she dabbed her eyes and finally broke a long silence. "You know, on that drive down to Henrietta's service, I kept telling myself that the promise I made Ruth and Henrietta decades ago no longer mattered, now that they were both gone. It's a terrible thing to see people you knew nearly all your life predecease you. It's like having pieces of yourself cut off and tossed aside." As she sighed, tears began to run down her cheeks.

Jeannie paused, dried her tears, and took a sip of tea. Holly hoped that Scott would remain silent so that without distraction, or excuse, Henrietta's friend could finally tell her truth.

"When I finally got to the reception, I knew this wasn't the right time or place. All the way back home, I thought how foolish I had been to imagine that I'd be able to free myself of this burden I've carried for so long. Back then, it all seemed so exciting! Your aunt—I mean your mother—Henrietta, was excited that she was going to have Max's baby, it was a small part of him she was carrying inside of her."

"When did you know that Henrietta was pregnant?" Holly asked.

"The two of them, Ruth and your mother," Jeannie said, looking directly at Scott, "involved me in their plan almost from the beginning."

Despite having met Mikhail, Scott was shaken by this additional evidence of a grand deception that profoundly affected the course of his life. Suddenly, Scott's mouth became dry; his feet and hands went cold. The confirmation that his mother was his aunt and his aunt was his mother overwhelmed him nearly to the point of tears. He knew from the moment Mikhail shared his story that this was a strong possibility. Still, Newberry's confession made it all the more real.

How could he have gone for so many years knowing none of this? Was he a fool, naïve, or just ignoring the obvious? The truth must have been hiding in plain sight: a possible reality Scott was reluctant to pursue.

Perhaps made uncomfortable by his shocked silence, Jeannie turned to Scott. "I think there are a few things you need to understand," she said softly as she took his hand. "Ruth and Henrietta were the daughters of a minister. In the Swedish community along the north coast of Mendocino, Reverend Bratten was a highly respected man. A scandal of this proportion would have ruined many lives! Looking back now, I can see how everything happened so suddenly. First, the reverend and his wife—your grandmother Sara— went back to Sweden for a year to work for their church in Stockholm. Ruth married Scott just before her parents departed. Meanwhile, Henrietta was engaged to Elijah, who was the most eligible bachelor in Mendocino County.

"When Henrietta had her affair with Max, Elijah knew nothing about it?" Holly asked breathlessly.

"No, he never knew about Max. And there was a good reason for that. Elijah's father had sent him to Japan to form a partnership and start a new tool manufacturing plant. Expanding the company overseas, particularly into Asia, was a huge undertaking at the time. Elijah's father depended on him. He was supposed to return to California within a year, but eleven months after he left, he wrote Henrietta explaining that he needed to stay another year. That put her into an emotional tailspin. She was nearly thirty, and she was horrified by the thought that if Elijah finally returned home and was no longer interested in marrying her, she might be too old to find a good husband. No one would think like that today, but those were very different times."

"How did Henrietta meet Max?" Holly asked.

"Believe it or not, Henrietta and Max met at Ruth's wedding," The irony of it all brought a smile back to Jeannie's lips. "Max was your father's best man!"

"My Dad's best man was my birth father?" Scott said, shaking his head in amazement.

"Ruth was the one who came to me first with the news that Henrietta was pregnant. Your father and I had the very same reaction. We were both shocked. Still, at the wedding, I can remember how those two hit it off. Sparks flew, to put it mildly."

"Was anyone surprised or concerned that Henrietta seemed to forget about Elijah?" Holly asked.

"Not really. Ruth felt horrible for her sister after Elijah had written telling her he needed to stay in Japan for a second year. I think she had doubts about his coming home and keeping his promise. In spite of her best efforts to remain calm and confident, Henrietta was unsure as well."

"How long did the relationship between Henrietta and Max last? I assume it was over by the time Elijah returned?"

"Max died two weeks to the day after the wedding."

"Wow," Holly said. "They must have really hit it off."

"Absolutely. Ruth moved into Scott's home on her wedding night. Just two days after the wedding, Sara and Johannes left for Sweden. That left Henrietta all alone in the parsonage with only Max to keep her company."

"Gosh," Holly said. "They certainly had the opportunity to..."

"Misbehave?" Jeannie said with a smile and a lifted brow.

"Absolutely," Holly said enthralled by the story of the two lovers.

"I'm a love child," Scott announced. He found a degree of

comfort in the fact that his life was the result of two star-crossed lovers.

"My amazing fifth-grade teacher! No one in my class would have ever guessed any of this," Holly said, shaking her head in wonder.

"What happened then?" Scott asked anxiously.

"Remember, it was Ruth, who was my earliest childhood friend. Henrietta was two years behind us in school, but she liked hanging out with the older girls.

"It was late on a Saturday afternoon; Henrietta, Ruth and I were out shopping for a dining room set for Ruth's new home. Her little 'love nest,' we called it. We were in Crowders, which back then was the only furniture shop anywhere near Fort Bragg. Some older gentleman walked into the shop and said to the owner, 'Did you hear about the accident up at the mill?' The color went out of Henrietta's face. Later I found out why. They had spent Friday night together at the parsonage, and she knew Max was working there the following day.

"Well, the poor dear ran straight out of the store as if a cannon had gone off! She headed up the road, toward the mill. It was more than a mile up there and most of that uphill. Ruth and I knew why she was in a panic. We jumped into a blue Thunderbird convertible that Scott had restored for Ruth and presented to her as a wedding present. It wasn't long before we caught up to Henrietta. She was still running along the side of the road and your mother—I mean, your Aunt Ruth—told her to try to calm down and jump into the back seat."

Jeannie's face clouded over with the memory of that sad day.

"There were many cars already at the mill when we arrived, there were also a couple of ambulances, and a dozen volunteer firefighters. You can't imagine what a wild scene it was! Both Ruth and I had our hands full just trying to calm Henrietta down."

"When did she learn that Max had died?" Holly asked, feeling a lump forming in her throat.

"Each minute felt like an eternity. It was probably an hour or less after we got there that we learned of his fate. Max was a big, strong man, but against a pile of unprocessed timber breaking loose, he and his two coworkers didn't stand a chance. By today's standards, mills were unimaginably dangerous places back then."

Jeannie used her handkerchief to wipe the corners of her eyes. "I've never seen a woman sadder than Henrietta was that day. It was just heartbreaking. Still, Ruth and I were thankful that we were there for her."

"When did Henrietta learn she was carrying Max's child?" Holly asked.

"Unlike Ruth, Henrietta was always slender as a young woman. She was also a picky eater. It was just her nature, I suppose. She had a history of irregular menstrual cycles, so she didn't pay much attention when she had gone over the time when her period should have come. But when she started experiencing some nausea and some tenderness in her breasts, she told Ruth. Together, they went south to the town of Mendocino to see a doctor. If indeed Henrietta was pregnant, they wanted to keep that news as far from Fort Bragg as they reasonably could.

"When it was confirmed that she was pregnant, Henrietta went into a complete panic. She was convinced that

God had punished her for the sin of having sex outside of marriage. God claimed his vengeance by taking Max. Then she wondered if being pregnant with Max's child was another sign from God."

"Really?" Holy asked.

"Holly, don't forget, Henrietta was the daughter of a preacher. She believed everything that happened to her was as a result of God's approval or disapproval. As great as the sin of having sex out of wedlock was, abortion was an even greater sin."

"I got lucky on that score," Scott said hoping to break the tension, if for only a brief moment.

"So they must have decided that they would pass the child off as Ruth's," Holly reasoned. "But how?"

"Believe me, it involved a good amount of scheming," Jeannie assured both of them. "I'll admit to playing an important role. Back then if you had a two-year associates degree, you could qualify for a teaching position in most California school districts by getting your teacher's certificate. I had registered for the program at Santa Rosa Junior College. It ran from September through January. Henrietta was due in the latter part of March…"

"As in my birthday," Scott said. "March twenty-third."

"Exactly," Jeannie said with a smile. "Henrietta left with me in late August, before she was noticeably pregnant. We moved down to Santa Rosa, far away from the prying eyes of our friends and neighbors back in Fort Bragg."

"But how did my mother—I mean my Aunt Ruth— convince my dad to go along with this scheme? And as far as the neighbors were concerned, how did she go from being 'not pregnant' to having a baby?"

"That was my next question," Holly added.

"Here's another little secret they kept from you. Your dad was in combat in Southeast Asia. He suffered a wound that left him sterile. Ruth very much wanted to have a child, but she also loved Scott. Before they decided to marry, they agreed that one day they would adopt. They had planned to wait at least a couple of years, but that changed when Henrietta found herself pregnant. Scott happily agreed to the scheme with two conditions. The first was that neither of them would identify to the child or to Ruth's parents, the child's actual birth mother. The second was that Ruth would join with him in the charade by shopping for pregnancy clothes and wearing them throughout Henrietta's pregnancy."

"Scott's parents, Ruth's in-laws, never knew either? Didn't he tell them about his wound?" Holly asked.

"They knew he had been wounded, but he kept the resulting sterility a secret. The family moved to Pasadena from Fort Bragg, when Scott was, what, ten?" Jeannie said, turning toward Scott.

"That's right. My dad's brother started a house painting business down there and invited him to join as a partner. They struggled for a time, but before long, the housing market was booming, and their business took off. So they obviously pulled it off. Ruth's and my dad's parents lived out their lives, assuming, as I did, that Ruth and Scott were my actual parents." Scott shook his head in awe. "Jeannie, don't you think what the sisters did was wrong?"

"I don't know how to answer that, Scott. Henrietta was going to have you in secret, and then give you up for adoption the day you were born. Who knows if you would have ever met Henrietta, Ruth, or Scott if you'd been adopted by another couple?"

Scott and Holly sat silently, thinking about the situation the sisters found themselves in.

"You're both forgetting one significant detail," Jeannie declared.

"What's that?" Holly and Scott asked in unison.

"The issue of Elijah. Before all this happened—before Henrietta met Max, before his death, her pregnancy, and all the rest—Henrietta was a young woman planning to marry the man who was undoubtedly the most eligible bachelor in the entire county! Elijah was selected at birth to be the third Hammer to lead Hammer Tools. He was rather shy, and so was Henrietta. Their relationship was the talk of Fort Bragg. When, after dating for nearly a year, Elijah invited Henrietta for a special dinner at a romantic restaurant down in Mendocino, we all thought that she would come back with an engagement ring. Instead, she broke the disappointing news to her sister and parents that Elijah was leaving for Japan, but he had pledged to return in a year and marry her. When he wrote to say his time there had to be extended, Henrietta was heartbroken. It was a perfect time for Max to sweep her off her feet. But when Max died so suddenly, and the evidence of their passion was about to be made apparent by your birth, Henrietta panicked. Ruth offered her a lifeline. I offered to help as well. At the time, it seemed like the best solution. Most importantly it allowed you, Scott, to have both your mother and your aunt close to you."

"But then," Holly said, "Something must have caused Ruth and Henrietta to become estranged. Scott tells me that after Ruth and her husband relocated to Pasadena, he hardly ever saw Henrietta, and Ruth rarely mentioned her name."

"As the great Scottish poet, Robert Burn, wrote, 'The best-laid schemes of mice and men often go askew, and leave us nothing but grief and pain.' That pretty much sums up the story of Ruth and Henrietta."

"How so?" Holly asked.

Jeannie reached again for her hankie so that she could catch a few more tears. "The girls' parents came back home a little over a year after they left. They were pleased beyond words with their handsome grandson! You were quite the stunning baby," Jeannie said to Scott.

Scott blushed, smiled and shook his head in embarrassment.

"Elijah came home just weeks after the girls' parents returned," Jeannie continued. "He was good to his word. He married Henrietta less than three months later. Henrietta, Ruth, and I stayed close friends. I took a teaching position in Mendocino. We saw each other regularly. Ruth often brought baby Scott along. We were all amazed at how quickly you grew. At this time, Elijah's father wanted to hand the company's daily operation over to his son. But before he did, he and Elijah decided that now that Hammer Tools was an international corporation it needed to be located in a city known around the world. Their choice was the one big city relatively close: San Francisco. Henrietta couldn't share with him her unspeakable pain over the idea of being so far from her son, so she shouldered on. She picked a house in Sausalito—the one that Henrietta died in so many years later, and she made certain that it had lots of bedrooms for all the children she and Elijah planned to have," Jeannie said with a tired shrug.

"By now, you can guess what happened. Babies have a way of coming into your life when the timing is…well, let's just say less than ideal. But when you're ready to begin a family, for one reason or another, things often don't go according to plan. As it turns out, Elijah suffered from low sperm count. That conclusion was two years in coming. He thought the problem was Henrietta's, but we all knew that wasn't the case," Jeannie added with a short laugh. "Today, they would have just taken his sperm and fertilized one of her eggs. But back then, that was the stuff of science fiction. As you can imagine, Henrietta grew increasingly disappointed—and I think a good deal bitter as well. The drive from Sausalito to Fort Bragg was nine hours round trip, and that was in good weather."

"This is where the grief and pain part comes in," Holly murmured.

"Oh yes my dear, you're right about that! Things only went from bad to worse. Ruth began to resent Henrietta's possessiveness when she came for a weekend visit to Fort Bragg. Your grandpa Bratten died suddenly of a heart attack, and your grandmother Sara moved in with you and your family. Then Scott, Sr. got the chance to sell his commercial painting business and become a partner in his brother's painting company.

"Henrietta was furious with Ruth for moving to Pasadena. Ruth would call me and say, 'What am I suppose to do? If it weren't for me, Scott would have been placed with an adoption agency, and she might have never seen her child again.' Then Henrietta would call me in tears declaring, 'I'm never going to have another baby, and now Ruth's taken, my only child!'"

"But I wasn't her child," Scott muttered. "She gave me away."

"Your right. Henrietta did—but only because she thought that it was what had to be done at the time," Jeannie reminded Scott. "As you can imagine, the divide and bitterness between the two of them only grew worse over the years."

"Why do you think Henrietta disappeared from my life for such a long time?"

"It was less painful for her to put you out of her mind than to see you and remember how her sister, as she now claimed, took you away from her."

"But that wasn't fair of her to say!" Holly exclaimed.

"No, it wasn't. But being bitter, and blaming Ruth was how she dealt with the pain of losing her only child. She rewrote the history of how it all happened. In her retelling, Ruth essentially schemed to take Scott away from her when she was too consumed with fear and grief to realize what was happening. None of this fit with the facts, but disappointment often moves us to rewrite the past.

"Henrietta pleaded with Elijah to adopt a child, or better still, two or more children. He was dead set against it. He insisted that only a child of his own bloodline could be the rightful heir to Hammer Tools. Maria, Elijah's sister, and her two sons, never had any interest in the business short of the profits that their share of the business earned every year. They agreed to sell their half of the business to the highest bidder when Elijah chose to retire. The Hammer family no longer had any connection to the Hammer Tool

Company other than the brand name the founding family left behind."

"Why did Henrietta choose to go into teaching?" Holly asked.

"She started teaching long before Elijah retired. It wasn't for the need of a teacher's salary. And let me tell you, Elijah was against her taking a job, any job! She spoke to me about that. I can remember her saying, 'If I'm not going to have children of my own, I can at least do something to improve the lives of other people's children.' It was a noble goal—at least it was at the start. But after a few years, whenever I came down to Sausalito, or she came up to Santa Rosa to have lunch, she would complain that she was very disappointed with her students. She would tell me that the children were disrespectful, lazy, inattentive, or all three.

"Having been one of those kids she was complaining about, I suppose she had a point," Holly admitted.

"Perhaps. But there is one thing you should never forget when you're a teacher: you set the tone and maintain order in your classroom while allowing children to behave like children. Kids sense when you don't like being with them and they push back."

"Wow!" Holly said. "Sounds like we would have been better off having you as our fifth-grade teacher."

Jeannie laughed. "In Henrietta's defense, I'm sure you and your fellow students were a handful."

"You don't know the half of it," Holly said with a smile that Scott found irresistible.

"But what about Henrietta getting her teaching certificate?" Scott asked. "She must have had some interest in being an educator to go through with the effort."

"Leaving home to earn her teaching certification provided an easy excuse for her parents and everyone else she knew as to why she would be away from Fort Bragg and spending so many months sharing an apartment with me in Santa Rosa. Henrietta would have taken classes in coal mining if it got her away from Fort Bragg and allowed her to keep the little secret growing inside of her. The plan was perfect, the result was less than perfect."

"Why didn't Henrietta quit teaching several years ago when her husband retired?" Holly wondered out loud.

"For a long time, their house was like the once-divided city of Berlin. I think both were disappointed with each other over not having children, and that big house they bought was a constant reminder of their unrealized dreams. But neither of them would give an inch. They were, as the expression goes, dug in."

"I'm surprised, that they didn't divorce years ago," Holly said

"Remember they were from a time and a culture in which divorce was unthinkable, so they clung to a failed marriage and waited for the other to make the first move.

"Not long ago, Henrietta called me. She wanted to meet for lunch. I said yes, and we met in downtown Petaluma, about halfway between Sausalito and Santa Rosa. Henrietta mentioned that she and Elijah were both happy and well. They'd finally settled their differences, and put all the bitterness behind them. She had quit her teaching job a few months earlier because they'd made plans to travel together. I was pleased to hear that they chose Japan as their first destination. Something about Ruth's passing and seeing Scott happy and successful with a good teaching position made her see the past in a more positive light. She was pleased with what she now thought was the excellent job your adoptive parents must have done in raising you." Turning to Scott, she added, "Her only real wish, was for you to have a happy life."

The three of them sat in silence for a brief time, reflecting on all the unexpected twists people encounter over a lifetime.

Finally, Jeannie said, "All this helped your mother to turn the page and look forward to a happier future. She called me after she heard your news that you had accepted a teaching position with Marin Academy. She was beside herself with anticipation. Then Elijah got so sick, so suddenly. Poor man! In truth, he was a good man. Henrietta did not want to acknowledge that for a very long time."

"The story would have had a happier ending if my real mother had revealed herself to me before she died," Scott said softly.

"I asked her at that last lunch we shared if she ever planned to tell you that it was her and not Ruth that brought you into this world. She said, 'As long as Elijah is alive I don't dare reveal that truth to anyone. You and I are the only two people left who know the whole story. It would destroy Elijah if he knew that I kept something like that from him all these years.'

"I then asked her if it was because Elijah was unable to make her pregnant or because she was determined not to admit that during his long absence she had a relationship with another man and had given birth to that man's son. She gave me a one-word answer: 'Both!'"

"You know, we hardly saw each other in the months

after I moved to Marin County. Then, shortly after Uncle Elijah's funeral, she called and invited me to the house. She explained that I was her only living relative, and she wanted to leave my name with her attorney in case anything were to happen to her."

"Were you surprised by that?" Jeannie asked.

"Not really. I thought that Uncle Elijah's death served as a reminder of her own longevity. I didn't mind. I was happy that she trusted me to be there for her if I was needed. For years our only relationship was a card on my birthday and one at Christmas."

"I guess that when her will is revealed, you won't be mentioned," Jeannie replied. "Henrietta never wanted Elijah to suspect she was anything other than your aunt. By keeping you away from the house, Henrietta kept you away from Elijah. It was clear to me that she was uncomfortable having you and him in the same room together. If Henrietta had lived longer, I'm convinced she would have revealed herself to you. It would have taken a good deal of courage. Admitting to your son you've lied to him his entire life is not an easy truth for anyone to own."

"I get the impression you didn't think very highly of my mother," Scott said.

"I had a bittersweet relationship with Henrietta. Growing up, she was my best friend's kid sister. When the whole world fell in on her—wondering if Elijah would come back, her brief, passionate love affair with Max, losing him so suddenly, and then the drama of her pregnancy, and the train wreck her marriage became…" Jeannie rolled her eyes at the thought of it all. "Other women followed television soap operas. I had Henrietta and Ruth."

The uneasy tension in the room broke when Scott laughed.

Holly and Jeannie joined in.

"No kid in my class ever imagined any of this drama was going on in Henrietta's life. I'm certain of that!"

"Trust me, my dear: no fifth grader has ever given serious thought to the fact that their teachers are real people with lives of their own. As a general rule, at age ten, life is not something that happens to others. It's something that happens to you."

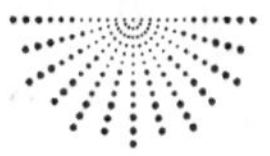

CHAPTER ELEVEN

Friday morning, Holly and Rob reviewed the news and feature assignments for the following week's editions.

To Holly, the process was akin to assembling a jigsaw puzzle. Its pieces were the photos, stories, and the all-important display ads that had to fit into each edition's final layout.

When they stopped working to take their lunch break, Holly shared with Rob portions of their visit with Jeannie Newberry. "I want to save the bulk of this story for when we're together this evening with Eddie and Bob Ivan, but there's just one thing I have to tell you now." Taking a deep breath, Holly declared, "Henrietta was Scott's mother."

Rob's eyes opened wide. "You're sure about that?"

"I know they'll probably have to dig her up and get some proof positive DNA test to make it a done deal, but the bottom line is that Henrietta, her sister Ruth, and that woman Jeannie were best buds growing up. Newberry held back at first, but bringing Scott sealed the deal. She let loose with a story that blew us both away! Poor Scott almost limped out of there. If he was a ten-pin set, she bowled a strike. No kidding, Rob. When we left there, I thought I'd have to help him back into the car."

"Wow! That bad?"

"Frankly, I'd say, that good—but just more than I think Scott was prepared to hear; even though we already had good reason to suspect that Henrietta was his mother."

"How was he when you got him back to his place?"

"His place? I took him to mine. If there was ever a guy who needed a good cuddle, it was Scott last night."

Rob frowned. "I'm not sure I was looking for that much detail."

"Man, you're such a small town prude!"

Chuckling, Rob placed his hands over his ears. "So, Mrs. Hammer had a love child!"

Holly nodded. "Yep. I guess she wasn't the old prude we kids imagined her to be."

"Talk about the story behind the story. This makes the Mulligan will look so uninteresting. Do you think we should use it next week?"

"Rob, given the fact that Scott and I have become a couple, I'm going to step back and let you make all the decisions regarding our coverage of the story. The last thing I want to do is have Scott think that I wanted to get close to him to have first dibs on this story."

"He's really become special to you, that's nice. No one deserves a guy like Scott more than you!"

This was one Friday night happy hour where Eddie, Rob, and Holly made it their goal to arrive on time. Drinks had been ordered, and a toast had been made when Bob Ivan, who was nearing eighty but looked ten or more years younger, walked over and said, "It must be ten years or more since I stepped foot in this place. Looks like the same old dump."

"It is that," Rob said as he stood to shake Bob's hand.

As was his habit, Bob wore a white button-down shirt with an open collar. Other than funerals and weddings, he hadn't worn a necktie in years. Bob's pants sat comfortably below his waistline to give his softening physique some extra room to breathe. In many ways, he was like an aging gothic church: unassuming on the outside, dazzlingly brilliant on the inside.

Bob had what many considered to be the most exceptional legal mind in Marin County. At various times he'd served as legal counsel and advisor to several of the towns in the county. By now, most of his colleagues had retired. But Bob feared that retirement would, in his words, "bore me right into an early grave," and so he continued to practice on behalf of a half-dozen clients that did not want to hear any of the hints he occasionally dropped about slowing down.

Like Eddie, Rob, and Holly, Bob was a native of Sausalito. Also, like them, he didn't hold back about its corrupt politics. When representing a client aggrieved by one of the city's less than rational zoning decisions, he called Sausalito, "The meanest little town in the West." His kids were long grown and out on their own, but he and his wife continued to live in the same house his parents purchased the year he started grade school.

He had a shock of white hair that stubbornly clung to the top of his otherwise balding head. Being always too busy with other matters, it was a rare occasion when Bob took the time to get his hair trimmed. As he leaned forward, he often brushed that one thick patch of white hair out of his eyes, which were bright blue, and surprisingly intimidating to a long series of hostile witnesses he had skewered on the witness stand over his long years in the courtroom.

"What are you kids up to these days?" Bob asked, happily.

He had earned the right to call them kids for two reasons. First, he was over forty years older. Second, in their time each of them rang his doorbell once or twice a year selling candy, cookies, or holiday wrapping paper to support their schools, their Scout troops or Sausalito's Little League team, the Shakers.

After greetings all around and a kiss on the cheek from Holly, Bob sat down and ordered a beer. "You know, with this damn medication they've got me on I'm supposed to have no more than two drinks a week. That takes a good deal of the fun out of life."

"So we've heard from our parents," Rob said with a laugh.

"Well, I hope you three listen and take good care of yourselves. Don't forget, aging is a direct result of not dying young."

"Amen," Eddie said as he tipped his glass slightly in acknowledgment of Bob's wise words.

It took nearly thirty minutes to catch Bob up on all that

had happened since the unexpected death of Henrietta Hammer.

"I read something about it in The Standard and in the county paper, Bob said. "I met Elijah a few times. Once he came to me to discuss a real estate deal, he was in a twist over. The man didn't suffer fools, I can tell you that. And he knew what he was doing when it came to buying and selling properties. He'd study a proposal, and say either, 'This makes sense,' or, 'It doesn't pencil out.'"

"Bob, what did he mean by 'doesn't pencil out?'" Holly asked.

"That just meant the numbers didn't add up, which was his way of saying there was little hope of ever realizing a profit given the asking price, the location and the condition of the property. Like I said, Elijah Hammer had a sharp eye for business."

"Just a few weeks ago the three of us were sitting here, toasting the memory of Henrietta," Rob said.

"Toasting, as in celebrating?" Bob asked with a raised eyebrow.

"Well, we remembered when we were her students and…" Rob said carefully hoping to find the right words.

"Hey, remember, I was a late bloomer, I didn't marry until I was in my forties. Both my boys had Mrs. Hammer as their fifth-grade teacher. They were scared to death of her. I'm sure she had some good qualities, but 'beloved teacher' would not be one of them."

Anxious to tell her story, Holly shared the details of Scott's Sunday discovery of Mikhail and their trip the day before to Santa Rosa. Her retelling of those two remarkable events took nearly thirty minutes.

Near the end, Rob could not hold back and said, "Henrietta—and a love child. Good gosh, this story is incredible!"

Eddie rolled his eyes. "We would have loved to have known about this twenty-five plus years ago when Henrietta was lecturing us on the importance of 'living an exemplary life.'"

"Everyone has their secrets," Bob countered. "But I have to admit, this story is right up there with those pulp fiction detective novels we all read when I was a kid!"

"I know," Holly said. "It's pretty nutty."

More than any other aspect of Henrietta and Scott's story, what stopped Bob in his tracks was the question of Henrietta's will. "If Scott is indeed the natural born son of Henrietta Bratten—the evidence clearly points in that direction—and he is not called out as such in her will, that would throw the entire estate into turmoil."

"I don't understand Bob. Why would that be?" Eddie asked.

"Because in California, any child of the deceased who is not identified as such in the will negates the validity of the will."

"What happens then?" Holly asked.

"Provided there aren't a half dozen more children Henrietta birthed, surrendered, and never acknowledged in her last will and testament, the value of her fortune—which is likely to be in the tens of millions, after taxes, and minus any liens or obligations against the estate—goes in its entirety to Scott."

Holly began to choke on one of the three oversized olives in her vodka martini.

"Easy, dear!" Eddie said as he slapped Holly on the back.

"My guesstimate of The Hammer estate would put it between forty and fifty million dollars. That being said, Scott is going to need more than what this Newberry woman shared with you. I don't doubt her story, but when you have that kind of money in an estate, everyone's motives for coming forward become suspect. Think of it as the legal equivalent of a fumble on the goal line: everyone on the field is going to try falling on that ball."

"Speaking of questionable motives," Rob added, "you should see the rogues' gallery of representatives from local charities that are waiting for the reading of her will."

"I wouldn't be surprised if one of them did her in," Holly said as she waved over Gail. "Any of you fellas want to buy a working girl a second martini?"

"It's on me. In fact, let me buy the drinks tonight," Bob said. "Hanging out with you three makes me feel forty again. And that's quite a treat."

"Thanks Bob!" Eddie, Rob, and Holly said in unison.

"Bob, tell us how this whole thing with 'undeclared children' came to be," Rob asked.

"It's not a situation that happens too often," Bob said. "But it was not uncommon for families to be separated back in a time when life in California was a lot less civilized than it is today."

"You mean the days of the Barbary Coast?" Holly asked.

"Whether you came here by boat or by land," Bob explained, "it was an awful journey. A lot of people died along the way. In addition to natural causes, they died in robberies, kidnappings, assaults, and more. I'm not sure there was ever a wilder place in the lower forty-eight than

San Francisco in the days before, during, and after the gold rush."

"But how did the state's lawmakers come up with something like this?" Eddie asked.

"It was pretty simple and understandable at the time. Families were torn apart for countless reasons. Could have been a blizzard coming over the Sierra, or a flood washing through the Central Valley. More often, it was because of a crime. Countless families were separated and never reunited. A parent who made no provision for their child or children, thought them to be lost, or most likely, deceased. In those days there was one horror story after another. Along the waterfront of San Francisco, where today you have high tech and financial firms, there were dangerous places like Shanghai Kelly's. A young man just arrived from back East, would go in there to have a couple of drinks. The saloon's operators would drug his drink. The next morning he'd wake up off the California coast on his way to China. Some eventually made it back. Others just disappeared and were assumed to have died or runoff. Believe me, this part of California put a lot of the wild in stories of the Wild West."

"I suppose," Holly said teasingly, "this was long before anyone thought about locating friends and families on social media."

"Hah! You're right about that, no posts, no shout outs, no tweets!"

"Bob, tweets? I had no idea you knew about tweets," Eddie said.

"Hey I may not have been to the movies since The Sound

of Music, but I keep up, man! I'm a lot cooler than you kids think."

"So, this law has stayed on the books all these years?" Eddie asked.

Bob nodded. "For whatever reason, a case of a past pregnancy might be something a mother chose not to acknowledge—possibly out of shame, or fear of losing a husband, or the fear of bringing disgrace upon her family. The list of reasons can be pretty darn long. After years of keeping the child's existence a secret, I would guess Henrietta didn't know what to do.

"But, if she intended to leave her child nothing, that would have been easy enough to do. In fact, in the month between Elijah's passing and Henrietta's death, she might have met with her attorney and amended her will."

"I'm not following you," Holly said as she glanced at Rob and Eddie both of whom shrugged.

"Henrietta simply needed to amend her will to say, 'I have a natural born child, Scott Silva, he is to receive none of the proceeds from my estate.' It's only when a natural-born child goes unacknowledged that the will is thrown into question.

"So there's a real chance that if she never acknowledged Scott as her natural born child during Elijah's lifetime, and it's easy to understand why she did not, and then failed to ask the will be amended during the brief time between her husband's death and her own, all her other bequests lose their validity."

"Amazing!" Holly said.

"It wouldn't surprise me in the least," Bob said. "Most people treat making an appointment to see their attorney with the same enthusiasm as they schedule a checkup with their dentist. There's an excellent chance Henrietta had no idea she was undoing the will's validity. People set aside the caveat that ignorance of the law is no excuse, but the law stands as written regardless."

"Bob, just one other thing," Rob said. "When I was doing that story about that crazy scribbled out will Mack Mulligan left behind, you told me about the case of Bessie Sanders. Could you share that story with Eddie and Holly? I could never tell it as well as you."

"Sure, happy to retell it. It's been one of my favorite stories from my years in private practice. I handled Bessie Sanders as a client. She was rescued from Leningrad as a young girl—perhaps ten-years-old when she escaped. A half million of her fellow citizens starved to death during the Nazi occupation and blockade of the Russian city we today know as St. Petersburg. Bessie was first taken to Finland and then made her way to America shortly after the war. Years later, she tried to hide from her second husband, an American, the fact that she had twin boys the result of an affair she had years before back in Richmond, Virginia. She put the boys up for adoption. I can remember to this day meeting with her and her second husband to draw up their wills. I asked, 'Bessie, you have no children from your previous marriage, and no natural born children is that correct?' 'Certainly not Mister Ivan,' Bessie says. We went back and forth on this point a couple of times. Something told the old prosecutor in me that Bessie wasn't completely honest. She was simply too emphatic in her reaction. I've got to give Bessie credit; however, she stuck to her story.

'No Mr. Ivan,' she said in a heavy Russian accent: 'Bessie have no children."

"One day, the twins now grown men, who've been told by the woman that raised them that they were adopted as infants, set out to find their birth mother. They tracked down a variety of leads, most of which turned out to be dead ends. But those two were persistent. Finally, they located her in San Francisco. Unfortunately, they were too late. Bessie had died a month earlier, which, sadly, her sons learned from Bessie's neighbor. The wealthy man Bessie had married had died two years prior. His entire estate had gone to Bessie. The court awarded the two boys, who she never acknowledged in her will, the remaining value of her estate.

The twins were pretty disappointed they never got to ask their mother why she had given them up for adoption. But the money and property they were awarded was a nice consolation prize for all their efforts in locating her. It came to about two million dollars. And that was back at a time when two million dollars was worth two million dollars. Pretty dramatic, wouldn't you say?"

"I'm amazed. I never knew any of this," Eddie said.

"Happens all the time Eddie," Bob assured him. "There's a lot of surprises buried in the law—particularly in tax and estate law. People live and die, never having the slightest idea it was ever there—unless, of course, they or someone they know runs right into the middle of a situation like the one your friend has stumbled into."

"I don't know if I ever heard the term, 'natural born child,' what exactly does that mean, Bob?"

"In a will, children are acknowledged in one of three

ways, they can be identified as adopted, or as the issue of a current or previous marriage. Scott would be referred to as a 'natural born child' because he was born to Henrietta out of wedlock."

"In other words, a bastard?" Rob said.

"Correct. Only the law preferred the softer tone of natural born."

"What should Scott do now?" Holly asked.

"Have him get in touch with me," Bob suggested. He pulled a dog-eared card from an old wallet that appeared to double as a personal filing cabinet.

"Bob, any idea who might represent the Hammer estate?" Rob asked.

"I've got a good guess, Nate Beasley. When I did some consulting work for Elijah, Beasley was involved. I think he's been the Hammer family attorney for many years."

"Beasley, that's right. I heard his name from Scott," Holly said. "Henrietta left Scott's name with him in case of an emergency telling him he was her nephew and had recently moved to Marin to accept a teaching position."

"If Henrietta claimed to Beasley that Scott was her nephew, there's a good chance she never came clean with him about her son," Bob said. "Good to know. Right now, moving forward, there is going to have to be a court order for an exhumation. We'll need to get Beasley involved in that."

"You think Beasley is going to try to block such a move?" Rob asked.

"I doubt that for two reasons. One, Nate's a good man. He'll want to see this set straight and done right. He'll be disturbed to learn that Henrietta deceived him, but he knows he's not the first attorney to have a client share less than the truth and nothing but the truth. Two, he's not going to get whatever final legal fees are due him until the will's validity is resolved and the estate is settled."

"Pretty wild stuff," Eddie said. "Those heirs in waiting are going to be in a twist if the will is ruled invalid."

"Oh what a tangled web we weave…" Rob said with a half smile.

As he looked at each one of them, Bob smiled and said, "Everyone has something to hide. Henrietta just had a bigger secret than most."

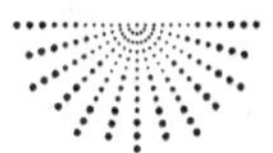

CHAPTER TWELVE

A request filed by Bob Ivan on behalf of his new client, Scott Silva, for the exhumation of Henrietta Hammer was approved one week later. Its specific purpose, providing indisputable proof that Henrietta was Scott's birth mother.

Tanned and rested from his family's Hawaiian vacation, Max Brownstein, the county's medical examiner, reviewed the court-approved order and gave his go-ahead shortly before he broke for lunch with his favorite sheriff's deputy detective, Eddie Austin.

They met at BJ's Restaurant and Brewhouse located less than a mile from their separate office locations. After sliding into one of the oversized booths, they ordered quickly: Eddie requested the North Beach mahi-mahi and shrimp, while Max ordered the jambalaya. The waiter asked if they wanted, "the recommended beer pairings with their entrees," prompting Eddie to say, "We'd love to, but we've got to get back to work."

Max rolled his eyes. "God, you're such a killjoy! One glass of beer couldn't take us too far off our game. Hey, with some of those chemicals I'm around in the morgue, I'm a little high most days anyway."

The waiter winced over what he had just heard and said, "I'll bring you the beer pairings," before hurrying off to grab orders from another table.

"What's he in such a hurry about?" Eddie asked with a raised eyebrow.

"When you just returned from Hawaii, everyone here looks like they're running at lightning speed."

"Really? Even in Marin County?"

"Eddie, compared to Kauai, downtown San Rafael, looks like downtown Los Angeles."

Eddie laughed over the comparison. "I haven't made it over to Kauai, is it quieter than Maui?"

"Way quieter."

"Wow. That's really peaceful."

"Big time, Eddie. But getting back to the land of the living and the recently departed, I got an exhumation order on Henrietta Hammer today. Isn't she the one you said you wanted to talk to me about?"

"Well, that didn't take long! Rob, Holly and I attended Henrietta's funeral just a few weeks back. If you can believe this, each of us had her as our fifth-grade teacher."

Max chuckled. "Having the three of you as students might, in and of itself be a cause of death. But if she survived these many years, I guess it was something else that killed her."

"Very funny. I'll have you know we were all good kids."

"There's a limit to how good ten-year-olds can be. The

wife and I lived in close quarters with our twin boys for the past two weeks. Only the instinct to pass my genetic code forward to future generations kept me from taking them out into the wild and seeing if they could find their way back to our bungalow. Want to ruin a fun family vacation? Bring your kids along."

Eddie shook his head and said, "That bad?"

"Kauai they say is romantic—but not when you have two ten-year-olds holding a late-night farting competition in the next room. And of course, laughing hysterically.

"I know the feeling," Eddie agreed. "I can't imagine my little Aaron times two!"

"So what was Henrietta's story? They're digging her up because of a claim against the estate?"

"Yes, from a nephew, Scott Silva. It seems pretty likely that in truth, he was her son. Of course, her DNA test will confirm or deny that. Apparently, she kept the child a secret from her husband their entire married life. And with an estate worth tens of millions of dollars, this is the kind of detail that's going to get a lot of attention."

"So, your sweet little fifth-grade teacher had a secret love child! That's a hoot. For a town of seventy-two hundred, Sausalito can produce more than its share of whacky stories."

"Just shake any tree in Sausalito and at least a few nuts will fall out," Eddie said with a mischievous smile.

"Who raised the kid?"

"The kid, who is now in his mid-forties, was raised by Henrietta's sister and brother-in-law. As best as we know, all three of them took the secret of his parentage with them to the grave. Pretty remarkable."

"Wow! The poor guy's head must be spinning. Who spilled the beans?"

"A friend of Henrietta's, with whom she spent her second and third trimester while they were both earning teaching certificates at Santa Rosa State. It was the best way to hide out from nosey neighbors in their hometown of Fort Bragg."

"Even today, Fort Bragg is a pretty sleepy little town. I can't imagine what it must have been like back then." As their oversized lunch plates and beer pairings were slid in front of them. Max asked, "Did we order all this?"

"I suppose we did," Eddie replied with a shrug. "And since my mother told me to finish whatever was put in front of me…"

"Did that rule include the beer?"

"It did, but that I learned from my old man."

They ate half of their meals in a hunger-fueled silence. Finally, Eddie said, "I don't think the coroner did much of anything to check Henrietta out. And I would very much appreciate you doing so after her exhumation."

"And I'd appreciate it if you'd invite me the next time Canning passes his Warrior seats onto you and you find yourself with an extra ticket," Max countered.

"With as good as that team has been in recent years, that doesn't happen too often. Still, I'll be happy to move you to the top of the guest list."

"Thanks! I could happily spend the rest of my day here. It's tough getting back into work mode after Hawaii."

"If you hadn't taken those two darling boys of yours, you may not have come back after two weeks."

"That would have been nice. Moving on to a less

pleasant topic, I imagine you think someone helped ease your old teacher's path out of this world and into the next?"

"You do have a flair for the dramatic, Max."

"Just trying to make a dull job a little more interesting. Why would someone be interested in the old dear making an early exit? Is this Scott fellow at the top of your list of suspects?"

"No, nothing like that. In fact, Holly was the one who stumbled upon a photo that caused Henrietta's love child secret to unravel. Up to that point, Scott didn't have a clue that his aunt was actually his mother. It comes down to two issues. First, the estate being worth millions invites the potential for mischief. Second, while there was nothing at the scene that looked suspicious, I don't think her body was given a close check when it arrived at the coroner. If she had been twenty years younger, there might have been more questions about the circumstances. I have several people who were undoubtedly awaiting her death. My gut tells me one of them might have gotten tired of waiting."

"You think it may have been Mrs. Peacock in the kitchen with a vile of poison in the blueberry muffins?"

"Yes, something like that. I arrived at her house shortly after a neighbor reported finding the body. She was sprawled across the kitchen floor. Nearing eighty, even I assumed she stroked out, or her ticker quit."

"She was a little younger than that. I noticed in the exhumation order that she was seventy-eight at the time of her death. Let me see what I can do when I get back to the office. If we're disturbing her eternal rest for a DNA sample, we might as well run a full toxicology panel on the body. It's worth finding out what exactly was in her system at the time of death. Make certain that nasty Mrs. Peacock didn't slip something lethal into her tea."

"Do you think there could be something the coroner didn't catch?"

"Always possible. Someone might have stepped in and done what nature might have taken ten or more years to do. There's also a chance she mixed one of these pills with one of those other pills and took her own self out of this world."

"Accidentally, not intentionally, correct?"

"Trust me, Eddie, if I had a hundred bucks for every time some senior took one pill from column A and one pill from column B and unintentionally caused their own premature death, I could buy that property in Kauai, not far from our vacation bungalow, that the missus and I were drooling over this time last week. Then you, Sharon, and Aaron would have to come visit to catch us up on all the excitement going on in Marin."

"Always happy to pay my favorite medical examiner a visit."

"Particularly when he's located in Hawaii."

"True that, pal."

"Eddie, I'll tell you one thing: there are too many prescription drugs floating around, especially for people of a certain age. There are guesstimates on how many accidental deaths they cause, and they're surprisingly high."

"I don't doubt it."

"Let me take a closer look, and I'll let you know what I find."

"I've got some more news on Henrietta for her two favorite former students," Eddie said when he called Rob. "Put the phone on speaker if Holly is there."

"Go ahead, she's right here."

"What's up Copper, aren't we seeing you tonight at Smitty's?"

"No can do guys. Sharon told me she's going to be late getting out of her dental appointment, so I've got to get Aaron from the after-hours program at Willow Creek School."

"We'll miss you, pal," Rob said. So what's up?"

"Max Brownstein signed off for Henrietta's body to be exhumed for DNA testing. Given her age and that there was nothing to raise a red flag in the police report, Max agreed with me that the coroner likely gave her a cursory examination. I'm happy to say that he's agreed to give her a much closer look."

"Does Brownstein think there might have been foul play?" Holly asked.

"I wouldn't go that far. However, Max feels as long as the old girl is being dug up, it wouldn't hurt to run far more detailed tests."

"What do you think he has in mind?" Rob asked.

"Principally, a full toxicology report."

"He suspects she ingested some toxin?" Rob asked.

"Anything is possible, although as Max explained, her death might be as innocent as her mixing up medication she was taking."

"Something tells me you helped sell him on the idea of foul play," Holly said.

"Guilty as charged. But I'll tell you this, getting her back out of the ground a second time after this DNA testing is complete, would be much tougher. Particularly, if we have nothing more to go on than a hunch. This was the time to pitch the idea that Henrietta's body needed a much closer look. To borrow a phrase, strike while the iron is hot."

"So, you do think someone might have nailed Mrs. Hammer," Rob declared.

"If I had to bet, I'd put my money on her stroking out. But some of those charity folks, particularly Phillips and Reese raise the hair on the back of my neck. The toxicology report is our best shot to find out if someone didn't want to wait a year, or a decade, for nature to take its course. Not to mention the convenient coincidence that Henrietta departed this world a little over a month after her husband's death."

"She's not the first spouse to go soon after the death of their partner," Rob added.

"True that, pal. This all could be as innocent as that. But let's see what Max finds."

"When will they know?" Holly asked.

"Probably four to six weeks."

"That long?"

"It's not like those TV shows, Holly, where detectives order a toxicology report in the morning, go out for lunch, and when they come back they find the results waiting on their desk," Eddie explained. "In real life, toxicology studies are a drawn-out process. That's why when some celebrity dies, and a lot of people wonder if drug use played a part, it's between one and two months before the ME has any real facts to share with the public. Forensic toxicology is a complex bit of business. I'm just happy that's a stone we're getting an opportunity to turn over."

"What about the DNA?" Rob asked. How long will that take?"

"That we'll have early next week," Eddie said. "If it comes in as a positive match with Scott—and the three of us are all laying odds we're going to get a positive match—have you given any thought as to how you're both going to cover the fact that dear old Henrietta had a love child?"

For a moment, Rob and Holly turned and stared at each other. They were somewhat surprised that they had not already discussed that all but certain twist in their coverage of Henrietta.

"We have to go with the story," Rob said after a moment's thought. "What other choices would we have?"

"Yeah, absolutely," Holly added.

"With an estate that size being upended in such dramatic fashion, this is going to seep out into the public one way or another," Rob said. "It's going to be embarrassing to some, and disturbing to others, but it's not a story we can sit on. The Independent will catch wind of this as well. A coroner's report and its impact on the estate won't take long to get out to the public."

"This story is going to be a bombshell to everyone who knew her," Eddie said. "Plus, if my crazy suspicion is correct and someone didn't want Henrietta living however many years she had left then that's going to be an even bigger bombshell."

"You've got to go where the story takes you," Rob said. "No matter how nutty it gets. If we get proof that Scott Silva is indeed Henrietta's child, Sausalito is going to know about it when our next edition hits. I'm not going to let the Independent walk that story out from under us! We started this story, and we're going to finish it!"

Holly listened to Rob's determination and knew he was right. What choice did they have? In a town where your lead story is about a drunk tourist falling off a ferry dock, Holly knew the infamously dour school teacher, and respected local heiress, having birthed a secret love child, is a once in a decade kind of story. Nevertheless, Holly was sure that Scott would be unhappy seeing the family's story turned into a public drama in which he played a leading role.

CHAPTER THIRTEEN

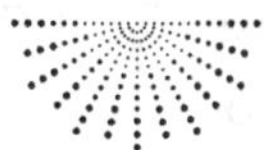

Shortly after nine the following Tuesday morning, Eddie bounded up the steps of the Standard's Victorian walk-up.

Rob looked up from his computer. "Eddie, what are you up to?"

"Holly! Get in here!" Eddie called out.

"What's up copper?" Holly said as she sauntered in from her office into Rob's.

"It's official. Scott Stephens is Henrietta's kid!"

"Oh, my God!" Holly said as she started to laugh. "What a naughty girl our Mrs. Hammer was!"

"We've got our lead for this week's Sausalito edition," Rob came out from behind his desk to give Eddie a fist bump followed by a bear hug.

"It's bigger than that. I spoke to Bob Ivan this morning. He and Beasley have already spoken. Beasley gave Henrietta's will a second reading and confirmed his recollection that she never mentioned a word about having given birth to a child. Scott's name never appears in the will," Eddie said.

"I'd like to be a fly on the wall when our local non-profits learn that Henrietta's will is going to be voided, and poor forgotten Scott is master of the House of Hammer," Rob declared with a laugh.

As Rob and Holly listened, Eddie gave them a summary of his conversation with Bob at the county courthouse that occurred an hour earlier.

When he finished, Rob shook his head in awe. "Thank you, Detective Austin! Now, get the hell out of here. We've got a front page to rework—not to mention a lead story to write."

Holly rushed over and gave Eddie a kiss on the check.

"What's that for?" Eddie asked.

"I just want you to know that if all this somehow leads to putting the Sausalito Opera Society out of business, you've made me the happiest girl in the world. Do you know that woman started screeching out an aria yesterday afternoon right across the street from my office?"

"Who were the unlucky victims this time?" Eddie asked.

"She cornered another unsuspecting tourist couple. I think they stopped to ask her directions. Most of the locals know to cross the street if they see her coming. I'm sure if I had a rifle with a scope, I could have picked her off from up here. Give her some old fashion Deadwood, South Dakota justice."

Eddie looked heavenward. "As I've previously suggested, Holly, I'd thank you for keeping your homicidal fantasies to yourself. I am a sworn officer of the law. I don't need to be hearing this."

"Eddie, don't worry. No jury packed with Sausalito residents would vote to convict me."

"Holly, here's an even better idea: call the Sausalito Police and report her for disturbing the peace. Maybe you'll get lucky, and they'll haul her off. It's not as if they have a lot of other police work to do around here."

"Wow, Laurie Chase thrown in jail!" Holly broke into a wide smile at the thought. "What more could a girl ask for?"

That night, Scott and Holly met at one of Mill Valley's most popular restaurants, Bungalow 44, for dinner.

Scott walked in just a few minutes after Holly arrived. After kissing her cheek, he exclaimed, "I love coming here. It's got such a great vibe."

Although it was just past seven, the restaurant was already buzzing at its usual busy pace. Patrons, standing two deep at the bar, pressed in closer as the hostess walked past with guests heading for one of the few remaining open tables.

After the two kissed quickly for a second time, Scott pulled back, took both of Holly's hands and looked at her and smiled.

As demurely as she could, Holly asked, "Did you have an interesting day?"

"Not so much interesting as intense," Scott said.

"I tried to call you."

"I got your message, but when you're in finals week, you have zero time for yourself. I spent my day jumping from one classroom to the next. On top of it all, I have all these nervous students wondering how they're doing. This whole 'make it into the best college or else' pressure that kids are under nowadays keeps getting nuttier with each passing year. Between students on edge, and faculty and staff trying to put out fires all day, things get pretty intense. On the upside, the day goes by in a hurry."

"And then on top of all that, there is the elephant in the room."

"What elephant?"

"You're kidding, right? Didn't you hear from Bob Ivan?"

Scott shook his head. "I saw I had two missed calls from his number, but we never did connect. I should have tried him while I was driving down here from San Rafael. Do you know what's up?"

"The test on your aunt came back," Holly said, more than a bit surprised that she would be the one to break this important news.

"So, it's official?" Scott said in a rush.

"I should have said the test results from your mother are back," Holly nodded and smiled.

Scott let loose with a low whistle. "Wow! I guess neither of us should be too surprised, given what we learned from Mikhail and Jeannie."

"You're right. Shocking at this point would have been finding out Henrietta wasn't your mother." Holly pulled Scott closer so that he could hear her above the din. "But there's even bigger news."

"What?" Scott asked, his voice also raised.

"Bob Ivan told Eddie, when they ran into each other this

morning at the courthouse, that you were not named in Henrietta's will! No mention at all."

"Yikes!" he exclaimed.

Holly had long heard the expression that there are more important things in life than money, but she wasn't sure if she had ever met someone who truly embodied that sentiment more than Scott.

If it had been me, and I found out that I was in line to claim the value of the entire Hammer estate, I'd be bouncing off the ceiling, Holly thought.

But Scott was silent. Apparently, lost in thought. Finally, he grabbed Holly's hand and said, "Let's get out of here and talk where we can hear each other."

"Sure, where are we going?"

"My mom's place," Scott said without hesitation. "I've been staying there the last couple of nights so I can get more of the house cleaned out. I know, you're thinking that I'm doing a lot of work for someone who forgot about me, but I'm convinced if Henrietta lived the years she anticipated having, she would have told me her story, and amended her will."

"Anything is possible. And the fact that you think, given time, she would have done the right thing, is just one of the reasons you're such a good person."

"I think you're pretty wonderful too."

"Do you want to stop and pick up some dinner?" Holly asked.

"Sure. Let's ask the hostess for something to take out. How about chicken, veggies, and potatoes?"

"Scott, we can pick that up down the block at Mill Valley Market for a lot less money."

"Yeah, but this place does killer chicken. And haven't you heard? I'm the only son of a very wealthy woman, recently deceased."

Holly giggled. "Now that you mention it, I did hear something about that."

Fifteen minutes later, with an oversized bag containing boxes of their food, Holly followed Scott as they drove separately down Blithedale Road to the South 101 entrance. They exited a few miles later off the steep grade that levels out briefly at the Spencer Avenue exit, high atop Sausalito. Not well lit, Holly had the taillights of Scott's car to help lead the way.

They drove down Monte Mar Drive, a steep, narrow road made all the more challenging by the lack of streetlights. For the uninitiated, driving this road after dark can be an uneasy experience. The Hammer estate sat up on a rocky bluff, which could be seen just before Monte Mar Drive ended at a switchback onto Currey Avenue.

Holly pulled up onto the property. She parked behind Scott. Together, they walked up the driveway to the front door of the old house. To her, the old mansion was, even more, forbidding at night.

For a fleeting moment, Holly felt a chill go down her spine as she thought she heard Henrietta whisper, "Stay out! You don't belong here."

Since first helping Scott, Holly had visited the house several times. Why then, she wondered, did it feel so unsettling on this occasion?

As Holly went through the front door, she did her best to ignore these uncomfortable feelings. She headed straight to Henrietta's kitchen to gather plates, forks, knives, and glasses for their meal.

Together they sat in the old massive dining room. Holly thought of the years Henrietta and Elijah faced off at opposite ends of its long mahogany table, rarely speaking to one another. Add to that their endless quarrels over her determination to remain an elementary school teacher, earning a salary that was, in Elijah's words, according to Newberry, "Completely unnecessary!"

She thought of Jeannie's revelation that Elijah's low sperm count, compounded by his refusal to adopt, crushed Henrietta's dream of filling this house with children.

At the same time, Elijah was wounded by her declaration that she would not allow herself to be, "a housewife, and a gracious hostess for corporate and civic gatherings."

Unlike the home's previous occupants, Scott and Holly sat close and held hands. To help celebrate the day's important news, Scott opened a fine French wine he had discovered in the basement during his first complete walkthrough of the house. Together, they toasted to, "New beginnings!"

Holly leaned in for a kiss.

"You know," Scott began, "even though I fully expected that I was Henrietta's child, there is a big part of me that still finds this whole thing hard to believe."

"That's exactly why I have been thinking about you all day. Each time I do, I return to the same question…"

"What question is that?"

"How would I feel if one day I discovered my mother was my aunt and my aunt was my mother? Beyond being shocked by the surprise of it all, I'd spend a lot of time thinking: What if?"

"I have done that! What would my life have been like if I'd grown up in this house? If Elijah had returned home early, within weeks of Max's death and Henrietta tricked him into thinking that I was his child. I guess I would have been president of Hammer Tools. To be honest, I think I much prefer being a math teacher."

"After our visit with Jeannie, I understood why Ruth and Henrietta made the decisions they did," Holly said. "But that doesn't make it right, or fair, to the person who innocently landed in the middle of their scheme."

"But when they came up with this grand deception, they were a lot younger than either of us are right now," Scott replied.

"I'm guessing, I would feel cheated."

"Cheated is probably the perfect word. If I said that to anyone other than you, they would probably look at me like I'm nuts! How many people go from a life lived paycheck to paycheck, to standing on the cusp of inheriting a fortune? Still, I don't feel like I won the lottery. I regret not having the time to really know my actual mother, or understand her life and how she saw the world.

"I know I have nothing to complain about. This should be considered a happy ending. I just wish it had all happened differently. Mostly that Henrietta had the time to share her true story with me."

For a time, they both ate in silence. Scott wondering what might have motivated Henrietta to tell him her true story, while Holly wondered how best to tell Scott that his story would be this week's lead in *The Sausalito Standard.*

"Scott, besides Bob Ivan, Rob was also trying to reach you today. He wanted to talk to you about the story we worked on for a good part of the day."

"Give him my apologies. I was just so busy with finals as I told you earlier. What story were you working on?"

"We're reporting the medical examiner's finding that you are Henrietta Hammer's child. In fact, you're tomorrow's front page lead."

"What? Why would that be a story?"

"Scott, seriously? This is a small town; stories like this don't come along every week. In fact, we never had a story like Henrietta's! A large estate, a lot of locals hoping to benefit from bequests, and a last-minute appearance by a previously unknown child; this story writes itself!"

Holly regretted those words moments after she spoke.

For too long, they sat in silence. Finally, Scott said in something of a low growl, "Holly, you haven't been using me to get close to a good story?"

"What? No, of course not! I like being with you. I love being with you! When I came here to help you start cleaning this place out, I wasn't going to write a feature for the paper about cleaning out my deceased teacher's old home. And when I asked about that photo of Mikhail, neither of us knew where that would lead. The only story anyone mentioned was Rob asking us to be on the lookout for old family photos we happened to find. Remember, he mentioned that to you at the reception? It's pretty routine stuff for any small town newspaper when a citizen of note passes to do a detailed obit. Just about everyone in town either knew Henrietta or knew of her."

"It sure as hell turned into a bigger story than that," Scott declared. "A few weeks ago when we were having dinner, and I said 'digging stuff up that other people would prefer to keep buried must be exciting,' I didn't mean stories about my family and me!" Helplessly, Holly shrugged and said nothing.

"I'm sorry to jump on you about this. It's just embarrassing to have the whole town know all these details, particularly the terrible story of my mother and my aunt deceiving me my entire life. People will think I'm a dope for not figuring all this out earlier."

"People will not think that! And Scott, if there had never been a Sausalito Standard, don't you think this story would have gotten out anyway? For one thing, your late mother's friends run some of the biggest organizations in town. The Sausalito Preservation Group and the Ladies of Liberty account for two-thirds of the gossips in this town! This is not the kind of story the Independent would have ignored. Just a reminder, Scott: That night at F3, you said it must be difficult for someone to be in the news business if they felt uncomfortable asking embarrassing questions. Well, you're right. It is hard! But if the only stories you ever write are stories people want to read about themselves, that's not news, that's public relations."

"I could make this less of a news story if I left all my mother's bequests just as she had them."

"That's your call. Personally, I think there are better charitable causes than those stuck up historic preservation people, or some crackpot woman who runs around town singing arias to unsuspecting victims. And as far as I can tell, that Sausalito Fine Arts Board is most likely a personal piggy bank for Chris and Ruby Reese."

"Holly, would you love me if I was just a math teacher, waiting every week to get my paycheck?"

"Hold on! First, you think I'm interested in you just for your story, and now you think I'm interested in you for your money? Well, I have news for you buster—right now I wouldn't be particularly interested in you for those reasons or any other!"

By now, it was apparent to both of them that what began as a celebration had gone terribly wrong.

"Maybe I should be going," Holly said, taking control of her anger.

"I won't try to stop you," Scott replied.

"Fine," Holly said as she tossed her napkin onto the table and turned to leave. As she reached the front door, she paused and wondered for a moment if Scott would call out to her.

The old house was filled with nothing but cold silence.

Holly opened the front door. It creaked with the pain of age. Now, angry and disappointed, she loudly pulled the solid wood door shut and walked back to her car on what had become a surprisingly chilly night.

CHAPTER FOURTEEN

Early the following morning, The Sausalito Standard began landing in mailboxes.

By noon, the paper's lead story was the talk of the town.

Ruby Reese's husband, Chris, knew something was terribly wrong when the teacup his wife was holding fell to the floor and broke into several pieces.

"I can't believe this," Ruby cried out, which quickly brought Chris to her side.

"What's wrong?"

"What's wrong?" she shrieked, "This is what's wrong!" Ruby's finger jabbed at The Standard's headline. "That nephew, we met at Henrietta's funeral turned out to be her son—and that seems to have invalidated her will."

"You mean all her bequests can all be revoked?" Chris asked in disbelief.

"Yes! And if they are, we'll have nothing to show for all the time we put into cultivating that wicked old bat. I hated her when I was a kid, and disliked her even more as an adult."

"Oh, my God!" Chris said in a hushed tone as he read part of the story while peering over his wife's shoulder. "That nasty old thing. I can't believe she had a secret affair. I can't believe everything we waited for could just vanish like this."

Francis Phillips, after a two-day revitalization retreat at a spa in nearby Calistoga, had just arrived back at his office. He was happily counting the receipts from the previous weekend's take at the society's visitor center when a board member called.

"Have you seen the front page of this week's Standard?" Phillips, a man with many secrets to keep, knew the news wasn't good when he pressed the caller for details and was told, "You better get a copy of the paper and see for yourself."

Five minutes later he stood on the corner of El Portal and Bridgeway holding a copy of the paper as tourists darted around him. His hands shook with anger and frustration as he read the headline:

Hammer Estate on Hold After Discovery of Previously Unknown Heir

Moments later, in the privacy of his office, he locked the door and read the story in full. The revelations it contained hit him like a bucket of ice water. The quotes of the two attorneys in the case were the story's most disturbing aspect.

Bob Ivan explained California's law regarding the discovery of an unacknowledged natural born child. Nate Beasley's comment was equally painful to read: "The validity of the entire will is in question after this revelation."

The Standard's story contained the basic outline of events. Before her marriage, Henrietta was believed to have had a brief, secret relationship with a Fort Bragg timber mill worker. "While the DNA link between Scott and his suspected father has yet to be proven, DNA testing has provided the essential proof that Henrietta Hammer was indisputably the mother of Scott Silva," Beasley confirmed.

Laurie Chase was listening to one of her favorite recordings of Tosca when she saw the white USPS truck pull close to her curbside mailbox. As usual, the driver flipped a few items into the box, pushed it shut and headed toward Laurie's uphill neighbor.

Moments later, Laurie sauntered down her driveway under a bright sun singing what is arguably opera's most beloved aria, Vissi d'arte, in which the title character expresses her desire to be a person who lives for the beauty of art and life.

Laurie's neighbors had long been accustomed to a variety of awful sounds coming from the Chase home. But on this occasion, the crescendo of her aria suddenly turned into a bloodcurdling scream as she pulled The Standard out of her mailbox and stared in horror at its front-page.

Amy Oliver was surprised, pleased, and honored when she answered her phone to hear the aging but still authoritative voice of Alma Samuels, on the line.

"My God, woman! Did you see this morning's Standard?" Alma barked.

"No," Amy admitted. "I've been outside pulling up weeds from my garden. Does it say something about the distribution of gifts from Henrietta's estate? I've been expecting to hear something any day now."

"Don't hold your breath! From what I can tell by reading that rag some fools call a newspaper, it's doubtful we'll ever see a dime of Henrietta's money."

"But that's impossible!" Amy protested while suddenly feeling one of her all too frequent headaches coming on.

"Well, get your head out of those weeds and read all about it," Alma ordered. "We needed this money to keep the Ladies of Liberty financially healthy. After all these years, it would be a shame if this organization fell apart during your term as president!"

With those chilling words, Alma hung up without wishing Amy a pleasant afternoon.

However this had occurred, Amy was confident of one thing: the Oliver name would be ruined in Sausalito if LOL collapsed and disbanded during her term of office.

For a small community where the installation of a new traffic light can be the talk of the town for several days, the discovery that Henrietta Hammer had a love child started eyes rolling and chins wagging.

The Standard's community reporter, the late Warren Bradley, often said, "Sausalito's hills are alive with the sound of gossip. The only thing this town has more of than tourists is rumors."

The news was most unsettling to those who were active members of one or more of Henrietta's pet non-profit organizations.

Additionally, there was the shock of fellow teachers and former students. Chief among those was the school's long-time principal who recalled numerous occasions when Mrs. Hammer lectured her on the dangerously loose morals and questionable judgment of today's children.

The only organization to have a measured response to the news of the day was the county's Animal Rescue Shelter. Based in San Rafael—some fifteen miles north of Sausalito —their director wrote to Scott to profess his deep sadness over the loss of, "A wonderful woman and a devoted supporter." He then concluded, "I would like to share with you the reasons why your mother so admired the vital work we do in the rescue, care, and shelter of animals in need."

Francis Phillips considered taking a similar approach, but for the moment found himself mired in deep despair over the potential loss of an estate gift that he described to supporters as, "A cash infusion that will redefine our future."

As for Henrietta's most eccentric suitor, Laurie Chase,

her anger lashed out against Henrietta's "charlatan son," and, "this wicked State of California for its insane laws." Chase's board, consisting mostly of aging acolytes, found these new developments challenging to follow. Nevertheless, they nodded their heads approvingly and applauded her enthusiastically.

Through all the tumult, there was no consensus amongst Sausalito's four charitable groups as to what if anything could be done to reverse these new developments. For several years each organization had confidently considered themselves future recipients of a significant gift from the Hammer estate. Henrietta's sudden death was greeted as a sign that this much anticipated day was finally at hand.

Perhaps there was nothing than to Scott and plead their case that if not all, then at least a portion of his mother's original bequests be honored. Even a reduced gift from the estate would help overcome the expected shortfalls they all now anticipated.

Scott's anger with Holly only increased over the following days. The Standard's reporting made him the key player in a family drama he would like to have remained out of the public eye.

Was he nothing more than a pawn in the realization of a scandalous story? Or was he overreacting, and in turn risking the loss of someone who had quickly become very important to him?

The path to finding the truth of his parentage started innocently. But now he wondered: was Holly's insistence that he meet with Jeanie Newberry, and then Bob Ivan, and her encouragement in locating Mikhail, the actions of a close friend; or merely the cultivation of what became an explosive story?

Scott was keenly aware of the curious stares, secret whispers, and raised eyebrows he came upon while walking along Sausalito's small residential shopping area. He couldn't help wonder if he was pitied as the object of a cruel deception, or an interloper looking to walk off with an undeserved fortune.

Do they think I'm a fool for having not figured this out much earlier? Scott wondered with an increasing sense of embarrassment.

By the end of the workweek, Sausalito was still buzzing over the story locals were calling, "Babygate."

Rob was pleased every time he heard those seven magical words, "Did you see The Standard this week?" On the other hand, Holly was far less satisfied. Perhaps, she thought, her little group's Friday night happy hour might be an excellent time to unburden herself and seek the advice of her two oldest friends.

They're men, perhaps they'll better understand what's going on in Scott's mind, Holly reasoned.

So after the usual chitchat and the request for two more beers and another Vodka martini, Holly raised her concerns.

"Wow, Holly," Rob began. "You certainly managed to

keep this to yourself. I had no idea Scott was so upset over our coverage. Doesn't he understand that the Independent would have jumped on this if we hadn't reported it first?"

Before she could reply, Eddie asked, "Have you tried talking to him since the night before The Standard came out?"

"I left him a message at home, and one on his voice mailbox at the school."

"…and nothing?" Eddie asked.

"Not a peep."

"He's just a little freaked out by all the attention. He's not the first person to get upset over a news story in which they play a pivotal role," Rob assured her.

Holly shrugged. "That's what I've been telling myself. I sure hope this isn't the end of the road for us. I really like Scott. He's a sweet, decent man. I even like the math nerd in him."

"Wow, Holly," Eddie said. "Sounds like you really fell for this guy. Good for you."

"Give him a little more time," Rob suggested. "He'll come around."

"No doubt he's more than a little embarrassed by the whole thing," Eddie added. "I can imagine if it had been me I'd probably want to disappear for a bit. Some people live to be the center of attention, and others hate it."

Just as he finished speaking, Eddie's cell phone began to vibrate its way across the small lament topped cocktail table that sat between the three of them. Eddie snatched it and said, "Eddie Austin." After listening for a moment, he said, "Hi Clarice. You're working late…"

There was a long pause as Eddie's eyes got bigger. "Oh,

geez, you have to be kidding! Okay, Marin General…I'm on my way. Thanks for reaching out. I owe you one, Clarice. You're the best!"

Eddie stood up. "Holly I think you better come with me."

"Why? What's up?"

"Clarice is an old friend. She works central dispatch for the sheriff's department. About twenty minutes ago Scott was found not far from here on the backseat of a car parked up on Glen Drive. The EMTs pulled him out, and they're transporting him by ambulance to Marin General."

"What?" Holly's response was just below a shout. "How the hell did that happen?"

"Come with me. We'll get a lot more answers up at the hospital than we'll get sitting here." Eddie said as he stuck his hand out and helped pull Holly up from her chair.

For a moment, she looked lost, but quickly, she gathered herself. "Oh, my God! Poor Scott!"

"Rob," Eddie said, reaching for his wallet.

"Get out of here. I've got this. But please, one of you call my cell and let me know how Scott's doing?"

Holly nodded. She knew Rob wanted a call as friend-to-friend, not a reporter to a publisher.

As she walked alongside Eddie, Holly could barely see through her tears. Eddie opened the door to his car and helped her into the passenger side. As he leaned in, he said, "Put on your seat belt. I'm going to break the rules and put on my siren so we'll get there just as fast as we can."

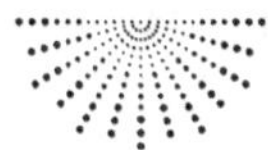

CHAPTER FIFTEEN

In six o'clock traffic, even with a siren and flashing red light on the dashboard of Eddie's unmarked vehicle, it still took nearly fifteen minutes to get from Smitty's to the hospital's emergency entrance.

Holly was silent the whole time. Unsure of what if anything to say, Eddie stayed quiet as well.

When they got to the hospital, they rushed in to find a Sausalito Police officer and a Marin County Sheriff's Department deputy in the hall leading to the operating theater. The two officers were reviewing their notes.

Eddie knew them both. He introduced Holly as a personal friend who was also a close friend of the accident victim.

"What's his condition?" Holly asked nervously.

"He's going to pull through," Officer Reed assured her.

"He took a pretty good bang to the head I don't think he would have had a chance if it wasn't for that safety helmet," Deputy Sanders added.

"Where was he when you found him?" Holly asked.

"Lying on the back seat of a car parked on Glen Drive, a little before Santa Rosa Avenue splits off going uphill while Glen goes downhill," Reed replied.

"How in the hell did he wind up on the back seat of a car?" Eddie asked.

"Well we've got a pretty good idea," deputy Sanders replied.

"It's just fortunate someone called it in," Reed added.

Sanders nodded. "A resident on Glen Drive was out walking her dog when she noticed a bike lying partially under a parked car that had a smashed rear window. A moment later, she heard someone moaning from inside the car, so she looked at the backseat. That's when she called 911."

"Where's the bike now?" Eddie asked.

"I took it up to the crime lab to have it checked out," Sanders responded quickly.

"Why?" Holly asked.

"When we looked at the bike," Reed explained, "both Sanders and I noticed the rear tire and back frame had been bent."

"Not consistent with the accident, I assume," Eddie said.

"Exactly. I thought we might be dealing with a hit and run situation."

"Smart move," Eddie said as he patted Sanders on the shoulder.

"He didn't bend the back of his bike riding headlong into the rear of a parked car," Reed added.

"Do you think Scott lost control of the bike when he was

struck from behind?" Eddie asked, while quickly writing in his notepad.

"That would be my guess. It looked to us like he went up and over the trunk of the car and crashed through its rear window?" Sanders explained.

"Agreed," Reed added. "Certainly unusual. Working patrol in Sausalito over the last twenty years, between the steep hills and the number of bicyclists I've seen some nasty accidents, but this one was a first for me."

"Doesn't sound like an accident to me!" Holly said, emerging from her initial shock.

"Let's follow the clues and find out where they lead," Eddie said in a low voice as he gave Holly's arm a reassuring squeeze.

As Sanders and Reed departed, Eddie quietly murmured, "Perhaps we can get in to see Scott."

"Seriously, Eddie—what the hell do you think happened?"

"We've got time to put all that together," he assured. "For now, the most important thing is that Scott's in one piece."

An hour after they reached the hospital, Eddie left to return to Sausalito. Holly assured him she was fine, but that she wanted to wait in Scott's room to see if he woke up before visiting hours ended at nine.

Holly talked to the nurse, who had Scott in his care until the overnight floor nurse came on at midnight. "I spoke to the doctor when your friend came out of the ER and went into the recovery area," the nurse replied. "He got a couple of nasty cuts—one on his arm and one on his right leg. It could have been a good deal worse, what with his flying through a car's rear window. The good news is that there's no sign of brain swelling or internal bleeding. Considering what his injuries could have been, he's a lucky guy."

"Do they have any idea when he'll wake up?" Holly asked anxiously.

"Between the trauma and the sedation from his surgery, I would guess between nine and eleven tonight."

"Oh…" Holly said, obviously disappointed. "I'd hoped it would be before visiting hours ended."

As he grasped Holly's hand, he explained, "We don't need to be too strict about that. You can stay as long as you want. I can get you a blanket and a pillow so you can rest a little. As the nurse left the room, he turned down the lights to a dim glow.

Holly moved the visitor chair next to the bed. Scott looked somehow younger and more peaceful than when she saw him last: that awful night at Henrietta's.

Hesitant to lower the bed's side rail, Holly instead reached her wrist through to hold Scott's hand. His palm was warm and soft, as one would expect of a man who had juggled numbers rather than tools all his adult life.

Holly leaned in and brushed back his long, straight blond hair. She was careful not to touch the surgical gauze and tape wrapped over the back of his neck and down along shoulders, which protected the cuts from shards of glass just below the line of his bike helmet.

He had a close call, Holly thought, as tears ran down her cheeks. Scott coming into her life, was a blessing. Perhaps someone else thought the exact opposite?

As Eddie exited 101 and headed south on Bridgeway, he rang Rob's cell.

"Are you finished with dinner?"

"Yep. We were just getting the kids ready for a story and bedtime. How's Scott?"

"Alive, thank goodness. But he took one hell of a wallop. You think your bride will let you out for twenty minutes? We need to talk."

"Sure, no problem. Karin knows about Scott's accident."

"Okay, I'm exiting 101 at Marin City, I'll be outside your place in five minutes."

Rob knew Eddie had something troubling him the moment he saw him. He recognized that far away look Eddie had whenever confronted by a puzzle that offered no apparent answers.

"How do you suppose Scott lost control of his bike, just before that curve where Glen Drive starts downhill and Santa Rosa splits off going uphill, and then crashed through the back window of a parked car? That's not the type of accident an experienced bicyclist is likely to have?"

"You're right," Rob conceded quickly.

Eddie then shared Sanders and Reed's assessment that Scott's bike had been struck from behind. "Along that stretch, it wouldn't take all that much to send a bike and its rider sailing off into the creek bed about fifty feet below the roadway. Racing bikes are light, and Scott is a pretty slim guy. I don't think this was an accident, particularly given the description the two officers gave me regarding the bike's condition."

"Maybe it was a kid with a learner's permit taking his parents' car out for a joy ride. He doesn't see the biker until it's too late, gets nervous, the car swerves and bangs into the back of Scott's bike."

"Yeah, that's possible."

"You're wearing your 'something is rotten in Denmark' look."

"I don't believe for a minute it was an accident."

Rob shook his head in wonder. "You think he was targeted?"

"I'm guessing he was biking away from Henrietta's old place, which is a two-minute drive from the site of where he was hit."

"You think that whoever did this had been laying in wait for him?"

"Sure!" Rob, if you were about to inherit a chunk of Henrietta's millions and Scott shows up ruining your payday, you might want him out of the picture."

"Not me, and not you, but you're right that some people would think that way."

"I'm guessing our suspect was shadowing Scott for the last couple of days—probably since The Standard broke that story about him Wednesday morning."

"Oh great—one more thing for Holly to be mad at me about," Rob muttered. Do you remember when we were teens, we used to walk the top of that curbstone that runs along the side of Glen?"

"It was our version of tightrope walking," Eddie

grimaced at the memory that went back twenty plus years. "It was a pretty dumb thing for us to do. Fortunately, that curbstone was a lot wider than a high wire. Gosh, the dumb things we did as kids."

"Anytime I think about some of our stunts, I find myself hoping that our kids are a good deal smarter than the two of us."

"Amen to that, Robbie boy."

"If you're right and someone was following Scott, they likely knew Sausalito well enough to realize that giving him a good push as he was approaching that curve could have sent Scott sailing over the curbstone and down into that gully! Forget a bike helmet," Rob said with a short laugh. "That drop would kill someone if they were wearing a helmet along with a suit of armor."

"Who would have thought that Scott crashing through the rear window of a car would have been getting off easy!"

Rob and Eddie sat silently contemplating what a gruesome ending Scott barely missed: plunging down a steep hillside with nothing but trees and rocks to break his fall.

"If you wanted Scott dead and you wanted to make it look like an accident, that's a great place to give his bike a shove," Rob offered. "But that leaves one thing I don't get.

"What's that?"

"Well, suppose the toxicology report comes back and proves that Henrietta was sent out of this world by something other than natural causes. Wouldn't this attempt on Scott's life make it rather apparent that the two are connected?"

"True, Rob. But you forget one thing. If Henrietta was killed, her killer had no way of knowing that in addition to a DNA test being conducted, a toxicology panel was performed on her as well. Look at it from their perspective. You go to all the trouble of arranging Henrietta's death, and it appears you got away with the perfect crime—only to have some guy pop up who discovers that he's not Henrietta's nephew, but her son. Now he's about to make off with the prize you planned on claiming for the past many years."

"Speaking of receiving a windfall, I know we all talk about this group of local organizations she supported, plus the animal shelter up in San Rafael, but is there anyone else in line for an estate gift that you should be looking into?"

"I asked Bob that same question. He told me Beasley made it pretty clear. Henrietta divided the estate equally between those five charitable causes. Bob guesstimates it's between seven and eight million each. Pretty serious money to a couple of working stiffs like the two of us."

"Certainly enough to be worth killing for particularly if you're badly in debt," Rob suggested. "At the very least, Scott's accident is going to make a great follow-up to this week's story on Henrietta."

"Just don't make it a headline, Rob. I think Holly is in enough trouble with Scott without another big story in The Standard."

"If I don't write another word about this story—and you know I'll have to— there is going to be plenty of ink spilled over Henrietta's estate, not to mention the investigation into Scott's accident. The Independent will make sure of that. And given the size of the estate, the San Francisco Chronicle will be sniffing around as well. In fact, Independent readers will have an account of what happened to Scott this afternoon before the next weekly edition of The

Standard comes out on Wednesday. Their Saturday morning edition is pretty well locked and loaded by now. But on Sunday, the Independent will probably give Scott's accident a pretty good play. 'Surprise heir in unexpected brush with death!' Rob said while making air quotes.

"I imagine you're right about that."

"Eddie, this story writes itself. I know that Scott and Holly would prefer less attention, but what happened today is not going to help. If they want less attention from the local press, they should move to Los Angeles."

"I feel sorry for Holly and even sorrier for Scott. Some people don't mind being in the spotlight. I'm pretty certain he's not one of them."

"Absolutely. But if you fall into the middle of an estate as big as Henrietta's in a town as small as this, you're going to get a lot of attention. Mulligan's estate was valued at a third of the Hammer's worth and look at the dust-up that caused. And as you know, Eddie, if Max Brownstein declares Henrietta's death a homicide, clear the decks, because this ride's going to get even wilder."

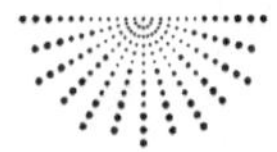

CHAPTER SIXTEEN

Monday morning Holly waited until she finished her large coffee before muttering, "Who could this son of a…"

"I've been wondering the same thing since Eddie filled me in on the details of Scott's accident," Rob said, interrupting her. "He thinks it's one of the heirs in waiting who wants everything to go back to the way it was before Scott stumbled into the middle of this."

"I've been thinking the same thing! Getting Scott out of the way would be the answer to all their problems—or so they think."

"That's it in a nutshell."

"Well, if Eddie finds the SOB, it would be nice if he threw him through a car's back window—just so he, or she, can fully appreciate the experience."

"Speaking of flying through car windows, what's the latest on Scott?"

"I'm going to go up there after work. I was with him last

night until ten. He's certainly a lot better. Friday night, he opened his eyes around midnight. When he saw me, he smiled, so I kissed him on the cheek. The nurses say he's going to be okay. But boy, it was sure hard to believe that with the way he looked that first night! On top of the impact bruising and the swelling, he had some nasty cuts, all of which required a bunch of stitches! It'll be two weeks before he's steady on his feet, but they're going to send him home tomorrow or Wednesday."

"Is he going to stay in Henrietta's house?"

"I think for now he wants to go back to his condo in San Rafael near the school. I didn't press him about it. I guess that he feels too much like a target in Sausalito. Not to mention every time one of the locals gives him a second glance, he feels uncomfortable. After the report in the Independent on Sunday, it will be that much worse."

"It had to take a pretty twisted mind to do something like that," Rob muttered as he shook his head in amazement.

Rob scanned the initial layout for the Sausalito edition, which is transmitted to the printer every Tuesday afternoon no later than four. But he stopped to open a topic with Holly he knew needed to be discussed. "Eddie told me that you were worried about how our coverage this week will impact Scott. Holly, you realize that, with a story like this, we're going to have to stay on top of it, right?"

"I was worried about it before Scott's accident. Actually, I don't know why I keep calling it an accident! I should say, after the attempt on his life," Holly paused for a moment and gathered herself.

"Scott is going to have to learn to live with seeing his name in the newspaper," Holly agreed. "Until this story plays itself out, his name is going to appear repeatedly. Our job is to report the story honestly. If we spend all our time worrying about how any story impacts the private lives of people involved, we're essentially out of the business of being journalists and into the business of public relations. We're not here to spin, we're here to report stories fully and honestly."

Rob put his arm around Holly's shoulder and gave her a reassuring squeeze, "I'm proud of you. We're excited to have interesting stories. It's what keeps readers reading. It's wrong to create sensational stories; it's equally wrong not to report events just because they are sensational."

"I think Scott's learning about the news business the hard way. He sat up on Sunday and read the Independent's coverage of his accident."

"I noticed they were careful not to make any assumptions, or draw any conclusions based on what happened to Scott," Rob said.

"But I think the headline"—Holly moved her hand across an imaginary front page—'Surprise Heir to Hammer Estate Victim in Hit and Run in Sausalito,' pretty much said it all."

"After the county crime lab looked at his bike and concluded that it was struck from behind by a vehicle and declared it a hit and run, their story pretty much wrote itself."

"I think someone at the Independent leaned on someone at the county to get that report expedited, so they could lead with it on Sunday. Perhaps it was Sheriff Canning," Holly suggested.

"That's okay. For a shoestring operation, we've got friends of our own in high places. And even if the county paper had held that bit of information back until today or Tuesday, they would've still had their story out a day before our Sausalito edition lands in mailboxes on Wednesday. We just have to do more with less. It's what we've always done."

Up at headquarters that same morning, Eddie was still simmering over what he reasoned with growing certainty was an attempt on Scott's life. He'd gotten a call twenty minutes earlier from Jack Canning's secretary requesting he report to the sheriff's office. Eddie was sure what the topic of the meeting would be. As he often told Rob, "If there's a crime story on the front page one day, I'm called into Canning's office the next."

Like any elected official—particularly one serving his fourth consecutive term—Sheriff Canning was not one to allow any news story to get out ahead of him. This was especially true this year when election day, for an unprecedented fifth term, was less than six months away.

No doubt, the Independent's story, in which it opined, "The sheriff's department is certain to ponder if there is a connection between Friday evening's hit and run incident and the revelation that Scott Silva is the heir apparent to the Hammer estate," prompted Canning's need to talk.

Not to his surprise, that was the newspaper passage that Canning stood and read the moment Eddie entered the sheriff's office.

"Well, Eddie, what do you think? Was this guy Silva really the target of a murder attempt?"

"I'm not a betting man Jack. But if I were, I'd go all in on that theory."

"How do you think it went down?"

"The driver gave him a push from behind, hard enough to bend the bike's rear wheel and fender hoping to send him flying off the roadway and permanently out of the picture. Once he goes head over handlebars, there wouldn't be much left of the bike or the rider after hitting bottom."

"How big a drop would he have had?"

"Fifty plus feet. The equivalent of driving a bicycle off the roof of a five-story building."

Canning gave a long low whistle. "Wow! The force of that crash would be game over."

"That was the hope! I think our perpetrator's plan was the impact on bike and rider would have been significant enough that any bang to the bike's rear fender or wheel would most likely have gone unnoticed after a drop like that. In fact, there's a decent chance Silva might have been impaled on a tree before hitting the ground.

Canning sat down, leaned back in his oversized leather swivel chair, and placed his snakeskin cowboy boots up on the edge of his huge desk. "So the plan went wrong when Silva crashed into the rear of a parked car.

"A professional killer would have known this plan had too many variables. A paid hit guy would have simply made Scott disappear. If we're lucky, the crime lab will be able to identify a small metal chip found embedded in the bike's tire with the make and model of the driver's car. It's a long shot, but the lab staff is accustomed to working long shots."

"That could make our job a lot simpler," Jack agreed.

"Did you check any nearby home security cameras to see if something was caught?"

"Most of those home video cams are trained on a smaller area around the immediate property, but it's certainly worth a try. I'll send out a deputy to do that this afternoon."

"Let's hope we come up with a result sooner than later. I hate when the Independent is looking over my shoulder," Jack muttered. "Not to mention The Standard," Canning added as he rolled his eyes. "So, where do you go from here?"

"There's a part of this whole Hammer business that you're not up to speed on. If you've got a few more minutes, I need to tell you this part of the story first."

"I'm all ears, Sherlock."

Eddie gave Jack a summary of what had happened since the afternoon of Henrietta's death. Most importantly, why he requested a toxicology panel be run along with DNA testing after the exhumation of Henrietta's body.

"When do you think Max will have some answers for you?" Canning asked.

"Hopefully this week or next."

"What can you do in the meantime to move this forward?"

"I'd like to take a closer look at the handful of players who stood to benefit the most from the Hammer estate before Scott Silva landed in the middle of this story."

"I thought they were all charities?"

"They are, Jack. But unlike the Animal Rescue Shelter or the Ladies of Liberty in Sausalito, they are relatively new non-profits that are closely controlled by one or two individuals."

"You know, Eddie, we have too many do-gooders in this county doing too many bad things. Don't quote me on that!"

Eddie grinned. "Sorry, boss, I missed what you said."

Three hours later, after having called and picked up sandwich orders, Eddie slipped into a parking spot a few doors up Princess Street from Rob and Holly's offices.

Holly had cleared the page layout table so that all three of them could take a breather on what was another busy workweek.

Eddie began by describing his morning meeting with Sheriff Canning.

"Jack's a good guy. I just wish he wasn't so tied to whatever story appeared on this week's front page."

"All sheriffs are also politicians," Rob suggested. "The good thing is his number one priority right now is the Hammer investigation and who was behind the attempt on Scott."

"If and when you find the jerk, I hope you give me the first crack at him," Holly said.

"Easy, Annie Oakley," Eddie warned. "I don't need you shooting any suspects."

"I'll behave, Scout's honor." Both Eddie and Rob found her promise to be less than convincing.

"As nice as it was for you to stop by, not to mention picking up lunch," Rob said, "You must want our help with something."

"Must I have a motive other than just spending time with my two best friends?"

"Yes!" Rob and Holly said in unison.

Eddied shrugged. "I suppose you know me too well."

"That's what friends are for," Rob replied.

"Okay, here's the deal. I told Canning that my top four suspects at this point are the individuals who run the organizations in line to get significant bequests from the Hammer estate. As I told Jack, we can probably eliminate the Ladies of Liberty. They're an established group, and I don't think Alma Samuels is out there ordering any hits. Also, we don't need to go poking around with the rescue shelter. But the characters that run the preservation group, that nutty opera lady that drives Holly up a wall, and the two prima donnas who operate that arts board all need a close look."

"Agreed!" Rob and Holly both exclaimed in unison.

"You two have worked together for too long!" Eddie said with a laugh.

"We've seen this sort of thing for years—not just in Sausalito, but a lot of the towns we cover," Rob explained. "Some of these generous folks are estate babies with nothing else to do. Others are prima donnas who just want to be at the center of attention, regardless of the cause du jour. But some, no doubt, are using a good cause as a means of supplementing their income. In some cases, it could be their only income."

"Eddie, what do you need from us?" Holly asked.

"Get down to city hall and pull up meeting minutes on those three groups along with anything else in the files that might be sketchy. Try to pull together old clippings about the groups in the library's storage area. The Standard probably has some old coverage of all three of these groups as well as the Independent. You might even find some stuff in the San Francisco Chronicle. The more we know about the people who run these organizations, the closer we might come to sorting all this out."

"That's going to take a good amount of digging. I assume you know it's going to be a job we'll have to tackle on Saturday," Rob responded. In truth, the last thing he or Holly wanted to do was give up one of their two weekend days. Still, Rob was aware that what they did could help drop the remaining pieces of this puzzle into place.

"I'm happy to do my bit," Eddie assured them both. "Just let me know what you need."

"I'm in," Holly said enthusiastically. "I'll do whatever it takes to help nail whoever tried to kill Scott."

"Good!" Eddie said relieved to get the additional help.

"I'm hoping it was the opera lady," Holly said in a low growl. "If it is, and she's found guilty, can we put her up before a firing squad? That would really make my year!"

"I know it would, dear." Eddie said as he patted her hand, "But except for Utah, firing squads went out of style a long time ago. The best you can hope for now is lethal injection, and that appears to be on shaky grounds, at least here in California."

Holly sighed. "Makes you miss the days of the old West. This town would be a lot more exciting, with an occasional hanging."

Two days later Scott was released from Marin General Hospital. He was well aware of the Independent's coverage of him as a hit-and-run victim.

Worse, in his view, was the speculation that he had been targeted because two days earlier he had been publicly identified as the rightful heir to the Hammer estate.

Scott confessed to Holly that he now understood that this story was not going away. All of its components were irresistible to reporters and entertaining to readers. "I suppose I'd have to live in a New York, Chicago, or Los Angeles, for a story like this to be cut down to a paragraph and buried on page eighteen."

Holly had no problem understanding Scott's hunger for privacy. It was something she had felt many times, growing up in a small town. Still, she was relieved that at last Scott understood the original story in The Standard—the one that left him so embarrassed, and triggered his angry reaction—would have appeared whether or not he had ever met Holly.

"There's no hiding a good story, is there?" He asked her.

"It's why people turn on the radio, the TV, open their laptop and check the headlines on their phones. We're all waiting to find out what happens next."

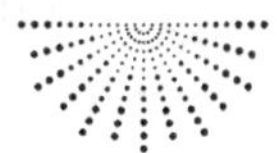

CHAPTER SEVENTEEN

On Saturday morning, Rob and Holly met at City Hall to go through the library's newspaper archives. The microfiche records captured local news dating back over the last one hundred and twenty-five years in a fashion more complete than any online files. Additionally, an extensive collection of binders held the minutes of all city meetings dating back several decades, much of which was also preserved on microfiche, and partially scanned for online access.

Their goal was to find out as much as possible about Francis Phillips, Ruby Reese, Chris Reese, and Laurie Chase.

"You start with Chase, your favorite diva?" Rob suggested. "Maybe you'll get lucky and find out she's an escaped con and we get out of here before lunch."

"That would make me so happy. Okay, I'm on it!"

The first significant piece Rob hit upon was an extensive biographical sketch written years earlier on Phillips by The Standard's gossip columnist, the late Warren Bradley. The article dated back to a time before Rob purchased the paper.

The piece began by detailing the mission of the newly formed Sausalito Preservation Group to "secure for future generations the rich and varied history of Sausalito's storied past."

Bradley, who Rob now recalled had been a regular at nearly all of Phillips' SPG meetings, wrote, "Mr. Phillips is a charismatic guardian of our cherished past. He holds his audience in rapt attention whenever he speaks of the individuals who chose to make this once desolate outpost their home."

As Rob read on, it became clear that Phillips a curious blend of facts and fables, all of which were bolstered by an eclectic mix of artifacts, gossip, and trivia. Phillips, who first came to Sausalito at age nineteen, was described by Bradley as, "A fresh-faced bohemian hoping to find a far more liberal environment than the one he left behind in his hometown of St. George, Utah."

Phillips raised just enough money, to acquire a shared space on one of the aging houseboats moored along A Dock, a long pier, which threatened to fall to ruin during each winter's punishing rainstorms. A few months later he met a young woman named Lily from the adjacent town of Mill Valley, who presented her parents, Bradley explained, with a choice: "Accept Francis as my life partner, or he and I will join an alternative community outside of Ashland, Oregon and you'll never see us again."

Reluctantly, Phillips recalled, he was accepted into the family. One day he and his young bride, who had changed her name to Francine so she and Francis could "experience a more complete blending of their souls," announced to her parents that they were expecting a third soul to, "help populate our family tree."

At that point, Francine's father, who ran a successful plumbing supply business in San Rafael, thought it was time to bring his son-in-law into the family business. But, as Phillips told Bradley, "I found working in an office and wearing a shirt and tie every day to be totally dispiriting. Remember, at that time, I was only a kid of twenty-five."

The baby brought a gift neither of Francine's parents had expected. As Francine explained tearfully to both of them shortly after their grandchild's arrival: "I want Fanny to have a blessed life. I know she's just twelve-weeks-old, but I see in her aura a wonderful future filled with amazing things. To help that come true, I've asked Francis to leave. I think he'll hold my baby back from fully expanding her chakras and becoming the person her birth karma intended her to be."

The world of plumbing, and office attire, now safely behind him, Francis once again embraced the life of Sausalito's houseboat community. It was two years later while working as a front desk clerk at Sausalito's small but well-appointed library that he struck on the idea of starting the preservation group. As Rob suspected, the personal benefits he might accrue by being a self-appointed guardian of the picturesque city's past were many. Sausalito may be a small town, but it was a place known worldwide to travelers as a popular day trip destination, which was easily reached by car, bus, ferry, or bicycle from San Francisco in thirty minutes or less.

Bradley's piece went on to explain that Phillips' library position put him in frequent contact with Peter Brock, a city hall clerk for thirty plus years. Peter had developed an abiding love for all things Sausalito. For decades, Brock had accumulated old books, documents, photos, and mementos that captured the history of European American settlers to this southernmost tip of Marin County.

The article detailed the circuit of meetings in which Brock, with his new protégé Phillips, were able to win the city's approval to convert two sizable adjoining conference rooms on the mostly vacated top floor of city hall into archives' storage areas.

Rob used this article to cross-reference dates of meeting minutes for various city council and planning commission meetings regarding the emergence of the new organization. In two years, the entity had given itself a name: the Sausalito Preservation Group.

Between Brock's long-standing relationships with council members and commissioners, and Phillips—whom when put to the task, could charm almost any audience— their requests were approved with relatively little delibera- tion, an unusual phenomenon in a city where the placement of new park benches could be debated for a year or more.

As with other incorporated cities and townships in Cali- fornia, elected city councils and their appointed boards and commissions all consist of five members. Every measure required a simple majority to move forward. Time and again, Rob was reminded of the old adage he learned long ago from Bob Ivan: "You can't advance projects, code revisions, or new laws in Sausalito if you can't count to three." Phillips must have grasped this essential lesson because he consistently secured three or more votes from every board he and Brock petitioned.

Soon after the SPG had its first formal board meeting and was gaining a broad base of support, Brock, a widower nearing eighty with a chronic alcoholism problem, was gently pushed aside by Phillips with a ceremony and the granting of an "emeritus" position.

Finally, Phillips possessed the unlimited authority Rob was sure had been his ultimate goal from the start.

Through the minutes of the group's meetings, Rob could see how Phillips positioned himself as the one indispensable ingredient in SPG's continued success. When motivated by self-interest, Phillips had the energy of a carnival barker, selling himself as the "lead visionary" behind this "exciting new project" when either speaking in front of the city council, or in public gatherings.

His last significant hurdle was to convince a group of downtown businessmen to help fund a new home for his growing organization. Carefully, he gathered the support of other town activists to share his vision of converting a small downtown building, previously occupied by the city as a tourist information center. It was situated just a few hundred feet from the city's principal point of entry for its lucrative tourist trade, the newly remodeled and expanded Sausalito ferry landing.

Transformed into an impressive glass and steel structure, it was, as the city council's proclamation declared, "an enduring symbol of pride in Sausalito's historic past and promising future."

A small revolt by nearby shop owners threatened to scuttle the downtown location when it was suggested that if the SPG was allowed to sell items such as T-shirts, calendars, and key rings, it could be in competition with numerous businesses selling Sausalito souvenirs. Phillips quieted all such concerns by insisting that any merchandise sold—books, maps, and such—would be restricted to items that honored the city's storied past and include in its price a small percentage for the continuing work of the preservation group. The city council and the planning commission readily accepted Phillips' commitment.

Rob scrutinized numerous photographs of the center's opening day ceremonies. Despite the many city and community dignitaries in attendance at its opening, Francis Phillips was undoubtedly the star. He was pictured with Henrietta Hammer and other enthusiastic backers of the project.

Within weeks of its opening, Phillip's pledge to sell a limited number of retail items to the tourist trade devolved into the sale of key chains, T-shirts, hats, and other keepsakes that carried the seal of the city and the year it was founded.

In a year, the SPG expanded the history center into a larger shop that sold thousands of dollars a day in souvenirs, each of which carried a small gold sticker that read, "Thank you for supporting the Sausalito Preservation Group."

Naturally, this enraged other merchants, as Rob recalled from a story, he wrote two years earlier. Privately owned and operated retailers vying for tourist dollars were now competing with a government subsidized, "non-profit" retailer.

Rob sat back and considered all Phillips had accomplished in a relatively short period: getting city and community support in funding what was primarily a closely held, "non-profit," enterprise. This was particularly ingenuous given Phillips' cadre of aging volunteer board members, none of whom had the time, energy, or inclination to follow the trail of money flowing out of tourist's pockets and into the coffers of Phillip's tightly controlled operation.

A multi-million-dollar gift from the Hammer estate would undoubtedly be Phillips' crowning achievement. The self-appointed guardian of the city's past had every reason, at least until Scott Silva's arrival, to envision a very prosperous future.

Rob took his notes and relevant photocopied documents on Phillips and the SPG and set them aside as he shifted his focus to Chris and Ruby Reese of the Sausalito Fine Arts Board.

Twice annually, in June and December, SFAB holds open studio events and encourages Sausalito residents to meet local artists and purchase their work. Advertising for these events is placed in The Standard, on banners hung on lampposts along Bridgeway, and in direct mailers sent to every area home.

In a presentation to the city council three years earlier, when they were seeking approval for their first open studios' event, Ruby and Chris explained how these events could provide a much-needed lift to the "struggling artists' community."

Ruby packed city meetings with sympathetic and enthusiastic supporters. Passionately she asked, "Where would our community be without the fine arts?"

It was her usual preamble, reminding her audience, "Sausalito has a unique history in fine arts. From houseboat studios to the artists' cooperatives that dot our picturesque waterfront, there is a magical vibrancy to this place that makes the hard work we do at the board more of a privilege than a burden."

Invariably, she made no attempt to explain to the city council and citizens attending what precisely that work entailed.

In color photos, Ruby's shock of red hair was in sharp contrast to the black outfits that draped her thin frame. Rob agreed with Holly's opinion that the severity of her appearance was intended to cultivate an impression that she was a creative soul; without becoming off-putting to the more conservative members of her community. In the search for donors, she cast a wide net.

Like Phillips, the Reeses were also featured in a story in The Standard. This time, the piece was a guest column by Betsy Baker, a stalwart of the Ladies of Liberty and a vocal booster of the SFAB.

You would think I'd remember some of these fluff pieces, but I don't, Rob thought.

The photo accompanying the article pictured Ruby and Chris arm and arm with Henrietta Hammer, who, like her, one-time student, was also smiling.

Chris Reese, described in Baker's piece as a "Sausalito-based painter," praised the work of his wife and her fellow board members in making the community a better place for all artists. "Ruby has really dedicated herself to seeing that artists like me get the financial support that we need to live and work in this special, but expensive, part of the world. The open studios' program helps make that possible. Equally important, it expands our community's growing footprint in the arts."

Later, Rob went through the SFAB's sales tax filings with the city over the last three open studio events. It did not appear that any of the events had been particularly profitable, causing Rob to suspect that half or less of their sales had actually been reported. Prices were likely reduced on the second and final day of each weekend, in exchange for the cash-only sale of artworks, allowing the revenue derived from a percentage of each sale to avoid notice.

Between that, as well as lottery ticket sales for several donated works of art, plus revenue for snacks, refreshments, and wine being sold at the events, there was a variety of opportunities for the Reeses to siphon off a substantial amount of cash.

That did not include the possible misdirection of money from grants and other community fundraisers.

As was the case with Phillips, both of the Reeses had access to funds they could have easily diverted for their personal benefit. Lax board oversight and insufficient financial reports for event revenue and ongoing support from patrons like Hammer would give the Reeses many chances to dip into monies that went under-reported or wholly ignored.

While Rob continued digging deeper into the Reeses, Holly took a close look at Laurie Chase's group, the Sausalito Opera Society.

Carefully she cobbled together a detailed portrait of the amateur diva she dreamed of putting behind bars. First, she learned that Chase's parents left her the home she lives in on Channing Way. Likely, it was unencumbered by any notes or liens. This question could be quickly answered through the county's property records.

Holly could find no reference to Laurie owning a business, being self-employed, or working in a government or private sector job. Realizing that there were no visible means of support other than a small monthly stipend she may or may not receive from the family's estate, Holly began to wonder if embezzlement from the organization Laurie had founded provided a needed source of income.

She does have that ridiculous vegetable garden, Holly paused to consider, but that can't take the place of having an adequate food budget. After all, how many zucchinis, carrots, tomatoes, and kale is one person going to eat in a single week?

Laurie's birth notice was found in a more than three-decade-old copy of the Independent. A photo of her parents, Carl and Carrie Chase, holding their new arrival was taken outside of the same aging home on Channing Way where Laurie still resides.

As Holly moved quickly through the records, she was shocked to find an article reporting the death of Laurie's mother in an accident on Highway 101 near the Rodeo

Drive exit. The Standard, which at the time was more discreet about personal details than the paper Rob and Holly published now, hinted that the late night accident at the bottom of the very steep Waldo Grade might have been connected to "cocktails the deceased enjoyed at a party earlier in the evening."

Wow, I never knew any of this, Holly thought. Maybe I heard about it as a little kid, and it just didn't register. It must have been rough on Laurie losing her mom at such an early age.

As Holly moved through past editions of the paper, she found nothing to suggest that Laurie had any siblings. Holly paid particular attention to the obituaries. There, she saw a death notice for Laurie's father, Carl. It was published nine years ago. He was sixty-one and died of lung cancer. The article mentioned nothing about his having any career or business endeavor.

Perhaps the family estate predates Laurie's parents' generation, Holly considered. She might have learned from her father how to make a fixed amount of estate money go a very long way.

Holly ran across articles in which Laurie spoke publicly of her intention to organize a "society of local opera lovers." In an article in the Independent dated five years ago, Laurie declared, "San Francisco and Berkley have opera societies. Now, with our new Sausalito group, there will be three opera societies in the Bay Area!"

Three too many, Holly thought with a laugh.

Holly moved on to review minutes of city council sessions and meetings of the parks and recreation commission. Laurie's proposals sailed through all these meetings.

When, months later, she returned to both bodies for permission to organize her Sunday afternoon Gabrielson Park events, city officials threw her softball questions interspersed by fawning praise for the society's "important work."

After their long day, Rob and Holly went back to The Standard's office to compare notes.

One truth was clear to both: There was enough information on Chase, Phillips, and the Reeses to call into question whether they were approaching their work as a service to the community or a form of self-enrichment.

Phillips' Sausalito Historic Preservation Center had enough money washing through it to make the organization, and him personally, financially secure. The Reeses' open gallery events also seemed financially self-serving, as did Chase's Opera in the park. While the concerts were free to the public, it generated substantial revenue from its VIP reserved tables in addition to beverages, food—and with the city's blessing—wine, beer, and champagne sales.

Add to this all of its local business sponsorships, and it became apparent that SOS was taking in a healthy sum from each of their special weekend events, including the recent addition of a holiday performance of The Nutcracker, staged at the Ladies of Liberty clubhouse.

To top it off, a quick search of annual revenue reports filed with the California Secretary of State's office showed that two of the organizations—Laurie's opera society and

Phillips' preservation league—had never filed a single tax document. Even more surprisingly, neither was registered with the state.

The only papers the Reeses' arts council filed were three-years-old. That report showed a negligible salary for Ruby of eight thousand dollars—and no compensation for Chris.

"Without salaries, how are they surviving?" Holly wondered aloud. "Are they lining their pockets with off the books' revenue?"

"At this stage, it's hard to say that definitively," Rob, responded. "All three organizations are led by individuals with easy opportunities to embezzle. Not taking salaries, and yet none have visible means of income: no reported administrative salaries from the non-profits they represent, and no other known jobs either part or full-time."

"At the same time," Holly added, "none are estate babies —well, perhaps Laurie. But from what I found, the Chase family money seems to have narrowed down to a trickle. I'm guessing at this stage, Laurie, minus revenue from SOS she might be pocketing, is house poor."

"But you know," Rob said after further thought, "there is one other red flag we see in the operation of all three organizations."

"What's that?"

"There's never any turnover at the top. If you or I were somehow roped into managing one of these groups, we'd be looking to pass control to someone else because it's obviously very time consuming, especially in light of the income it reportedly generates from a variety of events. But just like the Reeses, Laurie Chase and Francis Phillips all seem to control every aspect of their operations. In Phillips case, it's been many years since he pushed Peter Brock aside and took over sole control of the organization. Granted, you could say they don't want to see someone screw up what they took time and effort to build, but I think it's more than that. These organizations are their principal source of income, and they're not going to have someone get close enough to blow the whistle or demand their own cut of the take."

"I still think there's a possibility that Laurie Chase has family money," Holly countered. "But nothing that appears to be substantial. I drove up to Channing Way to take a look at her place. It's a valuable piece of property, but the house itself looks like it's been neglected for many years.

"As to what you said Rob about tight control, the opera society is all Laurie's baby. The board is there to cheer her on, not to audit her books once a year."

Rob shrugged. "Exactly the same case with Phillips board and the Reeses. Let's write up a report that we can give to Eddie on Monday. He's in a position to take any or all of our suspicions and turn them into possible criminal investigations."

"After reading about Laurie Chase, I'm going to see if I can interview her this week or next."

"Really? I never thought I'd hear you suggest that! What's your angle?"

"I'm not sure. I read that Laurie lost her mom when she was a little kid. Sounds like it was a DUI: she spun out one night and crashed into a tree near Rodeo Drive after speeding down the Waldo Grade."

"Ouch!" Rob said with a wince. "That's an easy place to

get yourself killed, sober. Wow, that had to be tough, especially on a little kid."

"I just want to learn more about her. I'm curious, I suppose."

"So you don't want to shoot her anymore?"

Holly grinned. "Well, I'll put shooting her on hold for now. You know, she's probably just a little nuts. If I started shooting people in Sausalito just because they were a bit odd, my list of victims would get pretty long!"

"If you're set on interviewing her, take the time to put together a profile piece on her and SOS. I'm sure it won't be long before we have another slow news week. Scott's 'Babygate' story will spin itself out soon enough, particularly without a new angle in the coming days. Before you know it, we'll be back to covering drunk tourists falling off the ferry dock and dog park improvement debates."

CHAPTER EIGHTEEN

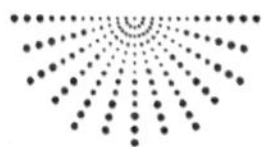

Rob's prediction proved correct. Within two weeks, life in Sausalito regained its equilibrium.

There was some buzz about a San Francisco dentist who died in a Sausalito hotel room of a heart attack at the end of a naughty weekend with his much younger dental assistant. A tourist reported having been the victim of a pickpocket, leading longtime residents to complain about "a crime spree." And the traffic light at one of the town's main intersections, Bridgeway and Bay Street, malfunctioned several times, despite attempts by the public works department to get it working correctly.

"Someone's going to get killed there," Alma Samuels wrote to The Standard's mailbag column. It was written in Alma's usually dour and overly dramatic tone.

"We could always wait a week or two and see if someone does get hit by a car at that intersection before doing another traffic light story," Holly suggested.

That idea was shot down by Rob, who explained, "A

fatality is unlikely, given the twenty miles per hour speed limit. But it's a slow news week so let's lead with the traffic light. Besides, it never hurts to throw Alma, our number one critic, a bone every now and then."

As Holly placed a photo of the traffic light in question on the front page, she grumbled, "Really? This is the best we've got for the Sausalito edition?"

"Perhaps we can tie it into other repairs by the city's public works department that have gone bad," Rob replied. "The only problem with that is I'll have no luck getting a city crew out to my place if we've got storm drainage problems this next rain season."

"You're telling me you'd let the chance of a backed-up storm sewer stand in the way of a free press?"

Rob snorted. "Yes, Holly, that's exactly what I'm telling you."

After a few minutes of silence, Holly had a different suggestion: "Let me call up my favorite diva and schedule that interview we were talking about a couple of weeks ago."

"You mean the one with the celebrated soprano, Laurie Chase?"

"The one and only. Maybe I'll get lucky, and she'll tell me who tried to push Scott into a gully!"

"Sure. Give it a try," Rob said with a smile. "When we're down to malfunctioning traffic lights for our lead story, the only place we can go is up."

Laurie was excited that Holly wanted to interview her about the founding, organizing and operating of the opera society. By the time Holly got off the phone, she had found herself reconsidering her earlier desire to pick Laurie off from her perch on Princess Street with one well-placed rifle shot.

The next day, with pad and recorder in hand, Holly parked her car alongside Laurie's vegetable garden, which covered most of the land in front of the old gray and white colonial-style clapboard house.

It was the right time of year for a bountiful garden—in Laurie's case, one overrun with zucchinis, strawberries, tomato plants, and carrots.

Holly wondered if she needed money, why not split the home's lot and develop it, or sell it with approved plans to build? That would generate two million dollars or more. Additionally, she has enough friends on the city council and the planning commission to get any building plans for the site approved.

As Holly walked through a shabby and somewhat over-grown patch of grass that led to the home's front door, she was struck by the thought that her assessment of Laurie's financial position might have been entirely incorrect. If she hasn't sold off that front lot, perhaps she doesn't need the extra money.

The front doorbell set off a full set of chimes that Holly could hear quite clearly standing on the opposite side of the door.

No answer.

Holly waited twenty seconds then rang a second time.

No answer.

She rang a third time as Holly began to wonder, in the twenty-four hours since they spoke, could Laurie have forgotten their appointment?

Still, she wasn't about to walk back to her car and drive off without another attempt.

The only number she had for Laurie was her home number. She pulled out her phone. Scrolling down through its directory, she found the name and tapped it. She heard ten rings both from her phone and inside the house.

With no answer, Holly angrily tapped the screen to end the call.

Now what? As depressed as Rob is over another slow news week, this was the perfect time to do a story on Laurie! I don't want to drive back down to the office and listen to more of his gripping, she thought.

Holly recalled how pleased Laurie was about being interviewed. This just doesn't make sense, she reasoned. Maybe the woman is half deaf. I would be if I listened to all that caterwauling on those opera recordings day and night. Perhaps I should go around the back of the house and see if she's just out of earshot.

Holly followed the path that led around to the back of the house. Reaching the back door, Holly knocked several times.

No answer.

She then tried turning the knob. As she anticipated, it was locked.

All this made Holly increasingly nervous. Still, she couldn't resist looking through the home's picture window, which had a view of the spacious patio and the bamboo covered hill behind it.

Holly cupped her hands on either side of her eyes to help her see inside and found herself looking at a dining room table. At the head of the table was a Chippendale chair that had fallen over on its side. Just beyond the chair, Holly saw a body lying face down on the floor.

Does she sit here all day and drink herself into a stupor, Holly wondered.

Or is she…

No, she can't be…

Immediately, Holly pulled out her cell again and tapped Eddie's number from her list of favorites.

On the second ring, she was comforted to hear Eddie. "Aren't you supposed to be up at Laurie Chase's place interviewing your favorite diva? You didn't kill her, did you?"

"How did you know I was coming up here?" Holly asked frantically. "Do you have a tail on me?"

"No, Einstein! I just called Rob a few minutes ago to see if he and Karin would babysit Aaron Saturday night. We've got some stupid sheriff's department function we have to attend."

"Well, I need you—and I mean now!"

"You mean at Laurie Chase's place?"

Holly explained her attempts to get Laurie to respond to her doorbell or her phone. "I went around the back to knock on that door, and now, through the rear window, I can see someone lying flat on the floor in the dining room. I don't know if she's dead or just dead drunk!

"Okay, don't panic. I'll call the EMT boys and the

Sausalito Police. What's the address, I know it's somewhere up on Channing—"

Holly gave Eddie the street number and then asked, "Aren't you coming too?"

"I'm over at the Marin City substation, getting in the car now. I'll head up 101 and be there in five." Eddie said and clicked off.

The Cavalry came within seconds of one another. First to arrive was the fire department. Then the EMT vehicle, followed by two patrol cars close behind.

Eddie's arrival, moments later, ended the parade. He appeared in his unmarked black car with a red light flashing on its dashboard.

Everyone present knew each other. Like Holly and Eddie, two of the patrol officers and two of the fire department's rescue team were natives of the town.

As they raced to the front door, Eddie warned them, "We'll likely have to pry the door open. Still, let's do our best to keep this place clean. It's possible that we're walking into a crime scene."

"Really, Eddie?" one of the officers asked.

"She's one of my suspects in the hit and run of Scott Silva last month, so I'm not sure what we might find here."

A window in the front door was broken to open the lock.

Once inside, one of the emergency med techs bent down

to place two fingers against Laurie's neck to check for a pulse.

"She's gone," he declared quickly. "And judging by how cold the body is, I'd say there's a good chance she died twelve hours ago, perhaps longer."

"Damn," Eddie said, shaking his head. "Okay boys, I've got a crime scene here. Let's clear out. However, I'll need one of Sausalito's Finest to hang in and handle any nosey neighbors. In fact, let's get some tape and put it around the perimeter of the property. With the lights and sirens show we just gave them, I'm sure some of them will come poking around any minute now. Also, let's get a call into the coroner's office. We need the deceased taken up to the medical examiner's office."

A moment later, Eddie was on his cell to the Sheriff's Department Crime Unit photographer, giving her the address so that she could document the scene as soon as possible.

Holly stood in the living room doorway, feeling less comfortable by the moment. Finally, she murmured, "Eddie, what do you want me to do?"

"I think you've had enough excitement for one day. Head back down to the office. I'll catch you there or at your place whenever I'm finished and give you an update. That'll probably take me two hours plus."

"Any idea what happened to her?"

"Not a clue, kiddo. Not a clue."

I t took Holly less ten minutes to head down the hill and walk back into the office. The second he saw her, Rob knew something had gone terribly wrong. "What's up? You look as if you've seen a ghost!"

Holly rolled her eyes. "Unbelievable!"

"She was that bad an interview?"

"I never got the interview."

Rob frowned. "Why not? Jeez, Holly! What are we going to do for our Sausalito lead?"

"You want a lead, Rob? Here's your lead!" Holly moved her hand across an imaginary front page: "Laurie Chase Found Dead by Standard Associate Editor Holly Cross!"

Rob's mouth dropped open in stunned disbelief. After a moment, he murmured, "Dead?"

"Yes, according to the EMTs I just left. Dead—twelve hours or more."

"Okay, let's get moving. Get that traffic light off the front page! We've got a story much better than that." When Rob added, "Great work!" Holly wasn't sure how to react.

But, with a deadline less than three hours away, there was no time for reflection. There was barely enough time to pull their new front-page together and transmit the newly revised edition to the printer.

H olly worked frantically during a period that felt to both of them like thirty minutes or less. After Rob uploaded the publication, they paused to take a breath.

Digging into the back of their small, crowded office refrigerator, Rob pulled out two chilled bottles of Dos Equis. He handed one of the beers to Holly.

"Breaking out the good stuff?" Holly smirked with a raised eyebrow.

"Hey, you deserve it, kid!" Rob replied. "I sent you up there to get a ho-hum interview, and you come back with one hell of a story! That part about going around the back of the house and seeing the body—wow! Just great! Really, it made me feel like I was right there with you!"

"You know Rob, at times it wouldn't hurt if you were just a touch more sensitive. You know, more like a normal person."

"Holly, need I remind you that a month ago this was the same woman you wanted to pick off with a rifle?"

"She was disturbing the peace!" Holly said as she dabbed with a tissue at the corners of her eyes." Don't tease me. I feel rotten enough."

"Oh come on, kid," Rob said as he put his arm around her shoulder. "Eddie will show up before long and tell us what really happened. Maybe she had a bad ticker, and you had bad timing."

"Maybe? I just hate the fact that I was the one who found her."

"Well, you did, and it saved us from running a story about a defective traffic light on the front page. So cheer up. You have to admit, your timing could not have been better."

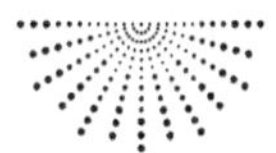

CHAPTER NINETEEN

Eddie called just as Rob and Holly finished their beers.

"I figured you two would still be at the office. Stay there. I'm leaving here, and I'll be straight down."

Not long after, Rob buzzed Eddie in through the front door.

He came bounding up their steep stairway two steps at a time. "Wow! What a day! Good work on finding that body, Holly."

Holly growled, "I wish you two would stop congratulating me on finding Laurie Chase."

"Hey, what did I do?" Eddie protested.

"She's just feeling a little fragile right now, you know finding a body and all," Rob said. But as he patted Holly's shoulder, she brushed him away.

"Hey, do I smell beer?" Eddie asked.

"Yes, you do," Rob assured him. "Dos Equis! Want one, amigo?"

"Absolutely!"

"So Eddie," Holly asked impatiently, "to what do we owe the pleasure of your visit?"

"Well that body you found earlier, you know the one you needed some help with…"

"Yes, I recall the circumstances."

"Turns out it might have been a case of accidental poisoning."

"Really?" Holly asked her curiosity now peeked.

"You better start back at the beginning," Rob said, sitting down at his desk prepared to be surprised.

"Just after Holly left I took a chance at getting a hold of Max Brownstein. If he was available, I thought it would be great to have the county's top forensics guy take a look at the body and the scene before we had Laurie moved out. I'm glad I did."

"Did you think something looked odd?" Rob asked. "When Holly got down here, it sounded like she had been eating dinner, got up from the table, and had a stroke or a heart attack."

"That was certainly my first guess."

"So what did Max think?" Holly asked.

"He looks at her dinner plate, sniffs it, then sniffs her nearly empty glass of wine. He then wanders into the kitchen and starts sniffing around in there as well. He's like a human bloodhound! Sometimes I think he has a sixth sense. Of course, I followed him wherever he went. He sees some of the food prepared for Laurie's dinner last night, sitting in a skillet on top of the stove. Max grabs one of those oversized Ziploc storage bags from a box on the counter, puts on a pair of blue latex surgical gloves, and places the skillet inside. Then he takes another bag, walks into the dining room, and does the same with her dinner plate. Well, at this stage it's pretty obvious what he's thinking…"

"Something she ate might have killed her?" Rob asked.

"Or so, Max thinks. I asked him why. He explains that it could have been a stroke or a bad ticker, but he didn't want a valuable piece of evidence to disappear if this turns out to be a case of food poisoning. He'll check the contents of her stomach, you can be sure of that."

"No signs of a violent struggle, a break in or anything like that, I presume?" Rob asked.

"As Holly saw, her house was clean. Nothing looked out of place. Whatever happened up there apparently happened quietly and quickly."

"Did Max have any guess as to the time of her death?" Holly asked.

"He estimated between six and eight o'clock last night."

"So, Laurie had likely been dead eighteen hours or more when I came knocking on her door."

"Right, Holly. Sorry, you walked into the middle of that."

"How long do you think it will take before Max has some answers?" Rob asked.

"He told me between thirty-six and forty-eight hours."

"Eddie, do you have any hunch as to what might have happened?" Holly asked.

"Not in the least, Holly. Outside of you, I don't have any idea who might have wanted to see her dead."

"That's true," Rob added as he turned to look at Holly with a raised eyebrow.

"Cut it out, you two! I did have my fantasies of picking

her off from up here, but that singing of hers would have been ruled justifiable homicide by any jury."

Eddie finished the last of his beer. "Well, Holly, you won't have to worry about Sausalito's songbird anymore. She's fallen from her perch."

"Which makes me think," Rob said. "Who will be there to sing at her funeral?"

"No one, I hope," Holly replied.

By the mid-morning the following day, as The Standard dropped into mailboxes, Sausalitans learned of Laurie Chase's unexpected death. Her group of acolytes, most of whom were thirty, or more years her senior, wondered what might have happened.

A candlelight vigil was planned for Friday evening at six, on the plaza in front of City Hall. On Friday morning, members of her board distributed flyers throughout the downtown and at other community gathering points to announce the event.

Holly found one of them on top of a pile of mail that the postman tossed onto the bottom step of the newspaper's Victorian walk-up. As Holly placed the flyer on Rob's desk, she asked, "What do you think, should we go?"

Rob winced. "I don't know. Karin expects me home right after tonight's happy hour, which usually breaks up a little after six."

"Well, I'm going. I am the one that found the body, you know."

"How could I forget? You've told me about it at least a half dozen times."

"I'm processing my feelings, Rob! It's upsetting finding a dead person."

"I've had the experience myself, you know. Let's not forget our dearly departed columnist, the gossiping gourmet. I suppose both of us have a knack for being at the wrong place at the wrong time. I'll go by the remembrance with you. It's on my way home. But when I do, I'm meeting, greeting, and getting the hell out of there."

"It's kind of you to go." Holly's eye roll indicated that, in her opinion, it was the least he could do. "You know if nothing else Laurie did provide you with a good lead story for this week's edition."

"You're right," Rob conceded. "For that, I'll be eternally grateful."

Eddie was already at their usual table at Smitty's when Rob and Holly walked in, a few minutes past five. He didn't notice them until they were about to sit down because he was looking at that small notebook he has with him at all times.

"Any news, for your favorite news team?" Rob asked, hoping for information on Laurie's autopsy.

"Good evening to the two of you as well," Eddie said with a forced smile.

"That's not your happy face is it," Holly announced. "What's up copper?"

"I just don't like when things happen that raise questions without providing any apparent answers."

"Such as?" Rob asked.

"For starters, the death of Laurie Chase being caused by aconite."

"Aconite? What the heck is that?" Holly asked.

"A highly poisonous herb that grows wild in lots of places around the world. It particularly likes a Mediterranean climate, such as the one we generally enjoy here in Northern California: warm, dry summers, chilly wet winters."

"She ingested it?" Rob asked.

"Yes. Apparently, it was mixed in with the rest of her food. Eddie replied. "In addition to her stomach contents from the autopsy, Max found traces of aconite in the pan Laurie used to prepare her meal."

"That explains why he was snooping around her kitchen," Rob said.

"I told you, the man has a sixth sense."

How do you suppose it found its way into her food?" Holly asked.

"Aconite deaths are not nearly as common as people accidentally poisoning themselves with wild mushrooms, but apparently it does happen. Max explained that generally, people pull it out of the ground, mistaking it for horseradish. It's a pretty innocent looking thing. Even has a root similar to that of a carrot."

"So, her death will be ruled accidental?" Rob asked.

Eddie shrugged. "Max is going to sit on the results for a while. The good news is the Independent has not been nosing around regarding Laurie's death. They know of her connection to the Hammer estate, but they must be working other stories. The press officer at the department has not received any information or interview requests from them. You might have another exclusive in the case of Holly's favorite songbird, come next Wednesday's paper. Max is thinking that he won't be ready to issue a full report until Tuesday, I'll keep you posted."

"So they think this stuff was growing wild in her garden?" Holly asked.

"That's where the story gets a bit odd," Eddie said. "In this region, if you were to stumble across aconite growing wild, odds are it would be up along some of the ridges of the Marin Headlands. The upper ridges get a good amount of winter rain, but the water doesn't pool along those ridges. Instead, it filters down through the soil. Aconite generally won't survive very long if excess moisture is present."

"But is there a chance it might have been out in Laurie's garden? I got the impression that vegetable patch of hers helped to provide a good part of her weekly food budget," Holly explained.

"Why would you think that?"

"I think she was house poor—you know, beautiful home, a wonderful lot, but that's all you have to your name. And a house isn't ready cash unless you're borrowing against its value. The kind of thing you see in a reverse mortgage. I've been thinking about that since Rob and I spent Saturday trying to learn more about Phillips, Chase, and the Reeses."

"But didn't you think she was skimming something off the top at the Opera Society?" Eddie asked Holly.

"With those concerts in the park, I have no doubt she had the opportunity. But until an audit is done of her books or the other two organizations, none of us can be sure where the money was going. That's why, after reading about her life—a single child who lost her mother at an early age, and her father was a bit of an odd duck—I had to know more. I actually wondered how much of her meals came out of that garden. I mean, no matter what you grow, there's, property taxes, insurance, and maintenance, not to mention a dozen different out of pocket needs."

"I never did know what got you so curious about Chase," Rob said to Holly. "I was just so desperate for a better Sausalito lead this week I would have printed an interview with a merchant about this year's best selling tourist items!"

"We haven't gotten that desperate yet," Holly exclaimed. "So Eddie, are you and the boys from Scotland Yard going to take a good look at Laurie's yard?"

"You bet. We're getting a crew up there to take samples from all over her garden. We're also putting that police crime scene tape all around the perimeter of Laurie's garden. That ought to stir up her neighbors."

"You think?" Rob said with a half smile.

"Someone is going to start the rumor that they're looking for bodies," Holly added.

"You think they're that daft?" Eddie said.

"I'll bet you a beer for you or a martini for me if we don't get one or more calls wanting to know what's going on, and asking if we're covering this story," Holly said with confidence.

"Okay, you're on," Eddie stuck out his pinky finger to seal the deal.

"Come on Holly," Rob said. "We've got a candlelight vigil to get to, down at City Hall."

Looking at her watch, Holly said, "Oh my gosh, you're right! Let's get going."

"What candlelight vigil?" Eddie asked.

"They're doing something for Laurie. Want to come along?"

"Sure." Eddie stood up and reached for his jacket.

"I didn't take you for the candlelight vigil type," Holly said.

"I'm not, but maybe Laurie's killer will be there."

"Are you serious? I thought the theory was accidental poisoning," Rob exclaimed.

"That's the working theory, but I'm open to other solutions."

"You really think her killer could be there?" Holly asked excitedly.

"Sure! It's like an arsonist waiting for the fire engines to arrive. Half of the fun is the thrill of it all."

Early twilight was descending on Sausalito as Eddie, Rob and Holly walked up the steep incline of Litho Street to the main entrance of City Hall. A group of approximately forty people had already gathered out front on the brick plaza. They were holding small white candles sticking out of white paper collars intended to catch the dripping wax.

It was Francis Phillips who handed out candles and said, "Welcome to our memorial celebration." The three friends smiled and nodded before moving toward the center of the gathering.

Within a few minutes of their arrival, Mayor Steve Herbert made his way up the steps of a small platform placed there for this event. "It's a joy to see so many familiar faces here tonight."

"It's Sausalito," Holly mumbled to Rob. "Once you get out of the tourist district, all you see are familiar faces."

"Laurie was one of Sausalito's treasures," the mayor continued.

Oh God, here we go, Rob thought.

"She worked tirelessly to bring the world of opera to our community. Her 'Opera Sundays in the Park' program thrilled us all."

"Not me buster," Holly muttered softly. Rob squeezed her arm as a reminder that she needed to behave.

"I was never a fan of opera," the mayor admitted, "But Laurie turned me around with her persistent love of Puccini, Verdi, Wagner, Mozart, and Bizet."

While the mayor continued, Eddie kept an eye on Ruby and Chris Reese, both of whom stood close to Francis Phillips.

My three favorite suspects. Anyone of them would have happily pushed Scott Silva into that gully, he thought. If one of them had, that same individual perhaps caused Henrietta Hammer's premature death.

All I need is more time and more information.

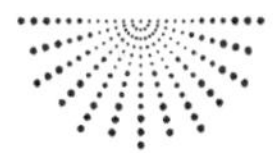

CHAPTER TWENTY

Saturday morning, the phone rang at nine-thirty, waking Holly out of a deep and much-needed sleep.

"What are you doing?" Scott asked in an excited voice.

"Making up for the sleep I missed all week," she grumbled.

"Sorry," Scott said, teasingly.

"Okay. Go on," Holly said, still half asleep.

"I want to know what you have planned for tonight."

"Not much of anything. Why? Are you working up to asking me out?"

"Yes, I am. Can you come up to my mother's house and meet me at seven?"

"Sure."

"Wear something nice."

"Don't I always?" Holly asked with an edge to her voice.

"Oh…yes! Absolutely."

"Okay. I'll wear something pretty, just for you."

"And be sure to get here by seven."

"Sounds like you're up to something."

"Get here by seven, and you'll find out," Scott said as he clicked off.

As Holly ran through her usual list of Saturday chores, she made sure to finish early to have a couple of hours to "beautify," as she explained to Eddie's wife, Sharon, when they ran into each other at the Golden Gate Market.

"What do you suppose he has in mind?" Sharon asked.

"I haven't a clue," Holly replied.

"Eddie tells me he's a good guy."

"He is. But he got real skittish about the news coverage over the whole Hammer estate thing, and blamed me along with everyone else in the news business," Holly explained. "He came to his senses after his accident—if 'accident' is the right word for what happened," Holly added with a raised an eyebrow.

"No story disappears just because it makes one or more people feel uncomfortable. If that were the case, what would we have to read and you and Rob would need to find a new line of work."

"I don't think any of us would mind waking up to find ourselves the heir to a fortune."

"From what I've heard about him, Scott has more love for science and math than money. There's certainly more to life than a healthy bank balance. Eddie and I would be satisfied if our income could keep up with our expenses."

"Tell me about it! And I work for Rob Timmons, the Ebenezer Scrooge of the newspaper business."

With that, both of them laughed as Sharon reached out and gripped Holly's hand. "Promise to call me tomorrow. I want to hear how your date went. You know Eddie isn't the only curious person in our family."

Precisely at seven, Holly arrived at the front door of Henrietta's old home.

As peculiar as it felt coming up here to clean the place out, for Holly it felt even stranger showing up dressed for a date!

A moment later, Scott came to the door looking like a man dressed to impress, with a sharp black blazer, white button-down shirt, a red tie with blue stripes, and tan slacks.

They kissed—lightly at first. But then Scott drew her in closer. They kissed more deeply until Holly pulled away. "Wow! What came over you, Romeo?"

"You did, Holly Cross," Scott replied as he pulled her in for another kiss.

Holly barely had the time to come up for air when from the driveway behind her she heard a car horn. Pulling back from Scott's kiss, she turned to find a black Lincoln town car in the driveway.

"Are you ready to go?" Scott asked.

"Sure," she said happily. "Where are we going?"

He winked. "That's the surprise."

A gold bucket of ice holding a bottle of champagne had been placed in the back of the Lincoln Town Car along with two champagne flutes.

"You do know how to show a girl a good time," Holly exclaimed as Scott popped the bottle's cork.

"No, I really don't," Scott replied. "But I'm trying to learn. Any suggestions are welcome."

The Saturday night traffic heading over the Golden Gate Bridge into the city was doing its usual crawl, but neither of the town car's passengers seemed to mind. As they snuggled up, Holly teased, "Seriously, Scott, I thought you had forgotten all about me."

"You're just about all that's on my mind day or night."

"You're saying all the right things," Holly said as she slid in closer for another kiss.

By the time they were off the bridge, traffic was flowing smoothly. The car turned onto Veterans Boulevard and headed toward the Richmond District.

"I haven't been in the city since our little adventure at the Russian Orthodox Church," Holly said.

"Same for me. That was one of the most memorable days of my life."

When the car pulled up to Katia's Russian Tea Room, Holly smiled. "I guess you really did like this place!"

"Are you kidding?" Scott said with a big smile, "I loved it."

For both Holly and Scott, dinner flew past. They started with Zakuski, the Russian version of what the Spanish call Tapas and in English, less romantically, "small plates." The dishes included eggplant caviar and marinated mushrooms.

For their entrée, they enjoyed blinis. Golden crepes filled with smoked salmon and salmon caviar.

Once they finished, the waiter brought out a chocolate walnut meringue torte to share, along with two cappuccinos. Scott took both of Holly's hands and said, "I know I apologized at the hospital and again, after I got home, for mistreating you. I think I was just overwhelmed by the whole situation. You know how there are people in this world that love to be recognized? I love not being recognized. I truly value being a private person. The whole Henrietta estate thing just freaked me out."

"I understand. Believe me, I would have been pretty unhappy if I was the object of all that attention."

"When I was a teen in love with science and math, I hoped that if I had a windfall, it would come from winning the Nobel Prize in physics, not because I was kept in the dark about my real birth parents. I'm lucky the press doesn't call me the accidental heir. I shouldn't say that it might happen any day now. I suppose I should just be happy and forget about how it all happened. It is like winning the California lottery without spending the buck to buy a ticket."

"Scott," Holly said as she placed her hand over his in the center of the table. "I have no idea how I would have reacted if I had been put through what you've been through. Probably not great—and I'm not even talking about your accident!"

"Yeah, but I took it all out on you, and I shouldn't have done that."

"In the past, forgotten! Let's just put it behind us. You were going through a lot of crazy stuff. I might have reacted the same way."

"Well, that's one of two things I wanted to tell you."

"What's the second?"

"I wanted to thank you. Holly, because of you, I'll forever know who my dad was."

"Oh, my God! Mikhail got his DNA test results?"

"Yes. At this point, it was little more than a formality, but still, it's nice to see it in print. The genetic match is so close! But just like in the match I would have with Ruth as opposed to Henrietta, not precise."

"I'm sure Max would have loved to have met his son," Holly said as she felt a few tears coming on.

Seeing one fall on her cheek, Scott said, "Don't start Holly, because I'll start too. And then we'll probably get tossed out of here."

On their ride back to Sausalito, Scott and Holly sat in silence. They demonstrated their satisfaction with the evening by holding hands as they watched the lights of the Golden Gate Bridge twinkling on a mild night.

Scott asked Holly to stay the night. More now than anytime in the past, Holly felt at home in the old mansion.

They never discussed their intentions for the future. They just went upstairs, got into bed, and held each other tightly as all the hurt dissolved into a new and more certain level of happiness.

Holly came into the office early on Monday morning. Sitting at her desk, she felt different from the person she was on Friday evening when she left work with Rob to meet-up with Eddie.

A sense of calm had come over her—something rare in Holly's life.

Sunday was spent in an almost dream-like haze. Scott was by no means her first relationship with a man, but this relationship was different from any other.

In recent years, the men in Holly's life, were, like her, in their thirties. All came and went with predictable regularity. On the other hand, Scott was ten years older. He had a youthful vigor and a curious mind. But he also had a level of wisdom that Holly had not experienced in previous relationships.

He was so worked up about their Saturday night date that throughout the evening Holly wondered if he was going to propose. She was glad he didn't. It would have been out of character. Scott was a more cautious soul.

Would I be happy being Scott's partner in life? Holly wondered, as she sipped coffee and looked out at the tourist shops of Princess Street.

She found a sense of calm in his arms when she awoke on Sunday morning. It gave her a rare sense of completeness. But Holly's nature always cautioned her. She wondered just how long this blissful feeling could last.

Rob came in at nine-thirty, having been "stuck," as he explained, at an early morning assembly at Willow Creek School watching with Karin as their son and daughter participated in a school play.

"What do you mean stuck?" Holly said as she reacted disapprovingly to Rob's assessment of the children's efforts.

"Oh you know, little kids being adorable, parents fawning over their every giggle. It gets a little too sappy for me," Rob explained, giving her a guilty half smile. "The play was called 'Awaken.' It was about welcoming the changing seasons. Let's just say it was lacking plot and dialogue."

"These kids are six, seven, and eight. You're just a nasty old curmudgeon!"

"I prefer to think of myself as a nasty young curmudgeon. Hey, what's come over you Holly? You were always just as big a grouch as me when it came to adorable kids, and cute school plays."

"We all have to grow up sometime, Mr. Timmons."

"I'd like to see how you'd feel spending part of your morning watching a children's play."

"You just have to enjoy the moment," Holly suggested with a smile.

Rob stared closely at Holly. "What's come over you? Sappy is not your usual modus operandi." Suddenly, Rob smiled. "Did you and Scott spend the weekend together?"

"That's none of your business!" Holly said in a huff. "And yes, we had a wonderful time," she added with a mischievous smile as she walked back to her office.

❧

The following morning, Rob and Holly debated how best to approach their story on Laurie Chase's autopsy.

They had another scoop since the Independent was still not paying attention to Laurie's death.

"We know the cause," Rob said. Still, it's hard to think of how the whole poisoning thing fits into the rest of the story,"

"Maybe it doesn't. There's a good chance that Henrietta's death and Laurie's death are totally unrelated."

"I know, but that's kind of a shame. The two were only weeks apart, and it would be that much better of a story if there were a link."

"As a general rule," Holly said, "I assume people who die because they unintentionally chopped a deadly mushroom or herb into their dinner is a tiny segment of the population."

"That's the long and the short of it," Rob agreed.

"The more I think about it, I really do feel sorry for the poor woman. She might have had her problems—and God only knows I thought she was a bit odd, but I'm sure she would have been happier having a life that was a good deal longer."

As Holly reached out for a relevant quotable source—in this case, an officer with the California Poison Control Center—Rob dug a little deeper into the statistical analysis of accidental poisonings on a national level. Just as they were both deep in thought knowing the clock was ticking on their next deadline, the downstairs buzzer rang: once, twice and then a third time in a frantic staccato.

Holly walked out to the steps and looked out through the building's wood and glass front entryway. It was Eddie.

Holly released the lock. "What are you so excited about?" she asked as Eddie came rushing up the steps taking them two at a time. "You're not going to believe this!"

"Try me," Holly said as Eddie rushed by and she turned to follow.

"You two are really going to flip when you hear this!"

"What?" Holly nearly shouted.

"You know we're on deadline right now," Rob said in no mood to chat about local gossip. "The Sausalito edition is due at the printer in less than three hours."

"Yeah, well contact the rewrite department because this changes your lead!" Eddie said, holding up a brown eight-by-ten envelope. Fanning it over his head, he said, "Hold on to your kibbles and bits people! I just got this from Brownstein's office twenty minutes ago. Care to take a guess what killed Henrietta Hammer?"

"Oh no," Holly and Rob exclaimed in unison. They looked at each other and then at Eddie. In unison, they said, "Aconite?"

Eddie grinned. "You two really do make a great team."

"Well, this throws everything into a different light," Rob said.

"How could that have happened?" Holly asked.

"I don't know," Eddie replied. "I've been asking myself that since Max handed me this report. In the county's records, we can locate one previous death attributed to aconite poisoning. Now we've had two in weeks! You guys are on a deadline, so I'll let you go. But tomorrow morning

I'd like to meet here at eight-thirty. Let's see what ideas we can gin up. Something pretty screwy is going on."

"Damn, Eddie! This is nuts!" Rob shook his head, still stunned by the news. "I assume I can use that report Max handed you?"

"Sure. It's a public document now." Eddie placed the envelope stamped Office of Marin County Medical Examiner, on Rob's desk. Chuckling, on his way back down the steps, Eddie called out, "This whole thing just keeps getting better!"

CHAPTER TWENTY-ONE

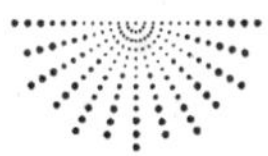

Both Holly and Rob were in the office by eight-fifteen the following morning, after a stop at the Starbucks across Princess Street to pick up coffee and pastries for their morning meeting.

They were still reeling from the news that Eddie delivered the previous day, which started a mad rush to edit the article on Laurie Chase's death before their printer's deadline.

Knowing that there were more questions than answers about how both Laurie and Henrietta died of aconite poisoning, they handled the story with great care. They were satisfied, however, that with a staff of two, and four community editions to get out every week, they had managed to plant a flag in the center of this story and again scoop the county-wide daily newspaper, which had a staff of over one-hundred.

By the time Eddie came in, put cream and sugar in his coffee, and took his first big bite from an over-sized cheese Danish, Holly and Rob were more than ready with their questions.

"Let me jump in," Holly started. "You both know how I love to do that."

Rob and Eddie nodded in agreement.

"The logical conclusion," at least to me, is that Laurie mistakenly added what she thought was an innocent herb, to a dish she made for Henrietta, and then for herself six weeks later. That's how they both ingested the aconite. I'm sure it came out of her garden."

"My thought as well," Rob said. "For all the sinister over-tones, perhaps we're dealing with two accidental deaths."

"And if all this was accidental," Holly continued, "then the idea of a spooked kid or some drunk driver hitting into the back of Scott's bicycle and then out of fear of the conse-quences driving off could be a real possibility. It wouldn't be the first hit and run in the Bay Area. They happen in San Francisco and Oakland on an almost weekly basis. Terrible, but true."

"Good points," Eddie conceded. "And remember: even if Henrietta's death was by accidental poisoning, that doesn't mean that one of my prime suspects would not be happy to see Scott out of the way. All three persons-of-interest— the Reeses and Phillips—had opportunity and motive to bang into the back of Scott's bicycle. They also had the opportu-nity, I assume, and the motive, to serve Henrietta a poisoned entrée."

"You're certainly right on that score," Rob said, as Holly nodded in agreement.

"Let me ask you both another question," Eddie continued. "Laurie is a single woman. As Holly suspects, she was probably living on a limited income. That being said, have you ever known a person like that to cook a casserole made for one? Wouldn't it be more logical that Laurie would have been poisoned within a few days of Henrietta? I suppose she might have frozen her portion, but still…"

"Hard to know," Rob replied. "The more sinister scenario is that whoever put the aconite in Henrietta's dish delivered the same dish to Laurie."

"That's possible," Holly said, "but what was their motive in getting rid of Laurie Chase?"

"Perhaps she was in on a scheme to get rid of Henrietta," Eddie suggested. "But now the killer saw her as a liability and needed her out of the way. Or maybe the murderer didn't want to pay her a share from Henrietta's estate, which I imagine will be greatly reduced, if not eliminated, thanks to Scott being placed into the mix. Of course, on the day Henrietta died, no one, including Laurie, knew what would happen regarding Scott Sousa."

"Did your crime lab crew finish their tests in Laurie's garden?" Rob asked.

"They've been analyzing soil samples from various parts of the garden. So far, they've found no aconite. At best, however, they've checked less than half the entire garden. Laurie had a good size piece of land up there. Finding the patch where aconite might have been growing is like finding the proverbial needle in the haystack."

"So, what will you do if you come up empty?" Holly asked.

"I can't say for certain. Aconite leaves a chemical signature in the soil, but if all that is there is a spare root or two, we don't have anywhere near the manpower to sift through every square foot of that garden. There's always a chance that she pulled some of it and put it in a dish she made for Henrietta, and then harvested the rest for the dish she made for herself."

"But there is one other twist," Rob added. "The killer may have planted the aconite in some corner of Laurie's garden, and harvested some of it to serve up to Henrietta."

"You're right," Eddie acknowledged. "That's an interesting scheme."

Holly shook her head. "Huh? You're losing me."

"Let's say that you plant the stuff in Chase's yard. Then you pull some of it up to kill Henrietta—but you leave the rest," Eddie said.

"Because if it's found growing in her yard, it's almost like leaving the murder weapon in the home of the person you're hoping to frame," Holly said with a self-satisfied smile.

"You then wait until the aconite is identified as the cause of death. Afterward, you make an anonymous tip about Laurie's garden being a possible source of the aconite," Rob added.

"But then you get a bad break," Eddie suggests. "Laurie digs the stuff up and throws it into her dish."

"If that scenario weren't so sad, it would be laughable," Rob said.

"But if it wasn't for your prodding," Holly said looking at

Eddie, "the likely outcome for Henrietta is that she would have been lowered into the ground and left there for the ages under the assumption that she was one more senior citizen who died of a stroke or a bum ticker."

"That would be fine with the killer," Rob said quickly. "If Eddie's suspicion from day one was right—that the killer was one of our original four heirs, Ruby or Chris Reese, Francis Phillips, or Laurie Chase—they still got what they wanted in the first place: Henrietta dead, and a multi-million dollar estate gift."

"What he, or she, didn't count on were the unexpected twists in the story," Eddie said. "The biggest of which was Henrietta's love child showing up! And poor, nutty Laurie Chase–digging up the aconite and accidentally poisoning herself."

"There was one other twist," Holly said. "It's that the three of us would not allow our former teacher to rest in peace. She might have terrified us when we were kids, but we became better people because of her."

"Hear, hear, Holly," Eddie said as he tipped the last of his coffee cup in salute to her. "I'm going to Laurie's service this afternoon. I imagine you two have to pass because of work."

"You know we both enjoy a funeral as much as the next guy," Rob said with a chuckle, "But we're slammed for the rest of the day."

Holly nodded, and then added, "I hope for your sake that one of her acolytes doesn't play a recording of Laurie's favorite arias."

Eddie's eyes got big. "You and me both!" If I'm lucky, the Reeses and Phillips will be there as well."

"As in the arsonist, staying around to watch the fire?" Rob asked.

Eddie nodded. "One thing my business has in common with yours is adherence to one simple rule: snooping isn't for quitters."

Four hours later, Eddie squeezed into the back pew for the one o'clock funeral service at the Presbyterian Church on Bulkley Avenue, just three blocks uphill from Rob and Holly's office.

After the service ended Eddie guessed that about one hundred plus people were heading downstairs to the church's community room for a reception sponsored by the board of the Sausalito Opera Society. With the Standard landing in mailboxes around town earlier that day, Eddie had no doubt that Laurie and Henrietta's deaths, having been attributed to aconite, would be topic number one.

"Do you think any of this was criminal?" One of Laurie's board members— the widower, Thomas Greer—asked a little too loudly into Eddie's ear.

"At this moment we believe it was just a tragic accident," he replied.

"Two poisonings of two well know residents in less than two months sounds a bit suspicious to me," Greer said firmly. The retired Chevron engineer had long been considered Sausalito's most eligible bachelor among the eighty plus set.

"We're looking into all the possibilities," Eddie added

just as the widow, Velma Beatrice, who was a member of Laurie's board, joined their conversation.

"Are you telling our boy Eddie some tall tales?" Velma asked Greer playfully while grabbing hold of his hand. It was no secret around town that she had set her sights on Greer.

"How are you, Mrs. Beatrice?" Eddie asked with the same forced smile he presented at all such occasions.

"I'm just fine. You know, I turned eighty last month. But I don't feel a day over seventy," Velma announced with a girlish smile and a wink thrown in Greer's direction.

"I was just asking this fine young man what he thought of Henrietta and Laurie both dying of that aconite stuff just six weeks apart. Of course, that's what it said on the front page of The Sausalito Standard. But I can't believe everything I see in print!"

"Isn't all this simply frightening?" Velma asked as she clasped her arm tightly around Greer's and pulled him in close for some much-needed protection.

"I agree, you can't believe everything you read in the paper," Eddie said with a laugh. "But in this case, the paper is spot on about aconite poisoning as the cause of both deaths. I've seen the medical examiner's reports myself. Since I have you here let me ask both of you a question."

"No, we didn't do it!" Velma said in a rush and then giggled.

"Oh, you're not suspects," he assured them. "At this point, I'm not sure anyone is. But I am curious about that large garden Laurie kept."

"You know, I use to come up and join her little gardening parties on Saturdays," Greer said. "In fact, I gave it up just a few months ago. It wasn't a problem for me getting down, but it keeps getting harder every year to get myself back up."

"Oh, don't listen to him. Thomas is such a natural outdoorsman! There's still a lot of pep left in this old boy," Velma insisted approvingly, as Greer winced with embarrassment.

"I didn't know Laurie shared her gardening space, although it's certainly a large enough garden that it makes sense," Eddie said.

"Oh, yes! We all enjoyed it," Greer offered. "Up in the hills, there is vegetation everywhere you look. But having the space for cultivating a real vegetable garden is quite a rare thing! Land has become too valuable over the last thirty years. Double lots like Laurie's have mostly been split and used for second homes. Not to mention Channing Way is far enough up that it's above the typical tree line, so it gets a lot of sunshine. Just about anything you plant up there does well."

"The few times I've seen community gardens they're divided in pretty obvious ways, usually by wood or sometimes brick dividers."

"You're right, Eddie, but all this was very informal, none of us marked off plots. We just used little flags to designate different plantings." Thomas replied. "Normally, we'd work there every Saturday in the dry season, and some other days of the week if we wanted to work, weather permitting during the rainy season as well. But everyone did his or her own thing. Laurie was always very welcoming. She was a lot like the hippie girl Velma once was."

"Thomas, behave yourself! Just because I'm a proponent

of free love, doesn't mean I'm still a hippie," Velma said and then laughed at her own joke.

"Did you get to keep what you grew?" Eddie asked.

"Oh, absolutely! But most of us gave Laurie some of what we grew just as a way of saying thanks. You know, she ate a little meat and fish now and then. But most of what she ate was vegetables from her garden."

"Laurie was such a wonderful person. And what a voice she had," Velma quickly added. "Oh, look, Thomas, there's Chris and Ruby Reese. Didn't they have a gardening plot up at Laurie's place as well?"

"They did," Greer responded. "And they've done very well with it, as I recall. They certainly both have green thumbs!"

The Reeses seemed a bit reluctant to join the group. Finally, they made their way over with smiles and handshakes all around.

Eddie, seizing an opportunity to see just how uneasy he could make the Reeses, quickly brought them up to speed on the conversation he had been having with Thomas Greer and Velma Beatrice.

"So, from what I've been told, you had your own plot up at Laurie's place?" Eddie asked.

"Yes. It's been fun, don't you both think?" Greer said. "In fact, these two might have been the best of all of us! Ruby and Chris had tomatoes, zucchinis, and kale. They both did a great job."

"We'll miss it," Ruby said in a quiet voice. "I imagine the property will be sold in the not too distant future."

"Why are the police digging up so much of the place?"

Greer asked. "I drove by there the other day and saw the crime scene tape all around the property."

"I don't think we had much choice. There was a reasonable chance that the garden is where the aconite came from. With two accidental poisonings in six weeks and with Laurie being a good friend of Henrietta's, it's plausible that Laurie prepared a dish for her and then later made one for herself, using what she assumed was the same innocent herb. Aconite, just like certain mushrooms, can look innocent, but it's not."

"Did they find any aconite when they dug up the garden?" Velma asked.

"Not yet. But that doesn't mean it was never there," Eddie explained.

"I recently read a book called 'The Garden of Deadly Delights.' It was one of those spy, suspense, romance things. I loved it, but it had nothing to do with any of this," Velma assured all of them with a shrug and a giggle.

"Well, whatever happens, I'm sorry to see the garden is gone now," Ruby insisted. "Of course I'm not half as sorry as I am over the loss of Laurie. She was a lovely person."

"That she was," Velma added, as Greer nodded in approval. "I don't think I have ever known anyone sweeter. And she could sing the birds right out of the trees!"

Eddie smiled. He wondered if Holly could have resisted saying something about Laurie's ability to make the birds take flight.

CHAPTER TWENTY-TWO

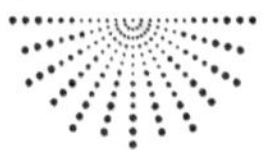

The following morning, Eddie had no trouble finding his way to Thomas Greer's front door.

Greer was one of many in Sausalito who'd paid Eddie to do a variety of odd jobs: mowing a lawn, fixing a door—or any other odd job. As he explained to Rob when they were both teens, "It's great having some pocket money for the movies and other stuff that you don't have to beg your mom and dad to give you."

Eddie was relieved to find Greer by himself.

Greer looked up from his newspaper when Eddie tapped on his screen door. "What are you up to?"

"I had something I thought you might be able to help me with."

"Sure, come right in son. Make yourself at home."

"I don't want to interrupt, I'll only be a couple of minutes. Ms. Beatrice isn't here, is she?"

"Nope." Thomas grinned. "She thinks she's got her claws in pretty deep, but I'm not ready to say, 'I do!'"

Eddie laughed. "Well, keep fighting the good fight."

"I don't know. It gets pretty lonely up here. My bride's gone seven years next month. I should be thankful for the nearly fifty years we had together. But, I'll tell you, Eddie, it goes by pretty darn quick. Enough about me; what are you up to?"

Eddie pulled a blank piece of paper out of his inside jacket pocket.

As he unfolded it and laid it down on the old fashion bar in one corner of the room, Eddie asked, "Is there any chance you might remember the layout of Laurie's garden? I mean, how the plots were divided up? We're just concerned there was more aconite growing there! When we find traces of the stuff, we'd like to inform whoever gardens that plot, to dispose of any vegetables they might have preserved. Two unintentional poisonings in six weeks are more than enough."

"Let me see if I can remember," Greer said as he sat down on the stool next to Eddie.

Greer thought for a time. Finally, he picked up a book and used its spine to draw straight lines both down and across the page.

When he was done, the page was divided into nine equal squares. Then he started writing names inside those squares.

"I was up here in the top left corner. Next to me was Velma. We had seen each other at some functions in the past, but it was up in the garden that we really became friends."

Slowly Greer filled in the other squares. Only when he

came to the bottom left-hand corner of the property did he write in the names Chris and Ruby Reese.

Once he had finished, Eddie patted him warmly on the back and thanked him. "This has been a great help."

Thomas squinted up at him. "Are you going to talk to each one of our little group?"

"Absolutely. We haven't found any evidence yet of aconite growing on the land, and there's a chance that poor Laurie harvested the last of it. Still, there's always the possibility that a spare root or two of the plant was left in the soil and will start growing back after the next rain season."

"We certainly don't want that!" Greer said with a grimace.

"Can't hurt to be overly cautious when it comes to something as deadly as this."

That afternoon Eddie updated Canning on his investigation. He knew that for now, Jack's interest had cooled since the Independent had not called his office in several days.

Still, Eddie wanted to be sure that Canning continued to support the soil analysis that needed to be done.

"Never hurts for us to take all needed precautions," Eddie emphasized, knowing that these words placed Canning in a box. If Jack shut down the soils testing project and another death occurred, it would be him the voters blamed.

At the same time, his budget had other priorities. Money

spent looking for what might be a phantom killer weed—was not something Jack was inclined to pursue.

"Okay, keep digging," Jack, instructed begrudgingly. "But let's get this wrapped up over the next day or two."

"No problem," Eddie assured him as he hurried to get out of Canning's office before he changed his mind.

He was determined to focus on the approximately twenty-five square yards of soil that Greer had labeled as belonging to Chris and Ruby Reese.

The following evening, Eddie joined Rob and Holly for their end-of-the-workweek cocktails.

Rob and Holly arrived first. They took their usual table. Although it would be packed with people in another four hours, right now the bar was quiet as a library.

"This place could never stay in business if it weren't for their weekend crowd, coupled with the handful of alcoholics who come in at noon, sit down at the bar and drink until dark," Holly proclaimed.

Within a quarter hour, Eddie appeared. He took off his jacket, revealing a sweat-soaked shirt underneath. Eddie placed it over the back of a dark wood captain's chair that likely dated back to the time when he, Rob and Holly were children.

"What have you been doing, running a marathon?" Rob exclaimed. "Sit down. I've already ordered you a Guinness."

"Thanks! Don't let anyone tell you that gardening is easy work."

"Happy to say I've never had the desire to put my hands

in dirt other than the occasional nasty rumor," Holly insisted as she reached for the vodka martini that Gail had just placed in front of her.

"Since when did you develop an interest in gardening?" Rob asked.

"Since I've been trying to find evidence of aconite growing in Laurie's vegetable garden."

"Any luck?" Holly asked.

"Yes, thanks to old man Greer," Eddie explained as he pulled out the map of the garden that he and Greer had created.

"Good old Thomas Greer?" Rob shook his head. "Man, I haven't heard that name in a long time."

"It had been a while for me as well. Then I saw him at the reception Wednesday after Laurie's service."

"Greer was one of the reasons Eddie and I had pocket money as kids," Rob informed Holly. "He gave us ten bucks each to clean up his yard every few weeks. How's the old guy doing?"

"He looks great for eighty plus. Unfortunately, Velma Beatrice has got her hooks into him pretty deep."

"Velma," Holly said a little too loudly, causing one of the two ancient mariners hunched over a beer at the bar to look back over his shoulder. "She's one of the nosiest of Sausalito's brigade of busybodies!"

Eddie shrugged. "He's been pretty lonely since his wife passed. Velma Beatrice was never one to miss an opportunity. Anyway, I learned from Greer that he and others, including Velma, worked up at Laurie's community garden. But more importantly, I learned that Ruby and Chris Reese worked a section of the garden." He pulled the paper with the plot outline from his jacket. "I asked him to draw out a map of the garden so we could alert all the volunteers to the fact that there might be aconite growing in their portion of the garden, under the assumption that Laurie harvested and ingested the poison unintentionally and they might do the same."

"Slick move," Rob said raising his right hand to offer Eddie a high five.

"Canning was getting ready to have the lab boys pack it in. I needed to find something fast or go home empty-handed. You know, twenty-five square yards may not be all that much soil to go sifting through. But when you times that by nine plots, it can be a project that takes a lot longer than Canning and his stingy finance manager were willing to support."

"Where in the garden did you find the aconite?" Rob asked.

"Here!" Eddie stabbed his finger at the square at the far corner of the property where Greer had written Chris and Ruby Reese.

"Have you picked them up already? Are they in the county lockup?" Holly asked excitedly.

"Not so fast, Annie Oakley. I've still got work to do. And, hear this you two: the fact that we found traces of aconite there is top secret! I don't want to read about this in the next edition of The Standard no matter how slow a news week you're having."

Rob made the Scouts Honor sign. "We hear you loud and clear. So what's your next step?"

"I need to dig down a little deeper—and I don't mean in Laurie's garden. Ironically, their plot of land was well situated, being right on the lower corner section of the property. It's very easily reached from the corner of Prospect and Channing Way.

"Why is that important?" Holly asked.

"Because I'm guessing that one or both of them harvested some of that stuff and delivered it to Henrietta, and then, possibly, to Laurie as well. They might have worked in tandem. However, there's also a chance that only one of them is the culprit. Until I get all that figured out, I don't want them running for the hills just because we found some of the stuff in their patch of Laurie's garden."

"So, one or both of them were likely behind the attempt to kill Scott?" Holly asked.

"That would be my guess," Eddie said. "If you wanted Henrietta out of the way, you'd certainly want Scott out of the picture!"

"Yet there is still the possibility that Laurie was foraging through different plots, came across the stuff, and unintentionally poisoned herself and Henrietta," Rob said.

"That's true. But all we found was a few torn roots of the aconite on the Reeses' plot. We had no luck coming up with it anywhere else. That's simply too much of a coincidence. They both had motive and opportunity to kill Henrietta and Laurie—and kill Scott as well. I'm moving forward along those lines. I suspect that when the story came out in The Standard that aconite had been identified as the cause of both deaths, one or both of them went up there and dug the stuff up. Or they did it after they got rid of Laurie. If you've killed off the two people you wanted dead, why leave any remaining aconite as evidence?"

"Ha!" Rob crowed. "They got it out of there never knowing that a few roots were left behind."

"If the Reeses were aware of the aconite growing in their plot, and they were innocent, they would have felt guilty but would have mentioned it to prove that they had nothing to hide," Holly pointed out.

"If either one or both, are actual gardeners, they would know that getting out every last bit of any plant is an iffy proposition—particularly if you're trying to do that without the benefit of full sunlight," Eddie added.

"Do you think they were doing a little night gardening?" Rob asked.

"My guess is after sunset, or just before sunrise. If I were the Reeses, I'd want to dig that stuff up with as few prying eyes as possible. You could work at night with a flashlight, but that's going to look pretty odd to any neighbor who happens to see you. Working in a garden at twilight or dawn makes you appear ambitious. Doing it in total darkness makes you look suspicious."

CHAPTER TWENTY-THREE

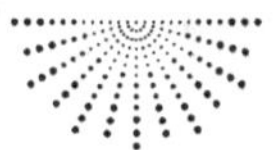

Back at work on Monday, two ideas came to Eddie.

First, people who walked dogs were his most likely observers, which is why he used his access to the county's rabies vaccination, tagging and licensing records to limit the scope of his search to dog owners within walking distance of Laurie's garden.

A search turned up ten registered dogs in what Eddie considered his most promising search area. He didn't worry about people out for long walks because they were far less likely to pass the garden at sunrise or sunset.

Once he defined the parameters of his search, Eddie's second premise came into play. In what had become one of the most valuable pockets of Sausalito real estate, many of the families he knew as a teen had moved away over the past two decades. But one still there was Velma Beatrice's younger sister, Kayla Campbell, who was the owner of a corgi husky.

Up and across on Channing there was one other

neighbor he knew well: the Spanos widow. Eddie had gone to both elementary and high school with her son, Nicholas —or Nicky, as he was known then. Nicky, like Rob, had been on the same high school basketball team with Eddie. He also knew Nick's dad had passed because he went to the service, but his mother, Angela, was still alive. According to the county licensing records, she had a German shepherd named Wolf.

To newcomers, Eddie was a tall man with a badge. But to these two women, Eddie was little more than one of the neighborhood kids who happened to work an exciting job.

Both would be happy to see him. He doubted they would hold anything back for fear of putting themselves into the middle of something. If nothing else, this was an excellent place to start.

Mid-morning on Tuesday Kayla Campbell reprimanded her corgi, Lucky, as he sniffed about Eddie's pants' cuffs and shoes. "Stop bothering Eddie, you old pest!" She told her dog sweetly as she reached up and pulled Eddie down for a kiss on the check. "You must come in for a cup of coffee or tea and a little something to eat. It seems like ages since I've seen you, and how are little Aaron and that sweet wife of yours?"

Before Eddie had a chance to answer, Kayla continued, "Velma mentioned that she saw you at poor Laurie's funeral. Oh, what a shame! Laurie was such a lovely person."

"Yes, I'm sure she was," Eddie responded with a forced smile.

"And that garden of hers! So many people enjoyed working up there. Some would be there at all hours. You know Eddie when you have a passion for something you keep at it."

Lucky continued to sniff about Eddie's shoes. "Stop bothering Eddie, you old pest!" Kayla said as she reached down to smack Lucky on the behind.

"It's interesting that people were so dedicated to working their gardens."

"Yes, wonderful. Laurie gave me cucumbers, kale, tomatoes—all sorts of wonderful things!"

"Who were some of the people you saw up there?"

"Well, let's see. Thomas and Velma just about every weekend. Also, Betsy Baker was a regular. As you know, her husband passed away last year."

"That's sad. I hadn't heard."

I ran into Ruby and Chris Reese a couple of times. What a couple of sweethearts those two are! Let me see... who else? Oh! How could I forget? I was so impressed. About a week ago, I was out walking Lucky, and I came across that wonderful man, Mr. Phillips. You know him, don't you?"

"You're talking about Francis Phillips?"

"Indeed, I am. He's the fellow who leads the Sausalito Preservation Group. Eddie, he's done a lot of good for this town."

Eddie shifted in his seat, not quite believing what he had just heard. After he gathered himself, he smiled. "Yes, I've met Mr. Phillips. I'm looking forward to seeing him again. Any idea how long ago it was that you saw him in the garden?"

"Why would that matter?" Kayla asked with a raised eyebrow.

"Well, let me tell you the whole story," Eddie said with a sigh. "There have been a few bikes stolen in this area over the last couple of weeks, and if it was within that timeframe. Mr. Phillips might have seen something suspicious."

"Oh my! I had no idea! I haven't been on a bike in as long as I can remember."

Eddie smiled and pressed ahead. "And you saw Mr. Phillips when?"

"Well…" Kayla said pausing and looking up toward the ceiling. "Oh wait…of course, I know! It was last Wednesday evening. I had dinner with Velma and Thomas down at Poggio's. After we ate, they took me straight home. That was about seven-thirty. A few minutes later, I went out to take Lucky for a walk. I hope that helps—and I hope you catch your thief." Kayla said as she pinched Eddie's cheek just as she did when he was a teen hand washing and polishing her car for five dollars.

Eddie, having heard the clue he needed, was anxious to get back to work. He felt sure that at any moment, however, Kayla was going to offer him cookies and milk. Before she could, he grabbed his cell phone from his pocket and looked at the screen. "Oh gosh, they need me back at head-quarters! You'll have to come down to our place and visit one day. Come and see our little Aaron. He's growing like a weed."

Kayla pulled him close to give him one more kiss on the check. "Don't be such a stranger!" she admonished Eddie as he moved toward the front door. "Come back and visit when you have more time. Maybe one day soon little Aaron will be old enough to come up and do some chores for me…"

Before doing anything else, Eddie decided to go up to the Spanos residence and see if lightning might strike twice.

Angela Spanos, who was in her late sixties, greeted him in a white silk robe that revealed more of her than Eddie wished to see.

In spite of her age and the rasp in her voice that revealed the effect of decades of smoking, the first thing she did after walking Eddie into the kitchen was light up a cigarette.

Wolf, her German shepherd, came bounding in, hoping to meet the stranger who had just arrived.

"Get outside," Spanos barked at the dog. She pointed toward the sliding glass door that led onto an enclosed porch ten feet off the ground. After he ran out, she closed the sliding glass door behind him and turned back to Eddie. "I can't believe what a big handsome man you've grown into! Can I get you anything, coffee, tea—or something a little stronger?" Her wink increased Eddie's unease.

He suggested that there had been reports of a night prowler in the area: a variation on the fantasy he concocted for Kayla Campbell.

"No prowlers," Angela assured him, "But I did see something strange a week ago. I was out on the patio, having a smoke. It was around nightfall, but I could see someone digging something up in the corner of that community garden Laurie Chase kept. Now that she's dead, I hope a new owner comes in and bulldozes over that garden. They can take that dilapidated old house of hers down while they're at it. It's not good for property values, you know?" As Spanos laughed at her own observation, she revealed her badly, smoke-stained teeth.

"Any idea what this fellow might have been up to?"

"I'm not sure if he was taking something out of the ground or putting something in. You work for the city. Maybe you can get them to put in some better street lights so we can see at night up here."

"Actually I work for the county. Any idea how long he was there?"

"No more than fifteen minutes. What do you suppose he was doing?"

Eddie feigned ignorance with a shrug. "Sometimes these prowlers will swipe something and then bury it quickly if they think someone is onto them," Eddie offered only too happy to lead Spanos astray. "Any chance he had a car nearby? I know it was dark, but if you could remember it might help us in catching this guy."

"Let's see if I can remember. I had a couple of vodka tonics in me. I'll make you one now if you're in the mood for a mid-morning cocktail."

Eddie gave a tired grin in return. "Sorry. I'm on duty. You say it was last week? Any chance it was last Wednesday night?"

"Let me think, you know I'm not as sharp as I use to be."

I don't doubt that Eddie thought while smiling innocently.

"Yes, that's right last Wednesday! I was getting ready to watch 'The 'Bachelor.' That's my favorite show" she exclaimed taking another drag off her cigarette. For a second time, the tie around her silk robe threatened to fall open.

Eddie thought it best to keep his eyes focused on the outside bottom corner of Laurie's garden.

"It was a big car," Angela added. "I'm guessing a Jeep Wrangler or something like that. Actually, I can't be sure. But, I do think it was white."

"Any chance you could make out his shape? I mean, was he tall or short? Heavyset? Thin? Average?"

"He wasn't heavyset. Not tall, not short. I guess you could just call him average size."

"Oh gosh, now what?" Eddie said as he grabbed his phone, looked at the screen, and then jammed it back into his pocket. "There's trouble back at headquarters! Thanks so much for your time, Mrs. Spanos," Eddie said, moving quickly toward the door.

"No bother Eddie. I'm always happy to see such a big handsome man, morning, noon, or night," Angela insisted as Eddie quickly went down her front steps. "Don't be such a stranger!" She called out as Eddie hurried to his car and drove away.

Back at his desk, Eddie checked the two different addresses for Francis Phillips that he had: one, the downtown location of the Sausalito Preservation Society headquarters and gift shop; the other, Phillips' houseboat, which was moored at A Dock, which is located on Sausalito's northern border.

Eddie then checked that with DMV records to see what if any car registrations were in their database for Francis Phillips.

"Bingo," Eddie murmured.

A white Jeep Wrangler was registered at the address for A Dock.

Angela Spanos' mind might be slipping in countless ways, but her vision was excellent.

It was time for Eddie to pay a visit to the trusted keeper of Sausalito's storied past—a history which included rum-runners, con artists, and one internationally renowned madam.

Eddie's first stop was the offices of the Sausalito Fine Arts Board. Maybe his day's lucky streak would continue, and both Ruby and Chris Reese would be in the office if only to update their two sets of accounting ledgers.

Eddie pushed open the door. He was delighted to find both Chris and Ruby were there and alone.

"Hi, remember me?" Eddie said while showing both of them his badge and photo ID. "Do you have a few minutes to talk?"

Annoyed, Ruby looked up from the piles of papers stacked everywhere. Eddie presumed the files were proposals from Bay Area artists eager to participate in their organization's July 4th art show. "Could we do this some other time, detective? We're kind of busy right now!"

"Well, it's important. I want to talk to you both about the murder of Henrietta Hammer."

"What do you mean murder?" Ruby asked as her voice deepened.

"Her case has been an open investigation with my department. We're close to making an arrest."

"That's insane! Who could have done such an awful thing?" Ruby Reese asked in what sounded like genuine shock. Chris, in stark contrast, looked at Eddie in stunned silence.

"Up until recently, I thought her killers were the two of you," Eddie proclaimed.

Ruby nearly leaped out of her chair. In a Wagnerian declaration that would have made Laurie Chase proud she shouted, "WHAT? I loved Henrietta! Why would I want to kill her?"

"Well, here's a thought." Eddie plopped down in the chair facing Ruby's desk. "You were tired of waiting for her to die. You wanted a substantial portion of her estate to help secure your futures."

"You're insane!" Ruby insisted.

"Really? Well, if both of you are so innocent, would you like to explain why aconite was found growing on your plot of land up at Laurie Chase's garden?"

"That's impossible!" Chris bolted up out of his chair.

"Why is that impossible, Mr. Reese?" Eddie said as he turned and faced him directly. "Is it impossible because your accomplice, Mr. Phillips, took the time to pull up all the aconite the night The Standard reported that Laurie Chase, like Henrietta Hammer, had died of aconite poisoning?"

"Chris," Ruby bellowed, "what in the world is this man talking about?"

"Call our attorney Ruby! We're not saying another word," Chris said, wilting quickly under pressure. "It's all just lies!"

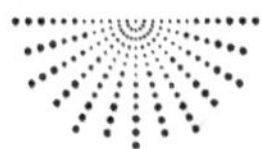

Several hours later, as Holly and Rob were closing up the office for the night, Eddie, exhausted but proud, pushed their office's front door buzzer.

As he walked up the stairs, he announced, "Francis Phillips and Chris Reese were both arrested this afternoon within thirty minutes of each other. They are scheduled to be arraigned in the morning, and are being held on suspicion of committing a double homicide."

"What? Wow!" Holly shouted with excitement as she dropped her bag with a thud on top of her desk before falling back down into her chair.

"How did you pull it all together?" Rob asked.

Eddie flopped down onto the office couch, tired but relieved. "Starting this morning, all the pieces began falling into place."

"Just like that?" Holly said, obviously stunned.

"Details," Rob insisted. "Details!"

Eddie nodded and smiled. "It was like that last section of

a jigsaw puzzle. You spend what seems like forever trying to get the right pieces to fall into where you think they will fit, but then they don't. For this puzzle, those little shreds of aconite in Laurie's garden were the key to unlocking it all."

Eddie took them back through his morning visits with Velma Beatrice's sister, Kayla Campbell, and explained that she was the first to confirm his suspicion: the reason they had come up with just trace amounts of aconite in a scattering of torn roots was that someone had removed what they thought was all of the deadly plants. That, someone, had also done their hasty gardening at twilight.

"But didn't you think that Laurie might have harvested what was left of aconite and put it in her veggie casserole?" Holly asked.

"I did, at first," Eddie conceded. "But when I thought about it a little more, I decided that didn't make sense."

"How so?" Rob asked.

"Two reasons: One, she was a serious gardener. If you're going to pull up the last of something out of the ground, you do it in the late fall—not in spring. If it was something new to her, something she had not tried before, she wasn't going to harvest it all with months left until the end of the season. That doesn't make sense."

"Good point," Holly said.

"More importantly, as Thomas Greer explained to me, everyone welcomed Laurie borrowing whatever she wanted from their yield. After all, they were gardening on her land. I don't think they would have felt that way, however, if she went into their garden plots and tore out entire swatches of plants. No, that aconite was there because someone wanted to cultivate it. That left the Reeses—and or a gardening buddy, who in this case turned out to be Phillips."

"How did you hook together Chris Reese and Francis Phillips?" Holly asked.

"Besides the fact that they are both greedier than they are bright," Rob added with a smile.

"Actually, a combination of factors," Eddie explained, "blended with a healthy dose of guesswork. To begin with, they both had priors, dating back many years. In a job just out of college, Phillips worked for a construction firm. He got caught embezzling. He did six months in the Colorado State Pen and a year of probation after that. Chris Reese was involved in similar shenanigans. He scammed an arts group in Taos, New Mexico. Both Chris and Francis managed to walk off with some pretty good money. And while I support the idea of finding an honest life after serving your time, both had a taste for taking money that didn't belong to them. A taste they apparently never got over."

Eddie then explained how he got lucky with the observations of Kayla Campbell, and Angela Spanos. "You know if you snoop around long enough, you might just get lucky. You see the same thing in the news business. In this case, I not only had a positive ID on Phillips but one on his vehicle as well."

"Do you think that Ruby, my old classmate, was involved in all this?"

"At first, I wasn't certain. That's why I decided to pay both the Reeses a visit before picking up that great guardian of our humble town's historical past."

"What did you do when you got to their place?" Rob asked.

"I strolled into their office, unannounced, and accused them both of killing Henrietta, and Laurie,"

"Boy, I wish I'd been there for that!" Holly said with obvious disappointment. "What happened next?"

"Ruby went crazy! She really went off on me. But while she fumed, I kept an eye on hubby Chris. Not to my surprise, he squirmed. It's a little something I learned way back from our old friend Bob Ivan, and his days as a county prosecutor. Think of it as shaking the branches of a walnut tree. You don't know what else might fall to the ground unless you give it a couple of really hard shakes."

"So, if Ruby wasn't skimming along with Chris, where did she think their extra cash was coming from?" Holly asked.

"That was actually the easiest part of Chris Reese's scam. Every couple of months he claimed he'd sold one of his dreadful pieces of modern art to a dealer in San Francisco. He'd then whitewashed the canvas that was supposedly purchased and start another one of his masterpieces."

"Good work, Detective Austin!" Rob said as he slapped Eddie on the back.

Holly gave him a hug and then asked, "How did you get Phillips?"

"I had an unmarked car waiting across from his Jeep Wrangler, which was parked in the lot outside of A Dock. You won't believe this one: Chris Reese, I suppose in a panic, texted Phillips and told him that he was being arrested along with his wife on suspicion of murder. He was going to need him to help arrange his bail! Then he adds, 'I would do the same for you!'"

"That was a pretty dumb move," Rob said with a laugh.

"Crooks are often clever, but rarely smart," Eddie replied.

"Do you think one or both of them gave Scott a shove through the back window of that car?" By Holly's tone, Eddie could tell she was ready for some swift frontier justice.

"Now that we have Phillips' jeep in property lockup, we're running a check on it. We did have a couple of paint fragments embedded in the bike, but none matched the manufacturer's paint. Turns out that Phillips car had been buffed down and repainted. It's almost certainly a stolen vehicle that our local historian got from some pal for undoubtedly an excellent price."

"I'm glad Ruby had no hand in this," Holly admitted.

"So it turns out, Chris, who enjoys making casseroles with toxic ingredients, asked his wife to deliver one of his creations to Henrietta the night before she died. My guess is she had it the following day for lunch. And that was where our story began."

"But that leaves one piece missing," Rob said. "Why kill Laurie Chase as well?"

"Remember Henrietta's housekeeper, Eloise?" Eddie asked. "Rob, you and I talked to her at the reception after Henrietta's service. She was the one who caught us in the act of demolishing that nice buffet Scott had arranged."

"Oh yeah, that's right," Rob said with a guilty smile. "Kind of an embarrassing moment—but worth it. Those were some of the best sandwiches I've ever had!"

"Eloise came to see me at my office a few days ago. She had just gotten back from a visit home to Sweden: her first in over twenty years. A friend called her up to tell her that she read in The Standard that both her late employer and Laurie Chase had died of aconite poisoning. The poor thing was beside herself."

"Why?" Rob asked quickly.

"It was after she heard that Laurie Chase had died of the very same thing, that she remembered something terrible."

"Oh no!" Holly said anticipating what Eddie was about to say.

"Oh yes," Eddie began. "She remembered Ruby Reese had dropped off a casserole. Henrietta, having eaten dinner earlier that evening, asked Eloise to cut it in half. Henrietta planned on having it for lunch the following day and suggested that Eloise take the other half home with her to have on Friday, her day off. But when Laurie Chase came to see Henrietta, later that same evening, Eloise suggested that Laurie take that half of the casserole home with her. She was going to take it for herself, but she was fond of Laurie, so she gave it to her."

"So that was how Laurie ingested the aconite. She must have put it in the freezer and then prepared it weeks later."

"Pretty sad. Eloise sat at my desk, crying and blaming herself."

"Good God! That poor thing!" Holly stuck her left hand up and put her right hand forward as if resting it on an imaginary Bible, and said, "I'm telling you both under oath, I'd give anything to hear Laurie across the street right now singing something from Rigadigalo."

"Rig-o-let-to, Holly!" Rob sighed after elongating the pronunciation of Verdi's famous opera.

"I just got a chill when you said opera!"

"Why is that Holly?" Eddie asked.

"Because at the reception after the funeral Laurie pulled me in close and said, 'Everyone thinks Henrietta died of something so mundane as a stroke, but in classic opera, she would have been poisoned by a jealous lover or a greedy, wicked man.'"

"You remembered all that?" Holly asked.

"What Laurie said spooked me enough that I scribbled it down on a sticky note and placed it up on my fridge. The night I came home after seeing Scott up at the hospital, I read that note a few times and thought about what Laurie said and wondered about what really happened to Henrietta. Then, of course, when I stumbled upon Laurie's body, I came home later and spent a good amount of time thinking about what she had said about a greedy, wicked man."

After a few moments of silence, Holly added, "I don't know about you two, but I think we've all earned a drink."

"But it's just Wednesday night," Eddie reminded her.

"Do we have to be creatures of habit?" Holly asked.

"Yes!" Eddie and Rob answered in unison.

"Fine. I'll call Scott and see if he wants to buy me a very dry martini. It's not as if we don't have something interesting to discuss."

"Is this relationship getting serious, Holly?" Eddie asked playfully.

"Eddie Austin, you're Marin County's best detective. See if you can figure that one out on your own."

EPILOGUE

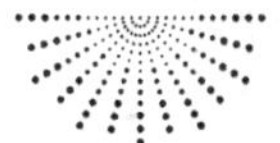

Tears came quickly to Mikhail's eyes and to those of his daughter, Rimma, when his wealthy nephew insisted on paying the cost of renovating and modernizing the family bakery.

"This is too generous," both Mikhail and Rimma protested.

"All I'm giving you is money. You gave me a large, loving family. I think I got the better of the deal."

The older man looked into his nephew's eyes. "Max would have been so proud of his son."

In time, Scott came to understand and appreciate how much children meant to Henrietta. He gave generously to children's shelters, healthcare, early childhood education, and development programs.

And to honor his aunt—the woman who raised him from birth—he established a children's daycare facility in San Rafael, naming it, "Ruth's House."

Over time, Henrietta's students—most of who were now grown with children of their own—came to see their old fifth-grade teacher through a more benevolent lens.

"She taught me not to settle for less than I was capable of doing," Rob said to a gathering of neighbors, old classmates, and city dignitaries at the dedication of the new Henrietta and Elijah Hammer Playground. It was built on one corner of the vast lawn in front of Sausalito's City Hall: a gift from the Scott Silva Foundation, it had a special climbing area for toddlers that Scott named, "Max's Place."

The Standard's new volunteer photographer, Walter Douglas, took pictures to preserve the moment. He had replaced Rob's previous star photographer, Michael Marks, remembered now as the "Phantom Photographer." Walter's photos showed parents holding hands with their children, as all anxiously awaited the cutting of an opening day ribbon.

The children were excited to stand on the deck of the pirate ship that rose out of a sandbox ocean, which served as the playground's centerpiece.

Scott and his dearest friend, Holly Cross, along with Eddie and Sharon, Rob and Karin, were content to watch their children and other families join in the celebration.

A bronze plaque, placed at the playground's entrance, was inscribed with the names of Elijah and Henrietta Hammer. It had a simple inscription:

"A place of happiness for children of all ages."

NEXT UP!

THE HORRIBLE HUSBAND
(Book 5)

William Bent, a.k.a. "Wild Bill," is the top-ranked morning host on San Francisco's KBUD. Known as the "King of Bro Talk Radio," he is also the husband of Barbara Bent, a longtime girlfriend of Karin Timmons, Sharon Austin, and Holly Cross.

When Barbara admits to Holly that her marriage is a disaster and she needs to create a life for herself, Holly suggests she apply for a position at KLIB, a competing station known as "Radio for the Modern Woman." Before long, "The Battling Bents" are Topic Number One throughout the Bay Area, and for good reason: the disdain between the soon-to-be divorced couple is obvious in their on-air barbs and very public slights.

When Wild Bill disappears without a trace, Barbara is naturally a suspect. But as Sheriff's Detective Inspector Eddie Austin digs deeper he learns that Wild Bill had a long list of men and women who would be happy to see KBUD's morning drive celebrity permanently off the air.

HOW TO REACH MARTIN

Martin Brown is an author and journalist whose articles on health and relationships have appeared in *Redbook, Playboy,* and *Complete Woman* magazines.

He and his wife, novelist Josie Brown, live in the city of San Francisco, where their grown children and granddog also reside.

For more Murder in Marin mysteries visit:
murderinmarin.com

Or go here to quickly sign up for Martin's newsletter:
subscribepage.com/MartinBrownEletterSignUp

You can also find Martin at:

facebook.com/MartinBrownCA

twitter.com/MurderInMarin